BLUE MAR

FRANCESCA G. VARELA

OWL HOUSE BOOKS

Also by the Author

Call of the Sun Child
Listen
The Seas of Distant Stars

CHAPTER ONE
LAUREL

L AUREL WOKE UP TO RED LIGHTS AND MEN'S VOICES. She jumped out of bed and, carefully, she peeked through the blinds. A patrol car and an ambulance were parked in the alley, their sirens silent. Two paramedics carried a thin, bearded man on a stretcher. His skin reminded Laurel of wet, ashy dust, but also of mud—of the cow fields when it rained.

The cops struggled to handcuff another man, this one with black hair down to his waist. He yelled into the air, something wild and indecipherable, and was quickly shoved into the car. They sped away.

What happened? A fight? A shooting? Why hadn't she heard the gunshot? Maybe it was something else, then. Laurel closed the blinds, crawled back into bed, and opened the news tab on her phone.

"Good evening, Laurel. Would you like to hear today's top stories?" her phone asked.

"Yes."

"Would you prefer to watch the local, national, or international bulletin?"

"Local."

"The local news has been interrupted by a special report. Would you like to see the special report?"

No, she wanted to hear about the shooting or whatever it was. But, still, she was curious. Special reports were usually big news.

"Yes," she responded.

"This is an active broadcast. Would you like the live version or the recorded version?"

"Live."

An image of the ocean popped up on her phone. *Great Pacific Garbage Island? On the phone: Dr. Ferris Thatcher, Political Advisor and author of 'And Then There Was Light: A Socio-Political History of the First Mars Mission'* scrawled across the screen.

"Well the thing is that it supersedes all borders. Do you create a new country, or do you declare this a territory of the United States? Does its jurisdiction lie in the hands of the government, or Lustro Corp? What you have to understand is that this is completely unprecedented."

"A bit like the space treaties?" the newscaster, Maria Gervais, said, and the camera flashed to her face. She wore almost no make-up, it seemed. Small wrinkles spread out from her eyes as she smiled.

"Quite a bit like the space treaties, Maria. Geo-engineering is the new space travel. It's the next frontier, and we're going to have to set up some ground rules because there simply *aren't* any."

Maria nodded. "Some experts are saying that the plastic-fusing technology is not advanced enough to absorb the smallest particles."

Laurel shook her head. "What is going on?" she muttered.

"The nano-particles of plastic, yes. Most of the Great Pacific Garbage Patch is made up of those tiny particles, so in order for Lustro to be successful, they're going to have to suck up quite a lot of nano-particles. But Lustro Corp says they can do it, so it's up to them to prove that they can, now that they have the permit. That's all there is to it, for now."

"Well thank you so much for your time, Dr. Thatcher."

"My pleasure."

"For those of you just joining us, this is a special late-night edition of the National News Bulletin. I'm Maria Gervais. Lustro Corp has just made history by announcing that they plan to engineer a brand-new island—out of plastic. That's right; plastic. Lustro's CEO, Phillip Stern, recently revealed plans to geo-engineer a large portion of the Great Pacific Garbage Patch using a machine they've dubbed the 'Plastic Originator'. Lustro plans to gather about five percent of the plastic in the Great Pacific Garbage Patch and transform the raw material into an island the size of Kauai. Lustro then plans to build a luxury resort on the island, with nightly rates estimated at a range of $1,000 to $10,000 per night."

The picture changed to a digital simulation of the resort. Bungalows, swimming pools, a concert venue, a racetrack, a golf course, a private airport.

"Construction on the island will begin at the end of this month. Many environmentalists are hailing Lustro's plastic-gathering technology as the solution to plastic pollution in our oceans, while others have already begun to criticize Lustro for keeping the 'Plastic Originator' under patent."

Laurel switched her phone to mute. How could they make an island out of plastic? It seemed impossible. Severed arms of Barbie dolls, Ziplock bags still smeared with peanut butter, misplaced buttons fallen from winter coats, bicycle handles smoothed by use, dilapidated shopping bags, scuffed sneakers, half-cracked ice cube trays—and all the tiny, microscopic pieces of plastic, too, all scooped up, broken down, and built up into an actual island? Impossible.

But, then again, the idea of a Mars colony had also once seemed impossible. They called it a suicide mission. In the weeks leading up to the take-off, the news had told the life stories of all the passengers, each of them getting their own five-minute profile at the end of the broadcast; their childhood, where they went to school, the families they were leaving behind, all with the quiet, thoughtful detail usually reserved for the recently deceased.

The launch itself had been during school hours. Laurel's teacher let them watch it on their phones. Laurel had expected the ship to blow up or something, but nothing happened. Back then she hadn't understood that people weren't skeptical about the ship taking off, but about it landing on Mars, and about the long journey over. How would the passengers react, being confined for so long? What if something went wrong? Any one, small thing, and they would be suffocated by the emptiness and density of space.

Two days later, the ship had made it past the moon and outside Earth's gravity. And then months passed, and Laurel had kind of forgotten that there were humans in space at all. Six months later, they landed and sent out robots to build the domes. A second mission joined them two years later with enough supplies to last a decade. The next shuttle was just sent up a month ago. Apparently one of the colonists was pregnant, now, too, and the baby would be the first human born outside of Earth. Space love. Love in space. Maybe that was the future.

Laurel tried to imagine what Mars was like. Of course she'd seen pictures and videos, but she wanted to know what it *felt* like. The red sunlight bleeding onto her skin. The brittle, recycled air circulating in delicate tufts of wind. The thick panes of glass, and her hand, there, against it, feeling the cold—sharp, electric, and uncontrollable.

Her parents joked that California seemed like another planet now, compared to how it was when they were kids. The fields used to be green. The river used to be full all year. She'd seen old pictures of her mom as a teenager, sprawled out on a beach towel with her friends alongside the river, their faces shimmery with sweat and sunscreen. Tall grasses and shrubs grew behind them. That shade of green didn't exist around here anymore.

It hadn't rained for an entire year. Half the businesses in town had closed down, partially because water was too expensive. And there were the shootings. It seemed like there was at least one a month. Nothing big—just random ones in the street, usually in tandem with botched robberies or car-jackings.

Laurel sat up in bed and re-opened the local news. Yes, it had been another shooting, but no word yet on who the two men were. Goosebumps rose on her arms. This was the first time something like this had happened so close to her apartment. Creepy.

In a few hours she left for work. The sun rose through the pale, limp clouds, painting them the color of red-delicious apple skins. Laurel walked slowly. One foot, then the other. The front steps were toothed with triangles of light. No blood on the ground, nothing wrong. But the world felt too still. She could hear the freeway, and the coughs of the city bus from the next block over.

Then she saw it. Down the street, near the laundry center, yellow police tape roped off a square of pavement. So that was where it happened. A woman stood next to it. She wore knee-length shorts and sandals, despite the chilly morning. Laurel had seen her in the laundry facility before; she lived in the complex.

"Morning," the woman said. "Did you hear it, last night?"

"I only heard the police."

"I heard voices, even before that, but no gunshots," she said. "They must have had a silencer on there. But someone heard it. Someone called the police."

"I'm surprised that sort of thing would happen here. This close to us."

"The way things are going—who knows." Laurel nodded.

"Do you carry pepper spray, hun?" the woman asked.

"I used to. It expired."

"Get yourself some more. It's always good to have on hand."

"Yeah. That's smart."

"Good luck, dear. I have to get to work."

"Me too. I'll see you."

Laurel continued on to her car. She couldn't afford the garage, so she had to park by the public charging station, about a half-mile down the street. Her car had more of a chance of getting stolen there, but, hey, that was why she'd bought a cheap used one that was already dented. It was the first and only car she'd ever owned. She'd bought it with the money she saved up in her first year working for Abuelo, which seemed fitting; he was also the one who had taught her how to drive.

When she was fifteen, he took her out to the edge of town, where the air smelled like cow manure. He taught her how to accelerate and decelerate, how to turn and how to slam the brakes quickly, but not too quickly. The wide, empty roads helped Laurel focus on handling the car, and get used to the feeling of driving. She remembered feeling like she was enclosed in a bubble, like the outside of the car was an extension of her body, facing the world for her, protecting her from its dustiness. She remembered it so well.

"Now go forty," Abuelo had said. "Forty miles an hour. *Despacio.*

Slow down a little. *Eso!* Here we go. Now we're cruising, Laurita." He'd turned down the radio. He always listened to *ranchera* music, since that was all they played on the Spanish-language radio stations. He had an old car back then—a blue one that still ran on gas—so it wasn't connected to satellite radio, and it didn't have Bluetooth. The local Spanish radio stations were aimed at Mexicans and their sad, lovesick ballads; so were the Spanish TV stations, and the Chicano newspapers. Mexican accents, Mexican slang, Mexican preferences. Nothing for Salvadorians.

"*Mira.* Now go sixty. On this straight shot here. Press hard with your foot, but little by little, not all at once. It should grow, grow, grow, and then you're going fast. Here we go. *Eso!*"

"When can I try the streets in town, Abuelo?"

"You must train, and then you'll be ready. You are not ready for that battle yet, Laurita." He'd grabbed her shoulder and pointed out the windshield. "This is your first challenge. *Mira,* look at this truck! Now stay calm. Stay in your lane. Here it comes."

She glanced out her side window as it passed. It was a metal truck with narrow, oval windows for the livestock inside. She saw a snout but couldn't tell if it belonged to a pig or a cow. The truck was so enormous it made its own wind, and she could feel its currents pull on Abuelo's car.

"Keep on straight. Keep doing what you're doing. Good. Good! You did it, Laurita! Look at that. Maybe you are ready for the city streets after all."

Part of her hadn't wanted to think of the future, of taking her driving test, getting her license. She'd wanted to keep driving with Abuelo every Sunday, just like that, out on the edge of things, surrounded by beige fields, the air smelly but brisk, the windows open, the *ranchera* music spilling out into the world, its steady bass rumbling through her chest.

Abuelo still had that same car. She imagined it, now, at this very moment, parked inside his garage, engulfed by a darkness that held ladders, cobwebs, plastic tubs of gasoline, and a broken computer monitor. He rarely cleaned his garage—had he ever?—but he wiped down his car with soap and water once a month. Maybe she would go over that weekend and wash his car for him; surprise him. Her mom kept an extra key to his house. Sometimes she stopped by after work and watered his plants; Abuelo was terrible at remembering, and his plants used to crisp up and die before she and Mom started helping out.

One plant, a coffee bush, was a birthday gift from Abuela, something to remind Abuelo of the coffee farm he grew up on. The plant's crisp and rubbery leaves curled at the edges, and in the sun they became a shimmery green that reminded Laurel of pine trees. Abuela told her that, in El Salvador, coffee grew in the mountains and the foothills, high enough where clouds and fog washed through the buttresses and lianas, through the ferns and the orchids and the ancient bromeliads. The plants grew little red coffee berries—Abuela called them "cherries" and Laurel wasn't sure if this was a Spanish/English mishap or if that was actually what they were called. But that's what Abuelo's family had grown, harvested, and sold.

"Do any of Abuelo's relatives still grow coffee?" Laurel once asked Abuela. "Did anyone keep up with it?"

"No. He moved here after the Civil War and you know your Tío Guillermo did too. Your Tía Roberta died in childbirth, and Tío Victor died when he was a little boy. So no one else was there to take over these things."

Laurel was glad she hadn't asked Abuelo about the coffee farm. It must make him sad to think of all his dead siblings. She'd had no idea there had ever been anyone else besides Tío Guillermo. It made sense, now, why her cousin's name was Victor. Tía Sandra named him that in honor of the uncle she never knew.

It seemed like a weird thing for Abuela to do, giving Abuelo a coffee plant. Would he really want to remember how much he'd lost? But Abuelo loved it. He arranged it on a stand in the front hallway, where the light fell in every morning and every afternoon. Abuela warned him that it would not grow cherries, that it would not grow coffee in this climate. It needed the hills and the fog, and the enormous rainstorms, to produce fruit. This little guy was just for show.

Laurel sighed. She wished she could see El Salvador. Just once. Just for a moment. But it was too dangerous.

She continued walking. Everything was still too quiet. Too empty. It gave her goosebumps. At last, she made it to her parking spot.

"Fuck!"

A long, pewter scratch spanned the whole side of the car, along with three ragged initials—RPE.

"Fuck." She looked around. Who would bother? Were they still there? Did they know this was her car, or was it random? What if someone was hiding, waiting to kill her? She tried to look inside, but the windows were fogged with spring dew. After three deep breaths she opened the sweaty door handle. Anyone? No. She crawled over the backseats to make sure they were empty, and then she locked the doors.

The radio turned on to its maximum volume. An early morning radio station playing energetic jazz. She hated jazz—found it too frenzied—but today she kept it on because it drowned out everything else, sort of like a white noise machine, a sheet of tin foil to cover the silent world.

As she drove through Main Street, the buildings loomed grayly on either side of her. The tallest of these buildings—the city government office—was probably only ten stories, but it seemed taller than that, or at least it had when Laurel was a little girl. There was something about its clean, white facade and copper-rimmed windows that had always felt futuristic. Her father used to work there before the lay-offs. Now he was the accountant for a construction company on the other side of town. She wondered if either of her parents were up yet. Had they heard about the shooting?

The saxophone sang. Up, down, ring-ring. It was way too brassy. She tried to listen. Her hands sweated as she waited at the red light. A shooting could happen anywhere. Dismal, empty street corners like this, at five in the morning, through tightly sealed windows—it could happen. In fact, it was *likely*. And what could she do? Her grip tightened. She dug her fingernails into the plastic steering-wheel fabric. What would she do?

On the edge of town, Laurel passed closed-down gas stations, abandoned department stores, 24-hour gun-and-pawn shops, craft microbreweries, and an old movie theater that opened up only on special occasions. This was the beginning of the wastelands—the lower-income suburbs—which were made up of several miles of one-story trailer homes. Most kept their yards pebbled, but some had careful rows of succulents or cacti on display. One house had even managed to grow a circle of dwarf orange trees.

Most everyone in the wastelands worked at the slaughterhouse. Beyond the last of the trailers, the land opened up into fields of dirt and dust. After the gray concrete of the city, it was a relief to see this chalky brown sea, and the blue sky above it. Laurel relaxed a little. No shooters would be hiding out here.

Cattle once roamed these fields. Laurel had seen pictures of them, many thousands of pure-black cows with their heads bent toward the grass. Now the fields were completely out of use, completely barren. When it rained they turned into swamps of mud and revivified cow poop. Big, dark birds with naked heads—vultures?—sometimes landed in the muck and pecked around. They kept their plump feathers spread wide and their wings long, and, without warning, they would take off into the sky with a surprising, lanky gracefulness.

Laurel looked for them but today the fields were empty. Maybe this was what it felt like to be on Mars. The sky and the dirt seemed just as deep as each other. Endless.

Out of this Martian landscape, just ahead, a square monolith appeared over the horizon. The slaughterhouse. It grew larger and squarer as she approached it. The wind picked up, suddenly, and brushed against her car. *Tink, tink, tink, click.* Dust wafted over the windshield. Like insects. Like pollen.

She parked, closed her eyes, and ran into the building. The dust stung her nose. Her teeth felt crusty.

Just inside the entrance, her boyfriend Evan was waiting for her. Maybe it was just her eyes adjusting to the light, but he seemed brighter than usual. His skin shone a healthy olive-tan that made his white shirt look crisp against his neck. Laurel's skin looked like that in summer, if she ever got out in the sun. For now it matched the gold-white inside of an almond.

"Is it windy again?" Evan asked.

"Again, yeah." She kissed him and then pressed her hands against his shoulders. "Weren't you just outside?"

"I got here early. I had that meeting with the heads."

"East coast time? How did it go?"

"Fine, I guess."

"You know how much Abuelo hates them."

"They're not that bad."

Evan kissed her cheek and put his arm around her. They walked slowly toward their offices.

"Did you see the news this morning?" she asked.

"The plastic island thing? How crazy is that? I don't see how the government's okay with it. New countries are going to be springing up all over the place. But as long as they're using plastic, everyone thinks it's fine, that they're doing a good thing—"

"Did you open up the local news?" Laurel asked.

"No."

"Something happened near my apartment."

"Is it your car? I told you the garage would be worth the extra money."

"No." She didn't feel like telling him about the scratches on her car. "Nothing happened to me. It was just a shooting."

"A shooting?"

"Near my place. I don't know what it was about."

He stopped walking. "Laurel, I told you you can move in with me. My part of town is safer. My apartment is safer."

"The east side used to be just as safe. The west will probably be hit next."

"That's why I bought that gun. And the security system. All I'm saying is you should think about it."

"I've been thinking about it."

"And?"

"I'm still thinking." She hugged him. His arms felt heavy on her back. "It's just the logistics, that's all. Your place is small. My place is tiny."

"We can move into a new place."

"More logistics. And isn't there a moratorium? For the water?"

"Not if we're already here. That's for new people."

They began walking again, through the blank, white hallway. Abuelo's voice rose through his closed door. English? Spanish? With his accent, Laurel couldn't tell.

"See you at lunch," Evan said when they got to Laurel's office. "And don't worry. Everything will be fine."

"I'm not worried."

"Everything will be fine," he said. He hugged her again, and then left for his own office down the hall.

Laurel closed the door and opened the blinds. She'd decorated this room herself when she first started. Her eighteen-year-old self had loved the bright blue walls, the framed vintage world map, the flower-patterned armchair that she'd found at a yard sale. Now it all felt a bit garish, and far too celebratory for a slaughterhouse. Within the next twelve hours, hundreds of cows would die right there, beyond those walls.

Laurel remembered the first time she ever saw the inside of the slaughterhouse. She was in middle school and her little sister, Paloma, was in elementary school. Abuelo owned the place back then. They'd been inside the front entrance, of course, and they'd seen Abuelo's office, but they'd never seen the inner workings.

It was a long summer day. They wanted an adventure, so they rode across town through the sun and the summer heat, and stashed their bikes in the empty lot next door. The entrance where the deliveries came in was wide open, and they sidled into the cool darkness, hoping to pop up behind Abuelo and surprise him. He'd long told them that it was an important job, but too dangerous for kids, and too bloody. That ignited a deep curiosity within them. They had to see it; they *had* to.

It smelled like an old garage, musty and wood-like, and just barely rotten. Their eyes adjusted to the dim light. Laurel discovered a red-orange slop of poop on the cement floor, and then another. The deeper they wandered in, the more it began to smell like animals. A plastic flap served as a door, and through the little clear window they could see steam, and cracks of light on the sides. They could hear a squealing, a high-pitched reverberating, men's voices. Laurel suddenly felt that they should not be there. She glanced at Paloma and saw the same feeling in her eyes, that crease above her nose that also appeared when they played with their Ouija board and she pretended not to be afraid of ghosts. They ran outside. The sunlight warmed their shoulders. Laurel was about to say that they should get their bikes when they heard Spanish voices. Around the corner came a man pushing a metal bin; a dumpster. Inside it were noses, ears, closed eyes, open eyes, plush pink tongues, snouts, necks gaping in blood.

"What are you kids doing here?" the man asked, his white jumpsuit somehow still white; bleach-clean.

"What is that?" Laurel asked.

"This, in here?" He waited stupidly for Laurel to nod. "This is what's left over after those steaks and hamburgers your parents buy. The heads. The insides."

Paloma ran first, and Laurel followed her. They hopped on their bikes as fast as possible and whirled home with sweat on their backs, somewhat terrified and also exhilarated, like characters in a movie one step closer to solving a mystery.

CHAPTER TWO
PALOMA

PALOMA SLOWED HER GAIT. She held her breath and listened to the meadow. The wind in the grass followed a rhythm—long, short, long, short. She closed her eyes. The sun picked at her forehead, right along her hairline. A single bird clicked in the bushes. *Chick-chick.* Or maybe it was a cricket.

Somehow Paloma was the only one on this trail. She continued walking with her eyes closed, listening for the crunch of her shoes against the gravel. The wind picked up, so she walked faster. Long, short, long, long, long, fast, fast, fast, a great gust at her back, on her bare shoulders.

What was she going to do? Part of her didn't want to go to medical school anymore. Her biggest role as a doctor would be to prescribe pills. At one point she'd thought she would be different, that she would be the one to change the system, but now she realized that that would be almost impossible. Why? Because she wouldn't learn how. Medical school would teach her about symptoms and pills. She would be in debt for years. She would have to take whatever position paid her the most money, and everyone knew that the only doctors who made good money were those who made deals with pharmaceutical companies.

But she'd already accepted her scholarship. And what else would she do with her biology degree? This had always been the plan. Graduation was in one week. Then she would go home for the summer, and then she would go to medical school in Washington. There was no use thinking about it. She told her thoughts to be quiet. She told them to shut up. Long, long, fast, fast. Her breath joined the wind. She went back to running.

When she got back to her apartment, her roommate, Kara, was sprawled on the couch, watching the news on her phone. "Paloma, did you hear about this?" she said.

"Depends what it is." Paloma knelt on the carpet and took off her shoes.

Kara sat up. "This whole island thing. Lustro is making a new island out of plastic."

"That can't be real."

"It is! Look." She handed Paloma her phone. "There's a print article about it too. Scroll down."

"Brave New World: How Lustro is Revolutionizing the Real Estate Game? Seriously?"

"Apparently they're using the plastic in the Great Pacific Garbage Patch."

"Well that's better than the whole thing where they were going to throw all our trash into space. Remember that?"

"Yeah, that was stupid."

Paloma skimmed through the article. "It says they're already shipping in workers. What do you bet they're either Asian or Latino?"

"Asian, probably. They're closer."

"Depends what's cheaper. Who's cheaper. With all the issues in Latin America these days, people are desperate for jobs."

"True. Your people." Kara laughed.

Her people. Honestly, Paloma didn't feel like they were her people. She felt more Anglo than Latina. But, still, she was asked all the time—"What are you?" And when she was younger she would answer, "Human," and they would roll their eyes and say,

"You know what I mean." Then she would feel pressured into answering them. "I'm half El Salvadorian. My grandparents are from there." And the other half? "My dad's side of the family is white. He's from here." This satisfied most of them. She was half Hispanic and half white and they could see it now, in the curve of her eyes and the warm glow of her skin. Others squinted at her, looked and looked but couldn't see it. "You must take after your dad, then," they would say, although if they ever saw a picture of her dad they would realize how wrong they were.

She'd inherited just two traits from her father—lighter skin—well, lighter than her mother's but not as light as his—and his nose, sloped up slightly at the tip, either delicate or pig-like depending on the angle. In every other trait she saw reflections of her mother. Her wide, horizontal cheekbones. Her small forehead. Her wide, half-triangle jawline. This was not the face of someone with one hundred percent European ancestry. Like most Latinos, there was probably some indigenous stuff going on in there, but no one knew how much or how far back it was. Oddly, her mother had blue eyes, bright blue like melted glaciers.

Eye color was something else Paloma got from her dad, or maybe from farther back on her mom's side. Abuelo and Abuela both had brown eyes, but theirs were darker than hers; she had light brown eyes, almost hazel, lighter than even her father's eyes. Laurel's eyes looked just like their father's.

"Would any of your relatives go to work on the island?" Kara asked.

Paloma laughed. "I only have one relative left in El Salvador. Everyone else moved a long time ago."

"Is it true that the gangs down there have vaporizing guns?"

"How would I know that?"

"Your aunt or whoever. I don't know."

"We don't talk to her that much. And she's my great-aunt."

"But you said you've been there."

"No I didn't. I've never been there, and neither has Laurel. It's too dangerous. I've just heard stories, but I'm sure it's changed a lot now."

"Yeah. The whole world's changing. And yet we just keep going. Living our lives like nothing's changed."

"See, your philosophy degree is already coming in handy."

"That's the only thing it's good for. Thinking. Wallowing about the state of the world," she said. "I'm going to be one hell of a professor. Kids, let's wallow together."

Paloma laughed again. Kara had been her roommate for the past three years, and they'd had a lot of conversations like this.

"You're right, though," Paloma said. "Just look at all the people out there who still have gasoline cars, all the people who still eat seafood. Pretending like they can keep doing stuff like that with no consequences." She handed Kara's phone back to her and stretched out on the carpet.

"Do you know it hasn't rained in two months?" Kara said.

"It hasn't been that long, has it?"

"It has. And it's only May. Usually the drought doesn't start until July."

"It's still better than at home in California. If we got half as much rain as Oregon—"

"It's always been dry there, though."

"Not the part where I'm from. There used to be rain sometimes. Now it's completely brown."

"Yeah, at least Oregon's still green," Kara said.

"For now."

"Browner. Drier. Deader. This is why I'm not having kids," Kara said. "Ever. What is there to look forward to?"

Paloma agreed that it didn't make much sense to bring a child into a dying, overpopulated world. Half the Earth was already undernourished or starving. If her parents wanted a grandkid, Laurel would have to be the one to do it. Paloma would just be an aunt.

"All those kids starving out there—no way am I having my own kids," Paloma said. "Plus we'll get the subsidies for it. The childless subsidies." Or maybe she would adopt. Someday, far in the future, when she was settled in her job.

"You know what you should do?" Kara said. "That Doctors Without Borders thing. You could go to Africa. You could help all those sick kids—"

"In six years? Will anyone still be living in Africa in six years?"

"Just be a whiz kid and get through medical school extra fast."

"I don't even know if I can get through it at regular speed."

"Oh, come on."

"I just—I don't know."

Kara stood up and stretched her arms above her head. "Maybe you're just nervous about graduating. Everything's going to change."

"Yeah. All those loans. All that debt. All that homework."

"See, you're just burnt out. You'll feel better once it's summer and you can have a break."

"Maybe."

Kara wandered into the kitchen. Paloma stayed on the floor. She laid so still that the motion-sensing lights turned off.

"Hey," Kara yelled from the other room. "Sam and I were thinking of going out tonight. You in?"

"I don't know."

"Come on. We don't have much time left."

"I need to study."

Kara popped her head back in. "You need a break."

"I do?"

"Yes."

"Okay. If you insist."

"Yes! Bailey and Chris are in, too."

"We should do the Ouija board again."

Kara laughed. She had a clear, musical laugh, probably because she did choir all through high school. "Oh no. I'm glad I missed your last seance."

Back during freshman year, Bailey, Chris, Sam, and Paloma had snuck into Portsman Hall just before it closed for the night, and they scrambled down to the bottom floor where there were no windows. With the room lit only by their phones and a dusty old candle from Chris's parents' house, they knelt around the Ouija board and drank cheap, warm beers.

"Dear spirits, awaken!" Bailey had said. Everyone laughed. She smiled and placed Paloma's fingers on the plastic indicator.

"Why do I have to do it?"

Bailey shook her head. "The spirits requested it. We'll take turns. Ghosts, we know you are in here! We've heard the stories. Please talk to us." Again, laughter, caught up, small and round, swirling over them.

"Please like us!" Sam yelled.

"Shh, you guys."

"It's moving!"

Paloma had always been afraid of Ouija boards. Abuela always warned her against them—she said not to mess with *los espiritús* because you didn't know if you'd get good ones or bad ones. Paloma wasn't sure what this one was, but her arms shivered with goosebumps.

"You're not moving it, are you? You swear you're not moving it?"

"I swear!" Bailey said. "I'm barely touching it."

The planchette dragged itself among the letters. It swirled, swung erratically, and then settled on a D. Paloma felt a tingling in her fingertips. She felt like someone was just above her, their invisible hands wrapped around her wrists, guiding her to the E, the A, and the D.

Paloma drew her hand back. "Dead?"

"You ruined it! It might've said something else."

"Aren't you guys creeped out?"

"Wait, wait, wait, try it again. There might've been something else."

But that was it; it didn't move again. Chris tried it, Sam tried it, but the spirits had nothing else to say.

"There's got to be more than one ghost in here," Bailey said "It's been around since the 1800s."

"That's all there is, I guess. That's all they have to say. Dead," Paloma said. "Done." Then, out of the corner of her eye, she saw the indicator move on its own, just slightly. Her muscles ran without her even thinking about it, and she bolted from the building. She waited outside on the dry grass, her hands on her thighs, her muscles still tensed, her breath hard.

Everyone else followed her.

"Paloma, what happened?" they asked.

"You didn't see that?"

"What?"

"That thing moved on its own!"

"No it didn't."

"Was anyone touching it when I was talking?"

No one answered.

"I swear it moved," Paloma said. "I swear."

They didn't believe her. They thought she was messing with them. Abuela would've believed her. She wondered if Abuela was a ghost now—a spirit who reached her delicate hands through Ouija boards. It had been six years now since Abuela passed away. It wasn't even old age but a car accident that killed her. Driving to the grocery store to buy rice for dinner. Missed a red light, straight on through, and immediate death. Knowing that she'd died instantly was supposed to be comforting, but it wasn't. Abuela hadn't even had time to realize that she was dying. She was just here, and then gone.

Ever since then, Paloma couldn't help but think of the Ouija board when she went to bio lab in Portsman Hall. Sometimes she heard a ticking on the ceiling. Their class was on the top floor. It could've been a squirrel or a bird or something, but it sounded too metallic, and too otherworldly, whatever that meant. She tried not to be afraid because Abuela had also told her that one should be more afraid of the living than the dead.

Paloma finally got up from the floor to start getting ready. She took her usual five-minute shower. The water shut off automatically when time was up. It had taken her a while to get used to it, but she could now wash her long, black hair in time to rinse out the conditioner. All the apartments around here had timers—on the lights, the water, the stove, even the front door so the air conditioning and heater wouldn't have to work so hard.

This was the kind of thing they needed at home, but nobody had enough money in Terrysville. Or, if they did, they wouldn't waste it on something so efficient. Some of the few rich families there even still had hot tubs.

When she got out of the shower, she checked her phone. Kara had sent her a text from the next room. *Bailey wants to know if we want to leave early and grab some dinner?*

Dinner sounds good, Paloma replied.

She'll meet us there.

'There' meant The Yard House, the vegan restaurant near campus. Kara and Paloma headed out, walking along the usual side street, past the frat houses and the abandoned gas station/car repair place. Today, an old man in a brown, corduroy jacket sat on what used to be the parking lot. No chair, no blanket, no cardboard, just his bottom on the cement.

"There's always someone there," Kara said quietly. "Have you noticed? It's always someone different."

"Homeless, probably."

"But there's only ever one person there at a time."

"I saw a couple there once—"

"The old couple with the matching sunglasses?"

"You've seen them too?"

"Downtown, by the bus station," Kara said. "I think that's where they live. They're kind of famous. I've even seen people take pictures of them."

"Someone should help them instead of taking their picture."

"Well you know someone gave them those sunglasses," Kara said.

"True."

"And they are pretty cute together."

"Oh yeah, homelessness is pretty cute," Paloma said.

"Sometimes."

"What kind of philosopher are you?"

"Hey, I have the unpopular opinion here," Kara said. "I don't think there's anything wrong with being homeless. We're all homeless, in a way."

"Yeah, okay. We need to get you a drink."

"Yes. Get me a drink stat, Doctor Paloma."

They walked past the row of houses with crumbling front porches; past the old fire station that was now a pot dispensary; past the 24-Hour-Diner where they sometimes got pie after the bars.

The road opened up into a four-lane highway. Countless cars wheezed by. It was easy to tell which ones were electric; they cruised along steadily, muffled and silent like the shooting stars Paloma had seen on camping trips—powerful, fast, and perfectly quiet. Paloma remembered when she was a little girl and most of the cars were gasoline. The roads roared, back then. Now it was mostly electric, at least in Oregon. In Terrysville, it was about half and half.

"What's going on over there?" Kara pointed down the road. At least thirty people were clustered in front of the discount supermarket. They chanted something rhythmic—was it a protest?

As they got closer, it became clear that the chanting wasn't rhythmic at all. It was many voices, stacked together at different pitches; a wave of polyphony.

Paloma picked out some of the comments:

"They can't expect us to take the bus across town. Not with bags."

"What if it's not just this one?"

"They better be open tomorrow."

"—pills for Michaela. Why didn't they leave the pharmacy open?"

A woman—overdressed in a puffy winter coat—folded her two young boys into a hug. A gray-haired man held up his phone and filmed the crowd. Paloma stepped in closer. The heat of the crowd rested gently on her skin. Someone smelled like citrusy perfume. Someone else smelled skunky, like weed. A neatly typed sign hung on the door: *We Are Closed Due To Shipment Delay. Will Reopen At 9 AM.*

"The news says it was open all morning," Kara said, her face turned to her phone. "Then they shoved everyone out about an hour ago."

"What about the other stores in town?"

"Everything's closed. I think only Lustro-Mart is open. How did I not see this on the news earlier?"

"Do you think the restaurant's open?"

"Let's go see." They continued down the street and around the corner. The windows were lit up and, near the front door, a little chalkboard listed the daily specials.

"Yep, it's open."

"Must be the benefit of using local food," Kara said.

"Hey guys!" Bailey waved at them from the front entrance. "I already got a table."

As they ate, they talked about the island, and about the pregnant lady on Mars, and about graduation. By the time they finished, the crowd in front of the market had dissipated, and the cars on the highway had thinned. They started the walk back to the apartment. Paloma pointed out the moon, but Bailey and Kara didn't see it. They glanced at the sky and then continued to talk about their dinner, how good the salad dressing was, how they'd miss the extra-crispy sweet potato fries. Paloma tuned them out for a moment. She watched the moonlight fall over the street. It seemed whiter than usual. Translucent, even. It seemed like she could break it if she wanted to. Like the moon was meek and threatened—like it was dying.

Back at the apartment, they pre-gamed before the bars. They took tequila shots and waited only ten minutes before taking another. Paloma usually didn't drink very much. How could she, when the negative health effects were always on her mind? Slowed metabolism, oilier skin, impaired detoxification, dehydration, moodiness—not to mention the headache, stomachache, and dizziness of a hangover. She usually had one or two drinks and left it at that, and in the morning she cleaned out her system with warm lemon water. But tonight she needed more than one or two drinks. She needed cloudiness; she needed the warmth of alcohol in her chest; she needed something to shield her from the future, something to slow things down and ease her mind, even if just for one night.

CHAPTER THREE
LAUREL

AUREL STARED AT HER LAPTOP SCREEN. When
did all the lettering get so small? Were her eyes going bad? Did
she have that rapid aging thing, where at 27 her body was actually 47? Or had a lifetime of staring at a computer finally worn
out her eyes? She sifted through her desk drawer and pulled out
her virtual reality glasses. The screen popped to life. Words ran
down the length of the wall. Her father had given her the VR set
last Christmas. She still wasn't used to it. The computer images
became 3D and life-size—bigger than life-size—and everything
else was tinted brownish-gray, like sunglasses.

She googled the plastic island. A tropical logo beamed onto the
wall. Lustro had named it Blue Mar. Apparently they'd already
sucked up all the plastic in their machine and were just about
to begin the island-morphing process next Monday. A video of
the plastic-sucking machine popped up. It was black and round,
and it floated like an enormous egg on the greenish water. Its

concave walls rattled as the machine filtered microscopic plastic from the ocean. How did it not suck up fish, and plankton, and all the little bacteria things living in the ocean? Laurel googled this question. A quote from a news article popped up.

"This is genius technology. It can detect, on a molecular level, the difference between plastic and everything else. Its sensors pick out plastic, and everything good is left alone."

That was Lustro's director. He was everywhere, it seemed. Friends with the president. Friends with famous actors like Tara Sanchez and Spence Herald.

"Our scientists are excited to share this discovery with the world."

Laurel opened up a picture of the resort. Everything was going to be painted turquoise, with big, white-rimmed windows looking out to the sea. The beaches would be plumped with real sand, and four lake-sized swimming pools would be filled with chemical-free saltwater. White cotton sheets. Flowing curtains. Green walls threaded with orchids and succulents. Fountains on each balcony. Beachside massages. Frozen drinks delivered by drone. What would it be like to afford a vacation like that? Blue Mar. Even the name was beautiful.

And what would it be like to get there first? To be the first person on that island? The first person on new land? Her footsteps against the hollow, fragile ground, on a drop of plastic in the center of the ocean?

Laurel jumped as someone knocked on her door.

"Yes?" She took off the VR glasses.

Abuelo stepped in. "You finish the shipment accounts, Laurita?"

"No. Almost."

"And the report. I sent you the email."

"Yeah, I got it." She closed her laptop and folded her arms on the desk.

"*Qué te pasa?*"

"Nothing. I was just taking a break." She rocked back and forth in her chair. "You've heard of this island thing, right?"

"*Claro que sí.*"

"What do you think of it?"

"I think it's a scam."

"A scam?"

"Islands cannot be built in the ocean. From *pedacitos de plástico?* No. They'll take your money and send you to some island that's already been there. They just want people to pay more to think they're on a new island."

"There's pictures, though. And videos."

"That doesn't mean they're real."

"What about Mars? Do you think that's real?"

"Maybe."

"But you've only seen pictures."

"Maybe, maybe—it's all a maybe. Everything." Abuelo laughed, a small chuckle that turned into a cough.

"You still have that cold?"

Abuelo waved his hand. "It's fine. Every day I drink tea and *jugo de naranja.*"

"Maybe you should take a day off. Rest a little."

His dark eyes looked flat, like they'd fallen deeper into his skull, and the blue-green veins on his forehead stood out.

"I haven't taken a day off in—"

"Ten years." She smiled. "That doesn't mean you can't now. You've had this cold for a few weeks now."

"I'll take a day off when I retire."

"Abuelo—"

"You can't just leave things, Laurita. Remember that when you take over. You can't leave things for others to do, not even the small things; you have to do it all yourself, all your duties—you have to supervise; you have to make sure things are done the right way. We are dealing with lives, here. We are dealing with worker safety, and *vacas*, too. The big people up there, they don't care as much."

Laurel nodded. How many times had she heard this same speech?

"And you are strong enough to do it. You know that, Laurita? You're strong enough to do things the right way."

"*Gracias*, Abuelo."

"But, I'm telling you, you need to work on your Spanish. *Todos los Mexicanos* in there will trust you better if you speak to them in *español*."

"I just said *gracias*!"

"You say it like a *gringa*. The 'r' is short. It's with the tongue on the top of the mouth."

"*Gracias?*"

"*Eso!* That's it."

"When are we going to do another Spanish lesson? A real one?"

"Whenever you want, Laurita. *Sábado?*"

"Okay. Yeah, *Sábado* afternoon."

"*Qué bueno.* And, listen, I don't think those books are helping. Watch a *novela*; remember what your abuela used to tell you— the more you hear the words, the more you remember them."

"But all the new *telenovelas* are so bad!"

"Hey, blame it on your mamá. If she had taught you as a little girl, you wouldn't have to learn now, eh?" He shook his head. "I told her to. *Cuántas veces.* Speak to the *cipotes* in Spanish, I said. It's a good skill to have."

Passing the language on had never been important to Laurel's mom; she wasn't against them learning, but she hadn't cared enough to make sure they did. There were a few words here and there—*noches, gracias, leche, feliz navidad, que te vaya bien*—that she had always used, but otherwise, the only Spanish Laurel heard was from Abuelo and Abuela. All her life Laurel had wanted to speak with them in bright, rolling Spanish, ever since she was a little girl.

Abuelo smiled. "You'll get it, Laurita. I have faith in you. You've been hearing this language since the day you were born." He tapped his forehead. "It's all in there."

Laurel hoped this was true. She smiled back.

"*Vamos.* Back to work, Laurita."

"Back to work," Laurel said, but she didn't, he couldn't, not with so much on her mind. She put the glasses on again. Blue Mar. Blue Mar. Blue Mar. For some reason, when she thought of them, out there, right now, building up the naked beginnings of the island, she imagined an empty field no bigger than the slaughterhouse. She imagined it to be silver, like a sheet of concrete, and so polished that the clouds reflected off of it. In her mind it was uninhabited, windswept, alien. In a way it was beautiful, but also terrifying. Absolutely empty. Pristine, untarnished by time and history, devoid of rock layers, and dirt, and footsteps. A piece of land made by humans yet free from human influence, out there at the edge of the world, thousands of miles from everything, where the waves sang of movement and silence.

*   *   *   *   *

That night, the mice re-emerged in Laurel's apartment. Just a month ago she'd given a quarter of her paycheck to the exterminators. A month ago! And now the mice had returned to their usual places. One lived in a crack in the bathroom wall. Another scuttled under her bed from time to time, its claws scraping like knives against the tile floor. One squeaked gently from behind the refrigerator. Laurel huddled in bed. At least the mice never came up onto the furniture; they were pretty polite, in that regard.

When her parents were young—and even when Laurel herself was younger—rats and mice weren't a big issue. They'd only become a problem in the last five years or so. That's when the whole thing with rodent-borne diseases started getting worse, too. Hantavirus, Tularemia, Plague, and all those other diseases that she couldn't even pronounce. For a while the local news reported new outbreaks, almost every day, it seemed, and then it settled down a little, probably because all the exterminating companies moved to town. They were one of the only businesses that were thriving.

Her phone vibrated. Evan.

"Hello?" she said, and the phone awoke to speaker mode.

"Hey, babe."

"Hey."

"What are you up to tonight?"

"Trying not to get attacked by mice."

"Are they back?"

"Yep."

"Already?"

"But not as bad this time. Well—not yet, at least."

"Why don't you come over?" Evan said. "I just ordered pizza and beer."

"It's already dark out. I don't want to walk to my car."

"I can pick you up."

"You might as well just hang out here, then."

"But my place is rat-free."

"Good point," Laurel said.

"I'll be there in ten to pick you up."

They drove through the empty streets. The last of sunset lingered at the zenith, a blob of hollow, orange dust against the gray night. Sunsets had always made Laurel sad, in a nostalgic, heavy sort of way. She wasn't sure why.

"Has the sky been looking hazier to you?" she asked Evan.

"Probably. Think about it—all those cow farts are blowing over from the slaughterhouse."

Laurel sighed. "I'm serious. Look at this place. Look at all this trash people have been dumping on the corners, too."

"It could be more wildfires down south, too," Evan said. "It did smell a little smoky today."

He parked in the garage and they started up the elevators. Evan was lucky enough to live in a Smart apartment, the kind with automatic appliances, a self-cleaning kitchen, a laundry-folder, and speakers inside the walls—soundproof to everyone else in the complex, but concert-worthy for the two of them. Evan's grandparents died a few years back, and they left him with enough money to buy a new car, pay off his student loans, and afford this rent for a while—well, until last week. Now he would finally have to live off of just his salary.

They sat on the soft, leather couch. Evan put his arm around her. "See, my apartment would fit the two of us just fine," he said. "Clean. Modern. Ratless."

"And expensive."

"Not with two people paying the rent."

She rested her head on his shoulder. "Maybe. Maybe." She wasn't sure what was holding her back. It seemed like such a big step to move in with Evan. They'd been dating for almost a year, but she wasn't in love with him yet. Almost, but—no, not yet. "You know what Abuelo would think of us if we moved in together?" she said.

"He'd be good with it, right? It's *me*."

"My parents would be good with it. But Abuelo would give you the eye. He wouldn't say anything, but he'd be weird about it."

Evan stayed silent. He breathed slowly, deeply. Laurel realized she'd been clenching the muscles in her shoulders for hours—for days, maybe. She tried to relax. She tried to concentrate on the warmth of Evan's body, and the dimmed lights, and the kind, yellow glow of the room. The pizza and beer arrived. Evan called for the door to open. The drone flew in, dropped the box on the coffee table, and snapped their picture to make sure they were old enough to drink alcohol.

"Mm, smells good," Evan said. Half pepperoni, half sausage. Laurel ate her pizza crust-first. She'd always liked the crust the best. She preferred bready foods in general—pasta, bread, bagels, tortillas. She'd never been a big meat eater, probably because of the slaughterhouse. It wasn't that meat scared her. She'd made peace with what meat was, and where it came from, and she believed that anyone who ate meat should come to terms with the reality of it. But sometimes the smell got to her. After enough trips to the slaughterhouse's inner helm, the place where the cattle were killed and cleaned, even cooked meat started to smell sharp, acidic, bloody. And any leftover meat that got thrown away was not just leftover food, but rotting flesh, there, in the trash can. She could easily horrify herself if she thought about that stuff for too long.

Evan grabbed his second slice.

"Do you ever wonder how we ended up here?" Laurel asked, suddenly.

Evan wiped his mouth with the back of his hand. He finished chewing. "What do you mean?"

"Working at a slaughterhouse. In this half-ass town where people get murdered all the time. Eating pizza on your electronic couch."

"This is our fate. The way things were always meant to be."

"Right." She gently shoved his arm. "I'm serious. Don't you ever wonder if this is—it?"

"It? Like, the end?"

"No, like if this is all there is?"

"Not really." He swallowed another bite. "Not when things are good." He clicked open a can of beer and handed it to her. "Cheers."

"*Salud.*"

"Nice little accent, there. *Salud.*"

Laurel's cheeks grew hot. She hated it when he made fun of her like that. He'd told her before—many times, in fact—that he didn't think of her as Latina. She didn't blame him; being half-Salvadorian didn't mean anything when you had dull-white skin and thin brown hair the color of mouse fur. It wasn't enough. And it wasn't just Evan; no one saw her as Latina, no one except Abuelo. Maybe if she learned Spanish, she would be able to claim her identity a little more comfortably, but probably not even then. She didn't look how she was supposed to. She was a white-passing woman with a *mestizo* family. That was all there was to it.

Evan opened two more beers. Laurel would be sleeping over. She'd brought extra clothes and a toothbrush with her. Evan would drive them both to the slaughterhouse in the morning.

The next day, at dawn, as she saw the slaughterhouse rise from the fields, as she smelled the musky odor of cows and the wide-open, dust-soaked wind, Laurel sighed. Working there had been the easy choice, a guaranteed job right out of high school, and it had made Abuelo happy. At the time it seemed like a good idea. Weird, yes, but also edgy. She was facing the reality of omnivory, working in a male-dominated field, and, as Abuelo told her on her first day, she would someday take over for him and be the manager. He'd never expected to pass it down, but he was glad to do so. Ecstatic. How could she ever leave now?

Evan parked carefully in his spot near the slaughterhouse entrance. They'd hardly spoken the whole ride over. Laurel cleared her throat.

"Don't let Abuelo know I slept over at your place," she said.

"What am I going to say, 'Hey Ramon, guess who slept over at my apartment last night'?" He opened the car door. Chilly morning air rushed in.

"You only gave me a ride over here, okay?"

"You're a grown woman, Laurel. And he knows we're together. He probably has an idea of what goes on."

"He's just super old-fashioned. He would be weird about it."

"Sure. I mean he *is* from the last millennium." He grabbed her hand, brought it to his mouth and kissed it. "You know, I can be old-fashioned, too. In a whole different way."

"Evan."

He dropped her hand. "Don't worry, I won't say anything."

Inside, the hallways smelled like bleach. The floors shined a perfect, stainless, ivory-white, illuminated by the overhead lights; a tundra of ice and snow. Evan headed straight to his office, but Laurel peeked her head through Abuelo's doorway.

"*Buenos días,*" she called.

"*Buenos días, Laurita, cómo amaneciste?*"

"*Bien, y usted?*"

"*Muy bien.*" Abuelo didn't look like he'd slept well at all; his skin looked pale, almost gray, and the dark circles under his eyes had darkened to a purple like red wine. Overnight, it seemed, the tufts of black hair around his forehead had palled to gray-white. Only a few stray, black hairs framed his upper lip and his chin.

She wanted to say something, but what was there to say? You look terrible? Abuelo coughed. The sound rose up from deep in his chest. He held a tissue to his mouth.

"Abuelo, you should be home."

"No, no, I'm fine. It's just a cough."

"Well at least go to the doctor this weekend. Get it checked out."

The cough resurfaced. Abuelo's shoulders shook. He buried his face back into the tissue and waved at her to go into her office.

"I'm serious," Laurel said, and she left the room.

In her office, Laurel searched for Blue Mar. A new video popped up; the plastic-gathering machine at work again. It turned out that they needed even more plastic, and there was still plenty left in the ocean. This would have been somewhat boring—somewhat repetitive—if it hadn't been for the sky; behind the egg-like machine, above the agitated waves, the sky furled into a nest of magnificent storm clouds. She had never seen clouds so mesmerizing. In Terrysville, the clouds were distant, insubstantial, annoying wisps. At best, they formed a bleak, dense sheet over the sky. But the clouds in the video—they hung low, heavy and ever-shifting. In their bellies they held grays and indigos and purples and even a sickly yellow that was somehow just as beautiful as clear blue sky. Laurel imagined the wind coming off these clouds. The smell, like soil after rain; the wild spray of water rising from the waves, how it would splash against her face, how she would squint into it and let her hair flow behind her like a kite, how, in the freeness of space, her arms would open wide, outstretched, as big as the sea—

Her door opened. "Laurita, I need to talk with you." Abuelo marched in, holding his morning mug of peppermint tea. He closed the door behind him.

"You can sit down, Abuelo." She pointed to the flower-patterned chair.

"No, I'll stand." He sipped his tea. "Laurita, do you remember what I told you about the new shipments?"

"The new shipments?"

"The new breed of cattle we have coming in?"

"They're coming from Ohio, right?"

"No, not those. The—" Abuelo coughed deeply. "The ones with the new genes."

"I don't think you told me about that. You mean they're genetically modified?"

"That's what the company wants to do. It's cheap. You get more for each cow."

"Well, you can't pick and choose whose cows you process, anymore. If they bring GMO cows in, that's not any reflection on you, or us."

"I am not going to allow those cows in here, Laurita. If I do, we'll only have GMO cows from now on. What I let in here is what I support, and those cows are not real cows. They have the DNA of all different animals. They're like DNA quilts. A little bit of strawberry, a little bit of fish, a little bit of monkey."

"It's better than lab-grown meat, though."

"It's not natural. These people are pretending they are gods. They don't know what they're doing."

"What are you going to tell the company?"

"That I've made up my mind. There are still people out there who want real cows."

Laurel nodded. She hoped that the company wouldn't fire him—or her.

"I want you to come with me to the meeting," Abuelo said.

"It's in person?"

"Two weeks from now, at their headquarters."

"It's that big a deal?"

"Yes. To me and to them, yes."

Laurel folded and unfolded the VR glasses. "We could market ourselves differently," she said. "As a facility that only processes non-GMO, organic cows."

"*Eso.* They might like that. The organic ones will pay more."

"And local—we could help the distributors make connections with local restaurants and stuff. So they can market it as a local product and get more for it."

"That's how it was when I first began. It was for the local farmers, for their cows. It was all local, everything. I never thought we would get to this point. This big." Abuelo coughed again. Some of his tea sloshed over the side of the mug. "*Gracias,* Laurita. Keep thinking." He continued to cough, out the door and down the hallway. Then—a plunk, a thud, and the crash of shattered glass. Laurel jumped up and ran into the hallway.

"Abuelo?"

He lay heavily on the tile floor, his face turned down, his arms splayed on either side of him like wings. Shards of the mug had sprayed down the hall, along with a dark rain of tea. Laurel gently rolled Abuelo to his back. His eyes remained closed. A red gash bled from his chin. She placed her fingers on his neck to feel his pulse. Was it there? She couldn't tell. Maybe that wasn't the right spot.

"Abuelo? Can you hear me?"

Nothing.

She ran back into her office, grabbed her phone, and called an ambulance. Where was Evan? Where was *anyone?* She ran back out. She held Abuelo's hand. It felt both cold and hot. Or maybe that was her own skin. Her entire body had thickened and numbed. She felt as though clay had solidified over her muscles. Panic, most likely. Fear.

"Evan!" she yelled into the silence. "Evan!"

She hovered her pal in front of Abuelo's mouth to see if he was breathing, but she couldn't tell.

One of the workers rounded the corner and rushed toward her. It was a young Mexican man whose name she'd forgotten. She recognized his face, though—his small, elongated eyes, and his thick, black eyebrows that joined together above his nose. Abuelo had introduced her to all the workers at one point or another.

"*Qué pasó?*" He knelt at her side. He said something else in Spanish. Too fast, too accented, too strung-together, each word rolling from one to the next.

"*Él está enfermo*," Laurel said.

He responded in fast-flying Spanish. She recognized the word *ambulancia*.

"*Sí, sí.*" She pointed to herself and to her phone. "*Teléfono.*"

Just then, two paramedics jogged in. A self-wheeling stretcher followed closely behind them, and they piled Abuelo onto it, his body limp, fish-like.

"Is he going to be okay?" Laurel asked. Her voice sounded deep, and distant.

"We'll get him in," one of them said—a woman with red hair tied back in a bun. "And we'll do all we can for him, okay?"

"You can ride in the ambulance with us or you can follow in your own vehicle," the other—a blonde man with a closely trimmed beard—said.

The stretcher powered forward, and the paramedics began to jog again. Laurel matched their pace. "But is he going to be okay?"

"Hopefully," the blonde man said, his voice jumpy with movement.

Laurel felt like she was about to cry. She glanced back.

The worker stood there, hunched, small. *"Voy a rezar por él,"* he called after her. By some miracle Laurel understood; *I'll pray for him.*

At the hospital, Laurel called her parents and then sat in the waiting area. She didn't know what the doctors were doing with Abuelo, or what was wrong with him. Had he tripped? Was it a heart attack? Something related to his cough?

For some reason, a memory popped into Laurel's head. She thought about a day in elementary school, so long ago, when the teacher brought in animal organs as part of an anatomy lesson. She wasn't sure how the teacher arranged it, or where the organs came from, but she remembered that she'd had to bring in a signed permission slip to participate in the lesson. Parent volunteers stood at different stations, different desks, and pointed things out with gloved hands. A cow liver. A pig heart. A pile of whole fish that could be dissected and slit open with pairs of scissors, with a sharpie line drawn on each belly to show the students where to cut. At each station there was a bed of newspaper. Most of the organs didn't faze her. The liver was purple-sheened and pillowy. The heart looked a lot like a boneless skinless chicken thigh, at least until the mom volunteer cut it in half, revealing the spindly, wiry, stalactite center.

The big draw of the day was the finale; as promised, a real-life doctor walked in with a plastic cooler. Everyone was called into a line and then, one by one, they were allowed to see what was in the cooler—a human brain. They were allowed to look closely, but not to touch it. The doctor stood, smiling, in her slacks and latex gloves, holding the brain on either side, like a melon, and turning it over so the kids could see the brainstem and the cerebellum. Laurel would never forget the smell of it—just like the animal organs, metallic, vaguely sour, like pickles and molding leaves.

When it was her turn to look closely, Laurel couldn't believe how small it was. She found it alarming that an adult human could fit in there. A whole being in such a small place. It was hard not to think of it as a USB drive, or a long-lost notebook or something—if you plugged it in, then, somehow, it would still have all the information in it, all the memories and feelings of a person. It was a house full of fantastic secrets, all the things that make one alive, locked up and impenetrable.

"Laurel!" Her mom fast-walked toward her, a rain jacket slung over one arm. "What did they say?"

"Nothing yet." Laurel hugged her mom's soft midsection. She smelled like the hippie rose perfume Paloma had gotten her for mother's day last year. "Is dad coming?"

"He had a meeting, then he said he'd be here."

Just then, the doctor came over. He shook their hands and made careful, prolonged eye contact. "We've had a look at Ramon. Has he been coughing or complaining of a sore throat lately?"

"Yes," Laurel said. "He's had a bad cough. For the last few weeks."

The doctor scribbled something on his tablet. "And has he had any stomach upset? Any complaints of aversion to certain foods?"

"I don't think so."

"I thought he fell," her mom said. "Is he sick?"

"We need to run a few more tests to determine the illness with any certainty, but, considering the coughing, and the loss of consciousness, it's looking so far like something called exitosus."

"Exitosus? That new disease?" Laurel had heard about it on the news. It had started out as a tropical disease, mostly in crowded, humid cities, and then it spread northward. She hadn't thought it existed this far north yet. Maybe this was the first case.

"It's a disease of the lungs. Some call it the new hantavirus; it begins as a cough and, eventually, it causes the lungs to fill with fluid. Typically it's accompanied by dangerously high fever and, in extreme cases, paralysis."

Laurel's mom crossed her arms. "How lon is the recovery time?" she asked. "If he has it."

The doctor's mouth tightened into a long, thin line. "We'll run those tests as soon as we can. Once we know what it is, we'll know what the treatment will be." He shook their hands again and told them they could go in to see Abuelo.

The nurse had arranged his arms at his sides and placed two pillows beneath his neck. The sheets made his skin pale, almost yellow. He looked uncomfortable. When he woke up he would have a neck ache, most likely, and maybe a soreness in his back.

"When do you think he'll be awake?" her mom asked the nurse, who spoke softly and breathily, almost in a whisper.

"We'll just have to see," she said. "We gave him some fluids. That should help. Could be any minute now." She pressed a button on the heart monitor and left the room.

Laurel's mom's face looked puffy, her forehead shiny. She sat in the plastic chair next to the bed. "I don't get it. He was at the house over the weekend. He was fine. How did this happen so fast?"

"He's had that cough for a while," Laurel said.

"A cough? A cough is a cough. You don't pass out from that."

"If he has exitosus, then that's why he passed out."

"I don't buy this exitosus stuff. It was probably the fall. He tripped and knocked himself out. Look at his face. They barely wiped off the blood." She pulled a tissue from her purse and rubbed at Abuelo's chin. The color lightened to a red-orange, like dried-up pasta sauce. She handed a fresh tissue to Laurel. "Here, put some water on this. That's a sink over there, right?"

"Yeah." Laurel wet the tissue with warm water.

"*Gracias*, Laurel." She said her name the Spanish way, separating the a from the u. Laurel loved when she said it like that. La-u-rel, the way her name should be. Her mom used this in place of a nickname. Paloma was Palomita, and Laurel was La-u-rel.

The blood receded. It was only a small cut. "Did they check for broken bones?" her mom asked. "How hard did he fall, Laurel?"

"I didn't see him. He was just on the ground, unconscious. But it sounded like a hard fall."

"But—oh, look, is he—"

Abuelo's eyes opened slowly, mechanically. He breathed deeply, in through the nose, out through the mouth.

"Papá, you're awake." Her mother said something in Spanish. Abuelo replied gruffly, his voice cracked and dry. They talked for a long while until, finally, Abuelo's eyes shifted to Laurel.

"Laurita," he said, and he held out his hand. "I need you to watch over things at work."

"Of course."

"You know what to do. I'll be out of here as soon as I can."

"You take it easy, Papá," her mom said. "You do what the doctors say, okay?"

"They—no, I'll be fine. I'll see if they will let me go tonight or tomorrow."

Laurel glanced at her mother. Should they tell him about the exitosus possibility? Could he feel that it was more than just a cold—the heaviness in his chest, the sour taste on the back of his tongue, the cloudy, balled-up pressure behind his forehead?

"You get out of here and you're going to take a vacation," her mom said. "You've earned one, by now."

"*Jesús.* Where would I go, Alma? The only place I want to visit is home to El Salvador, and—"

"I've told you. The gangs are worse than ever. Sandra says it's run-down. No one has jobs, there are shootings every day—it's not how it used to be."

"*Cálmate,* Alma. I was going to say that I want to go home but I can't. It has never been the same, not since the *guerra civil.* Even you haven't seen it the way I saw it. The way it was. We used to wander around the *hacienda,* all day as children, and run through the orchards, climb the trees, reach up, grab the fruit and eat it right there, the *naranjas* and the *guayabas,* and the *parchas* on the vine, and we would ride the horses down to the neighbor's, and out into the *selva* to watch the *monos,* to look for *pumas.* We tried to climb the big trees, too, but we couldn't do it." He laughed into his chest. "You could go anywhere, back then. And it was so natural, so green; you should have smelled it, after it rained, after a big rain, with lightning and thunder and the rain coming down, wham. The smell of the grass. And all the *pajaritos* would come out, and they would all sing together, all around you. The cows, too. The cows sang after it rained."

Laurel's mom smiled tightly. "Papá, maybe you should rest for a little bit. We can talk about this later."

"*Sí, hijita,*" he said, and then he closed his eyes.

CHAPTER FOUR
PALOMA

PALOMA SAT ON THE CARPET, PULLED HER KNEES TO HER CHEST, AND LEANED BACK AGAINST THE DOOR. She stared at the computer at the end of the hall. *Prime Gate Apartments. Do you have a question? I can answer it!* These words revolved across the screen in dense, bright bubble letters, again, and again, and again. Paloma ran her fingers through her hair. She stood up, and then she stretched into her favorite yoga pose, a forward fold. For a moment she stayed like that—fingers to toes, hair draped over knees, neck exposed. Then she checked her phone. An hour had already passed. She sat down again.

At last Laurel lumbered down the hall. Paloma stood up quickly.

"Laurel, you're home," she shouted.

"Paloma?" Laurel smiled briefly, and then her eyes fell to the floor. She stopped just in front of her. "You're back," she said, and she pulled her into a weak hug. "What are you doing here?"

"Waiting for you to come home from work," Paloma said.

Laurel squinted at her. "Yeah, but why?"

"I just wanted to see you. To say hi."

"Why didn't you come by the slaughterhouse?"

Paloma forced a smile. "I haven't even been home yet. I came straight here."

"You mean your stuff is still in your car?"

"Yeah. But I just couldn't—"

"You know your stuff's going to get stolen."

"It's fine."

"It's fine if your stuff gets stolen?"

"I just wanted to hang out for a little bit. Just a half-hour?"

"Go put your stuff away at Mom and Dad's and come back," Laurel said.

"No, it's fine. I don't care that much."

"Paloma, that stuff costs money. Take it home and come back."

"I don't care about my stuff. Any of it. It's fine."

"Okay," Laurel said. "Okay. Fine." She opened the door. "You shouldn't have been sitting on the floor, you know. There's rat poop all over the place. Even in the hallway."

"Again?"

"Yep."

"Have you tried that mint essential oil spray I told you about?" Paloma asked.

"It's too expensive." Laurel let the sink run. "Do you want any water? Or beer?"

"No, I'm good." Paloma leaned against the counter and crossed her arms. "But the spray, you don't need a lot of it. And I've heard it works super well for deterring rodents."

Laurel sipped at her water. The whites of her eyes were veined with red, and all traces of last summer's tan had faded. Her hair formed a stark, dark-brown halo around her face. She sat on the edge of her bed, her back turned to Paloma.

"So how's work been?" Paloma asked.

Laurel turned around. "I can't even think about that right now."

"I was just trying to make conversation."

"Well I know how much you *love* the slaughterhouse, so let's not get into that."

"That's not what I meant."

"It's fine. Tell me about school. You're all finished?"

"Yeah. Except the ceremony. But it would've been a waste of time anyway. A whole day of strangers walking across a stage."

"I mean, you could've done it if you wanted to."

"Who wants to walk if their family isn't there? No. And I want to be here for Abuelo." Paloma paused. "That's why I stopped by your apartment first. Abuelo—even though he wouldn't have been there anyway, it just seems like the house will be emptier—I don't know—"

"Think of mom and dad. They want to see you." Laurel stood and walked to the sink.

"You want me to go?"

"You can do whatever you want."

Paloma breathed in, a deep-bellied meditation breath. She sat in silence for the next few minutes. She waited for Laurel to say something—anything, but her sister kept her head down in the steam of the sink, and she continued to wash her instant cooker pot insert, probably still dirty from last night's dinner.

"All right," Paloma finally said. She waited for Laurel to turn the water off. "I guess I'll go, then."

"Okay. I'll see you tomorrow," Laurel said.

"Why, what's tomorrow?"

"I'll see you at the hospital."

"Right. Okay. Tomorrow." Paloma waved at her sister and escaped into the hallway. The screen now read: *¿Tiene preguntas?¡Puedo contestarlas!* Again, and again, and again.

*   *   *   *   *

"Now, there *is* a new drug we could try," the doctor said. "It's still in the experimental stages. But at this point, we don't have many other options. There are few methods for treating exitosis."

"What does the drug do?" Paloma asked. "What are the side effects? And the success rate?"

"We've only tried this on one other patient, and their success was moderate—"

"We? Who's we? You don't mean they tested it here, do you?"

"No, I mean the drug. It's been tested only once. Anywhere." He turned to Paloma's mother. "In full disclosure, Mrs. Monti, I would say we have a five to ten percent chance of success."

Her mother covered her eyes, and her father put his arm around her. Laurel gazed at the floor, her eyes unmoving. Paloma shook her head. Nothing felt real. She leaned back against the wall. A nurse passed by, with a self-wheeling cart of cleaning products at her heels. A message rose from the intercom, but Paloma couldn't understand the words. It sounded like a roar, a rising flood; something about to burst.

The doctor folded his hands in front of him and stared at Paloma's parents.

"There has to be a better way," Paloma said.

"I'm sorry," said the doctor, his fat shoulders slumped, concave, rising and falling with his heavy breathing.

"Let's try the drug," her mother said roughly. "If we have a chance, it's worth it."

"I don't want to get your hopes up—"

"We understand that."

The doctor nodded, shook their hands, and walked away, whispering intensely into his watch.

Paloma led the family into Abuelo's room. His eyes opened, and he smiled through his teeth. "Palomita, *la doctora*. Someday soon you will be the one helping people like me, eh?"

"I think I've got almost another decade until I'm a doctor."

"And then she'll be rich," Laurel said. "And when she's rich she can take you on vacation, Abuelo." Her gaze met Paloma's.

"Right," Paloma said, trying to keep the sadness from her voice. "Anywhere you want to go."

"You'll finally be rich, Paloma," Laurel said.

When Paloma was younger, in middle school or so, she used to joke that she would marry a rich guy, and, if she didn't, she would make sure to work at a high-paying job. Either way, her goal in life was to be rich.

And she still wanted that, in a way. Money wasn't the only reason she'd decided to become a doctor, but it was part of it. Who wouldn't want to have enough money to be comfortable? Money meant freedom—freedom from worry, freedom to travel, freedom to live wherever you wanted. And doctors helped people. How amazing was that? You could get rich by helping people! Sure, it would be hard work, and long hours, but it would be worth it. At least, that's what Paloma had thought when she was a teenager. It had been such an easy choice back then, when her whole future was spread ahead of her, clearly mapped out, step one, step two, step three. Full scholarship for undergrad. Partial scholarship for medical school.

It was too late to change things now. She'd already accepted the school's offer. She'd already picked out an apartment and signed the contract for fall. Her parents—and Abuelo—were unbelievably proud of her. And, honestly, part of her did still want to go. But this new part of her, whatever it was, it made her feel restless. Like something was off. Sometimes, at night, her stomach ached for no reason, and she sat awake and stared into the dark air above her bed. She tried to see her future, all clean and simple—med school, graduation, residencies, a house near a river, with big, broad shade trees in the backyard, and a deck with a lounge chair, and solar panels and a brand-new car. She tried to see all of it as vividly as she once had, but now it was fuzzy. These felt like the dreams of someone else, an old friend or a movie character. The worst thing was that if she gave up on becoming a doctor, she would have no idea what to do with herself. The world was crumbling, and, meanwhile, they all went on, day by day, moment by moment, pretending that nothing was wrong, pretending that the drought would break next year, next spring, that the rivers would return, that the water bill would go back down, that the supermarkets would always have affordable food and bottled water. Paloma once thought this way, but, throughout her life, things had only gotten worse.

Laurel turned on the TV. "I can't believe they still have cable in here," she said. "Ancient."

The news flashed to a live shot of Blue Mar. The island itself had been finished for a few weeks, but no resort, not yet.

"They're still building that thing?" Paloma's father said. "What's their estimate?"

Laurel turned up the volume.

"—because of Lustro's involvement in the agricultural sector, they've experienced declines in revenue related to the hurricanes in the southeast and the Caribbean. That sort of thing takes a toll on all their sectors. A big project like this has to be the first thing they abandon, because the costs behind it are absolutely unprecedented. I mean, nothing even compares to this; nothing on the historical record. The costs are monumental."

"Thank you, Steven," Fernando Montoya, the newscaster, said, in his round and pleasant voice. "We've just received word that Lustro's board will be voting on whether or not to abandon the Blur Mar project. No details yet on when that vote is to take place."

"Seriously?" Laurel clicked the mute button. "They've come this far. They can't just not build it."

"I don't mind," Paloma said. "The last thing the world needs is another rich-people resort."

"Why not? You'd be the one going there, right?"

Paloma knew her sister was joking; she knew she was supposed to laugh, but she couldn't. She felt heavier each day, like her mouth was regressing into stone, or plastic, or metal, unable to move in either direction, unable to smile or frown, just a straight line, just an evenness like the unwrinkled bedsheets stretched taut over Abuelo's frail body. He no longer seemed like a body at all, but a sculpture. A sculpture of a deflating man, the same heavy eyebrows as Tía Sandra, bleached to pure white, the same round belly as Tío Marco, now concave, flat, dipping in, a crater, his skin no longer red-brown like her mother's but worn, faded as a cloth left out in the sun.

Abuelo began to speak. His voice waxed and waned, growing stronger and weaker every few words. At times he paused and his chest shook. Lately he'd been rambling for long tangents. Sometimes he made sense, and sometimes it was as though he'd forgotten how to string words together. The doctors said this ebb and flow was normal for exitosis patients; the stress on the brain, the swelling, something about oxygen flow. Sometimes he even forgot how to speak English, but not today.

"We used to wake up at sunrise," he said, his eyes cloudy, dim. "The roosters, *ki-kiri-ki*, every morning. And then we helped harvest the cherries on the coffee bushes. We grew some cacao, too, just a little bit of it. You should have seen it, Laurita. The *vacas* they had there. So skinny compared to the ones here, but, mmm, *qué rico*. We helped butcher them at the neighbor's house. We knew where our meat came from. We knew where everything came from. That was before the war. I married your abuelita after. We didn't feel much of it. We stayed out of it, we stayed inside as much as we could and we didn't go down into the valley on weekends anymore. There was less food. The *mercado* closed down for three weeks once. We had some stored, and some growing, but then we ran out, and we had no food for five days. I'd never felt so much hunger. Painful, deep hunger. Your abuelita, in the valley, her cousin was shot, out in town one day, and her friend's house was burnt down. They tried to stay out of it too but it came to them. She saw a man get his head cut off in the street one day. Sometimes she dreamed about it, years later, decades; *pesadillas*, and she'd wake up shaking and crying. It was a bad government, that was what it was. I didn't want nothing to do with that. No. Politics, religion, none of it."

"Papá, why are you thinking about this kind of stuff now?" Paloma's mother asked.

"It's always there, *hijita*. *Por dios*. Can you stop treating me like a child? *Como un bebe?*" He spat something else in Spanish. Her mom's eyes rose.

"Maybe we should let your father rest, Alma," Paloma's dad said quietly. "We don't want him to get worked up."

"*Puedo oírte*," Abuelo said. I can hear you. But then he closed his eyes again.

"You guys can go. Take a break. I'll stay with him a little longer," Paloma said. She'd spent the least time with him; she'd only gotten back from school a week ago. "Really. I'll keep him company for another few hours."

They left. She sat carefully in the plastic visitor's chair. The news was still playing. She took it off mute and turned the volume low. Nothing interesting. Nothing more about the island.

"Palomita."

"What is it, Abuelo?"

"*Quiero pedirte un favor.*"

"*Qué?*"

"I want you to go there. Someday. For me."

"Go where?"

"El Salvador. I want you to go back. When things are better. I want you to see it. To hear the birds in the forest. The green fields. The rain. And go to the ocean. The dark sand, the waves. You can surf, there. And all the ladies in their bikinis. The sun is strong. In the summer we used to go on *vacaciones* to the *playa*, and we would stand on the dock and catch the fish for dinner. And get the coconuts from the trees, right there. Drink the milk straight from it." His chest sputtered. He coughed bitterly, sharply, too weak to bring his hands over his mouth. "Palomita. It will get better someday. It won't be the same, but it will be better. There will still be parts of it, parts that will always be how they used to be."

"Of course I'll go there someday. I've always wanted to."

"Go there and think of your abuelita, huh? And your abuelito." He laughed painfully. "Think of us. That way you will bring us with you."

"Don't say that. You'll be there, too." The moment she said this she realized it wasn't true; Abuelo would not be going anywhere. Not now, not ever again.

Abuelo fell asleep. His hands lay cupped but peaceful, arranged delicately at his sides, his knuckles rivuleted with greenish veins and sunspots. But his eyes—they looked anything but peaceful; his eyelids were stretched taut, as though he were forcing them shut. Like he was getting ready to fall. Getting ready to jump. She kissed him on the cheek before she left.

That night, at home, after her parents had gone to sleep, Paloma re-watched the news segment about Blue Mar. She wondered what it would be like to stand on that island. Plastic transformed into—what? Soil? Bathroom tile flooring? Sand? She had a hard time picturing her feet on that ground. It seemed almost like another planet, icy and cloudy and completely blank. Just wind. No insects, no fossils, no leaf litter. No led or mercury embedded in the ground, no abandoned gasoline cars or ditches lined with plastic grocery bags. Just dark blue storm-winds and cracks of lightning. A tropical iceberg. The smell of a new car, mixed with seaweed and dead fish, maybe a few seagull droppings staining the interior. She would run for days without seeing anything, hear only her breathing, feel, suddenly, all of her body's intricacies, the forward and down propulsion of her thigh muscles, the arched bridge of the bones on top of her foot, the balled-up pressure as her bare feet hit the ground, the pinch of her fingernails against her palms, clenched in, fists, as they pumped at her sides. For some reason this was much easier for her to imagine; much easier than picturing herself sitting or standing on the island; easier, even, than imagining the island from a bird's perspective, completely empty.

The next day, Paloma needed to get out, so she took the bus to the wastelands to go for a walk along the old gravel road, the one that led past the abandoned cattle fencing and what was once a slow, muddy river. No one else walked out there. No one even drove on it anymore. It was way out there, miles from town.

Paloma walked for hours. The clouds grew yellowish and pale. They were high-up clouds, the kind that didn't bring rain, the kind made of dust rather than water. It would be dark soon and she would be out here all alone. Maybe that's what she wanted; to recreate an earlier time. To hold on to something.

She had been there before. Once, when she was twelve, she ran away because some kids at school had started calling her Mexican, and saying that she belonged at the Spanish-Language high school on the other side of town. She told them she was El Salvadorian, not Mexican, that she was only half, and that she didn't speak Spanish, that she didn't even think of herself as Latina, just look at her sister, her sister looked white as anyone, but they didn't listen; they told her what she was, and they laughed at her.

After school she'd started walking until she reached a bend in the river, a place with high grass. By then it was completely dark except for the light of some industrial building, and the dull glow of the city behind her. She'd heard a deep grunt. Her arms had grown limp with panic. She lit up her phone. Several eyes shined back at her, scale-blue, green-blue, like aliens, or fish. Another grunt, and then she'd realized they were cows. They'd torn a hole in the fence and escaped. None of them had made it very far, just to the edge of the water. She could only see two cows, the ones right there in front of her, but she knew there were more. She could hear their huffs of breath, feel their heat, the lumps of their bodies in the cooling darkness. Something about this had comforted her. She'd hoped there were thousands of them; that they would run away and become feral.

She'd stayed out with the cows until her hands numbed. Midnight or so, when all the heat had risen from the dirt. The walk back had taken her so long that she only had time to shower, eat, and leave for school. She told her parents she'd been at a friend's house. That's what they'd thought. They weren't even worried. "Just tell us next time," her dad had said, and that was the end of it. Laurel was still living at home back then, and she'd thought Paloma was with a boy. "What's his name?" she'd whispered, but Paloma didn't answer.

The river itself was different now. It had become a channel, a canal, completely empty, the mud compacted on the sides into walls of clay. The mud smelled vaguely of manure, even though the cows were long gone.

Paloma couldn't bring herself to sit down. How had everything changed so quickly? She stared at the mud, trying to find shapes in it. A star. A—rhombus? Was that what they were called? She knew the cows were dead now and had been slaughtered, likely in Abuelo's slaughterhouse. Maybe one got away. Just one cow who made it far enough that no human ever found him. Maybe he was in the Sierras somewhere. A mountain cow. Or maybe he'd made it beyond them, into the great basin—dry, cracked, windy—and he slept in respite from the desert in a grove of cottonwood trees.

She sighed. What was she going to do with herself this summer? She looked up, and there was *la luna*. The moon. She'd learned the Spanish word first. It was always *la luna* in her head. Abuela told her that they used to plant crops by the phases of the moon. The sugar cane had no rhythm to it, since they kept it going all the time, but they rotated the crops in the garden.

"Some things we planted on the *luna llena,* and some things we planted on the *luna nueva.*" Abuela had laughed. "They used to say the moon would heal you if you went out in the light."

Did this count? The pale, early moon? Malformed, blurry with whatever pollution particles made the sky milky? Would it heal her?

La luna llena. She'd always thought that sounded beautiful. What must the sky look like in El Salvador? She imagined it bright, spiraling, so full of stars that there was hardly any black behind them. That's how she imagined the sky above the plastic island, too. Empty and full all at once. She'd just read something about how there was more plastic in the sea than visible stars in the sky, and that wasn't even counting the plastic used for the island. Countless pieces of plastic were still out there, broken up into little tiny pieces. They formed constellations in the deep, filmy ocean, and glinted dully, there in the long, filtered light, in the bellies of fish and fish-eaters. The petroleum in the plastic was once dead plant matter. Then it was heated and compressed, and it became a cup, or cling-wrap, and then it was tossed into the sea, and swallowed by whales, who washed up on shore, their intestines distended, grotesque, spilling open with chewed-up bits of plastic inside them. Constellations.

What would Lustro Corp do, Paloma wondered? Would they lease out their technology to others, so all the plastic in the oceans could eventually be picked up? Or would they keep it to themselves, and hold on to it desperately as they drowned? Probably the latter. Or maybe they would rent out the machine for inordinate sums of money. Maybe the island would sit there, abandoned, for decades, centuries, even, until Lustro went out of business and some other company inherited it. All those trillionaires would be so disappointed that their resort never got built.

Maybe one of them would buy it, and he'd live there, all alone, in a small, glass mansion full of potted plants and bonsai trees. Once a month he'd throw enormous parties for his rich friends with private planes, and they'd throw their waste straight into the mouth of the sea.

The sun puffed away, its light caught in the ropes of dust on the horizon. Paloma began her walk back to the bus stop. Her skin felt gritty. She crossed her arms and watched the day fade into early evening. A single star blossomed above her head. After half an hour the bus picked her up, and she kept her eyes on the star through the window. They passed the wasteland trailers. The movie theater. By the time they made it to the old mall, the star had sunk into the gray-brown sky of the city.

A woman on the sidewalk yelled. She was thin and tall, with brown hair tied up neatly in a bun. A man with his hands in his pockets stepped closer to her—too close—and said something quietly. The woman lifted her phone from her purse.

"I'll call the police!" she shouted.

The man grabbed her wrist. He turned his head—his blue-green eyes met Paloma's through the window. Such watery eyes. Not watery like he'd been crying, but watery from irritation, or tiredness. Maybe from dust. He faced the woman again. Paloma wondered if she should say something to the bus driver, or maybe call the police herself, but then the bus started moving again. What if it had been nothing? What if the two knew each other and it was just a misunderstanding? It was better not to get involved.

When Paloma walked into the house, her dad rose from the kitchen table.

"Where have you been?" he asked.

"I went for a walk."

"You've been gone for hours." What was with the sternness in his voice? Hadn't she just graduated from college? Did he think she was still a kid? "Where did you walk? It's dangerous to be outside in the dark. Your sister doesn't even like to *drive* alone at night."

"Why? What's so dangerous?"

"The shootings have picked up around here. There's one every other night, it seems."

"Every other night? The whole town's going to be killed off soon, at that rate."

"This isn't a joke."

"I wasn't joking."

"When there's hard times, people do what they need to do to survive. They need money, they're going to take it."

She thought of the woman on the sidewalk. "You don't have to kill someone to take their money."

"You do if you don't know what you're doing. If you panic."

Paloma paused. The woman might be dead.

"Just please be more careful, Paloma. Think of your mother. She has enough to worry about right now."

Paloma nodded. Her father hugged her briefly and then retreated into his room. The house wrapped silently around her. She sat on the couch, her hands placed primly on her knees. For some reason she thought of a story Abuelo had told the other day; well, not a story, exactly, but a string of memories from his childhood.

Every summer, Abuelo's family spent three weeks at the coast. They stayed at the *hacienda* of a distant relative, Don Alberto, who was so rich that his servants lived in their own *casitas* behind the big house. The yard was a spacious field of neatly trimmed grass, rimmed by coconut palms and bougainvillea. Beyond the hedges, the ocean curled into rhythmic waves perfect for surfing.

In the front room of his house, Don Alberto kept two pet monkeys named Mona Lisa and Maurice. They lived in cages and wore silk ribbons around their necks. He also owned a baby ocelot—a tiny, fuzzy kitten that he called Gatito. One day, Gatito turned against him and bit his finger, drawing blood and severing his fingernail. Don Alberto scooped him up, drove him to the exact same spot in the rainforest where he once killed his ocelot-parents during a hunting trip, and he set Gatito free.

But that was not what Abuelo remembered the most. No— it was the ocean. Every day, Abuelo and Tío Guillermo roamed the beaches from dawn until dusk. They became friends with a group of local boys, who taught them how to surf, and how to fish for lobsters using a sharpened rebar and the innertube of a tire. They caught lobsters as big as their thighs—enormous, bright red, perfect lobsters that they took home at night to cook over an open fire in the sand.

They became expert divers, leaping from the fishing dock to search for oysters, or to catch fish with their rebar spears. Abuelo and Tío Guillermo never sold what they caught; they brought it home, or they gave it to the local boys, who were generally poor; their parents worked in restaurants, or hotels, or as servants for people like Don Alberto.

In the ocean, they swam with dolphins, and sharks, and turtles. Abuelo learned to hold his breath for minutes at a time, and to open his eyes in the saltwater. In his mind he mapped the currents, and the timing of the tides, and he grew so comfortable in the water that he began to think of himself as part of it. He loved it. The water, warmer than his skin. The waves as they coursed like wind. The smell of sun on salt. Those were the best days; swimming, surfing, fishing, lying on the humid sand at night to watch the stars billow up from the horizon.

One year, Abuelo found a splotch of turtle eggs nestled on the beach. The local boys told him he could take some, but only some. In order for there to be eggs next year, hundreds of baby turtles needed to scuttle through the moonlight and into the warm, kneeling ocean.

Abuelo's parents were surprised when Abuelo and Tío Guillermo each came home with a handful. Turtle eggs tasted dense, like chicken eggs and like seaweed. They were a delicacy.

The next summer, Abuelo's parents told him he was too old to play with the local boys. They weren't the right kind of people to be friends with. They were *sucio*; *pobre*. And so he stopped. And that was where Abuelo had ended his story—his train of memories.

Paloma wasn't sure why she'd thought of that. She pressed the button on the curtains behind the couch, and they opened slowly, steadily, unveiling the yellow lamp-light on the street and the blue silence surrounding it. Paloma stretched forward to peek at the sky. Nothing. Absolutely nothing.

CHAPTER FIVE
LAUREL

WORK FELT EMPTY WITHOUT ABUELO. Laurel hated how quiet the hallways were. Without Abuelo's voice leaking from his office, she could hear the dim thud of the workrooms, and the wind as it scraped against the side of the building, and her plastic heels as they clicked against the hallway tiles, and her breath as she walked, how it burned through her nostrils. She tried to focus. Office. Sit down. Open laptop. Databasing. Financing. Paperwork. Emails.

She worked as long as she could stand it, and then she opened the news to check on Blue Mar. Every day she looked for updates. Now that Lustro had abandoned the island, what would happen next?

Today the first headline read—Blue Mar Island Execs Issue Warning to Pirates. Now there were pirates involved? She clicked on the link to a written article.

At Lustro's New York headquarters this morning, Richard Ainsley spoke to the press about Lustro's bankrupt business venture, the Blue Mar Island Resort. "This is a temporary pause, a glitch in the funding, that's all," Ainsley said. "We plan to revive Blue Mar Island within the next five years, and, unless these pirates are willing to pay for their use of the place, they have no right to it whatsoever."

What pirates? Laurel clicked on another link below the story. Planet's Pirates Take Over Blue Mar Island.

A group of radical environmentalists has occupied the abandoned Blue Mar Island resort in the mid-pacific. Planet, one of the country's largest environmental non-profits with membership numbering around 150 million, has claimed the group of radicals as their own affiliates. Planet's executive director, Paul Shreifer, stated that, "Our goal here is justice. This island belongs to no one and to everyone, and we're going to make use of that. We don't need another resort, especially one for the super-rich. We need more land for the disenfranchised; more land for the people who are impacted by the gluttony that would have been celebrated on that resort. So we bought the boats. We chose the leaders for each boat. We told them to create a new world populated by the people who need a new world. And then we left it in their hands."

According to Shreifer, the pirates have set up a camp on the island with the essentials, including solar electricity and desalinated water. They plan to set out to sea in the next few weeks. When asked whether he considered his affiliates to be pirates, Shreifer said, "Yes, I guess you could call them pirates. Pirates in the best way possible."

Laurel sat back in her chair. This didn't even seem real, but it was from News Today, one of the more reliable news sites. She plugged in her headphones and watched the video that went with the article. Paul Shreifer looked old for a guy in charge of such a big organization. The lines on his forehead pulsed up every time he raised his eyebrows. Abuelo didn't even have wrinkles like that; just some small lines around his mouth and on the outsides of his eyes.

"We're always looking for more volunteers, here at home or abroad. Donations, spreading the word, everything helps," said Paul Shreifer.

"Now tell me, Paul, what's going to happen next?" the news guy asked, tilting his head and folding his hands together.

"What's going to happen next? Our plan is to make good use of Blue Mar Island. To make it a home for the people who need it."

"And what about the legal mplications of all this? Any worries there?"

"We've got a great legal team and, you know, I think people will see we're doing the right thing."

Laurel glanced up from the screen, and there was Evan, waving his hand at her face. "How loud do you have the volume, babe?" He laughed.

"Sorry." She closed her screen. "What did you say?"

"I said there's a new Thai place that just opened up. Want to try it for dinner?"

"Yeah, sure."

He held up his phone. "According to the review they have actual cloth tablecloths and real candles. And flowers on every table. This is high-class Thai. It's Thai for refined clientele."

"Like us?" Laurel laughed.

"Hey, we're important people. They probably buy our beef. Without us they wouldn't feed anyone."

"We should ask for a discount." She smiled. Her molars hurt. She must've been grinding her teeth the past few nights.

Evan smiled back. "Great," he said. "Tonight, then?"

"I'm visiting Abuelo tonight. You should come, you know. He—" No, she couldn't say it. It hurt to even think it—that Abuelo didn't have much time left. She tried to push it away; to go numb.

"We can go before dinner."

"Okay. Yeah."

"Great," he said, and he lingered in the doorway. Laurel lumbered up from her chair and kissed his cheek. He'd just shaved. He smelled like shampoo, the berries and mint kind that he bought from the Lustro-Mart down the street whenever they were having a two for one deal. He downloaded coupons too and sometimes he got an extra one free.

She pulled away and Evan's eyes followed her lips. He looked like he was about to say something, and she worried he'd ask how Abuelo was doing. That was a question she was tired of hearing. It made her stomach hurt to think of an answer.

"Do you want to sleep over, after dinner?" Evan asked. The way he said it, with some hesitation, reminded her of a high school boy asking a girl on a first date. Probably because she hadn't slept over in weeks.

"Yeah, sure," she said. They talked for a few more minutes, and then he left for his own office.

Laurel thought of the first day she met him, three years ago. That was the first day the new contract started taking effect, the day that Abuelo became the manager and not the owner of the slaughterhouse. He'd hated signing on with Bradley & Bradley. "*Qué lástima*. But I had no other choice, Laurita. No one is buying from the small guys anymore. Our prices are too high and if we lower them, we're gonna sink." So they became part of the big guys, an arm of the multinational Bradley & Bradley corporate lifeform.

Evan was what Abuelo called "the company's live-in spy," the one who communicated with the heads and who made sure the slaughterhouse was up to the corporation's standards. Bradley & Bradley was one of the better corporations out there; they gave a big part of their proceeds to charities, and they made sure all their factories and slaughterhouses and trucks and drones and retail shipment centers were completely solar-powered.

One of the first things they did was tack solar panels onto the roof. Laurel had never seen solar panels like these; they were purple, and shaped like rhombuses, and they rolled out flat on the roof like part of the tile.

She tried to hate Bradley & Bradley but they did bring in a lot more business. Instead of just California livestock they had access to farms all over the country, enormous, sprawling beef farms that sold their animals for hardly anything and shipped them over for free. They hired almost one hundred new employees. Bradley also bought new machines for them—electric butcher's knives and an automated thermostat that somehow kept cold air on the meat and not on the workers. All down the line everything was stainless steel, strong and brand new. By now the steel appeared rusty with blood but a good scrubbing revealed the glamour underneath. That stuff would last for years.

Best of all—although he'd never admit it—Abuelo's risk was gone. Money was not his concern anymore. He was an employee of Bradley & Bradley, and he would get paid no matter what. He didn't have as much power as he once did, but he was still in charge of the slaughterhouse's day-to-day workings. He was still the boss. He still hired and fired the workers, and he still enforced the rules, even if he wasn't allowed to make them anymore.

Abuelo introduced Evan to everyone in the slaughterhouse that first day, saving Laurel for last. He shook her hand with a tight grip. Laurel felt the calluses on the back of his knuckles and wondered if he was a boxer or something. She tried to grip his hand just as tightly, but her muscles felt limp. She cut the handshake short. "Nice to meet you, Mr. Miller," she said.

"Evan," he said. "Mr. Miller is a little too formal."

"Okay, Evan, then."

"Will you give him the tour, Laurita?" Abuelo asked.

"Sure."

"Good. I'll leave you to it, then," Abuelo said, and he retreated to his office.

"Laurel, you said?" Evan tried to pronounce it the way Abuelo had when he introduced her—the Spanish way, La-u-rel—but his tongue caught on the roof of his mouth and the whole thing was mumbled.

"Laurel," she said as flatly as she could. "La-u-rel, Laurel. Same thing, different accents."

"So is your grandfather from—?"

"El Salvador."

"Really?" Evan looked at her closely. She felt him analyze her face. "And the other side of your family?"

"My dad's family is Scottish and Italian."

Now Evan nodded. "Okay, yeah. You have Italian features." He placed his hand on his chest. "My family's Italian. And English."

"That's where Miller comes in."

"Yeah. Which is weird because I'm like ninety percent Italian. That little eighth bit of me has me labeled as a British guy. But we're definitely Italian. The food, the music, everything. Both my grandparents were from there, and my grandfather on the other side."

"I don't know much about my Italian side. My relatives came over in the 1800s so it's pretty distant. And here I am with an Italian last name. Monti."

"Well it matches how you look. Italian."

"I guess so."

"We're both M names, huh? Miller and Monti."

Looking back she realized he'd been flirting with her. At the time she thought he was just filling the air, one of those people who needed constant conversation.

"You know I did one of those DNA tests?" he said. She'd always liked his voice. It was smooth, young, much higher in pitch than her father's or Abuelo's. "The ones that say where your family is from? No surprises, everything on the dot, except that I'm two percent Black."

"Isn't everybody? Because humans came from Africa?"

"No, they don't go that far back on the test. Two percent would be a great-great-great grandparent. Or maybe great-great? Not far enough to go back millions of years."

"Interesting." What would hers be? Quarter Scottish, quarter Italian, half El Salvadorian? Was El Salvadorian an option? Or maybe it would be more general, and just say Hispanic? Paloma used to get mad at Laurel when she said their race was Hispanic.

"That's an ethnicity, not a race," she'd say.

"So what's our race, then?"

"White, I guess."

"You think Abuelo and Mom are white? No one would ever call them white."

"Well they're probably part Native or Black or something, but we don't know for sure so we can't claim that on forms or anything. And you and I have the white from Dad's side. So it's safe to say we're white."

"White and Hispanic just don't seem like the same thing."

Laurel looked white, and the world saw her as white, but that didn't mean that was all she was. She was white-and-Hispanic. Just white, to her, meant plain American white with no connection to any other culture. For most white Americans, the old traditions from Europe—the foods, the songs, the languages—were lost generations ago, and replaced by general Americanness; patriotism, American flag barbecues, hot dogs, football games.

"They're different kinds of white, I guess," Paloma had said. "Anglo white and Latin white. Different cultures, same race."

"What's that word? The Spanish word that means mixed?"

"*Mezclado?*"

"No, the one just for—*mestizo*! That's it."

"Yes. *Mestizo*. Mom and Abuelo are most likely *mestizo*."

"And so are we."

"We're half *mestizo*."

"So we're more *mestizo* than they are."

"That's not how it works, Laurel. We have less non-white blood than they do."

"So we're super mixed."

"We're a little mixed."

Laurel stopped arguing at that point. Paloma always thought she was right about everything. Even when they were younger, back before she was the first one to go to college, Paloma was a little bit full of herself.

The first place Laurel had taken Evan was to the viewing corridor. It was a walkway separated from the butchering floor by a thick pane of glass. Inside, the floor was a deep, dark red, and shining. Small ponds of blood mixed with the hose water that had failed to wash them away. Yellow lights shined crudely on the workers' foreheads. She could see the sweat glisten on their skin. They strung up the first cow by its back hoofs, so it hung upside down. One machine held the cow's head, while another slit its throat with a sharp, square knife. Blood gushed forth, its steam rising like smoke toward the light. The cow's eyes remained open. One of the workers closed them, one by one.

Laurel pointed out the bulk of the cow's muscles; how that specific breed had been bred to grow massive in only one year. "The cows we had before were just normal cows," she'd said. "Slow growing."

"We hooked you up, then," Evan said.

"Bradley & Bradley did, yeah."

"Are they GMO?"

"No. Just specially bred. Abuelo hates GMO's."

"Why? Bradley & Bradley is into GMO's."

"I don't know. Ask him sometime."

They followed the cow down the line. Laurel nodded to two men with hairnets, who had already begun to cut through the string of tendons and remove the cow's head. Farther down, they separated the cow's abdomen into portions—ribs, back, offal. The ribs had always bothered Laurel; they looked just like the bones in her own chest, only bigger, and thicker, and exposed, red-pink and tipped by dark, scabby bone marrow. She turned her attention back to the workers. "Abuelo knows everyone's names," she'd told Evan. "Sometimes he sits with them in the break room and talks with them in Spanish."

"A lot of Mexicans here," Evan said. "Before this I worked in one of the drone shipping ports, and it was mostly Blacks."

Laurel didn't like the way he said that. Blacks. Not Black people, just Blacks.

"Yep, everyone is Mexican here," Laurel said. "Almost everyone."

"Do you ever feel like you're in another country?"

"No. I grew up here, so I'm used to it. There's always been a lot of Mexican people. There are even two high schools, one for English speakers and one for Spanish speakers."

"Why didn't they just make them learn English?"

"Because you can get by without English."

"It's probably because they're not sticking around. They're here to make money and then go back to Mexico."

"Some of them, yeah. Things just keep getting worse down there, though. Their droughts are more extreme than ours."

"But they don't want to stay here. They don't want to be American."

American. What did that even mean? Was speaking Spanish any less American than speaking English?

"Do you speak Spanish?" Evan had asked.

"Just a little. My mom never taught us."

"Why not?"

"I don't know. She grew up here before they had two high schools, so she spoke English with her friends and Spanish with her family. I guess she didn't speak Spanish with us because my dad doesn't speak it. It would've left him out."

"How about Ramon? Didn't he want to teach you?"

"He's the type of person who thinks I'll pick it up just by listening to him, but I think I need to have it broken down a little more. I've learned a lot from him, though. Numbers. Food. Swear words. I learned those by accident, though. Abuelo thinks I don't understand him so he swears all the time. That's how I picked them up." Laurel laughed. "Back in high school, I used to swear at people in Spanish. I thought I was so cool, and so sneaky, and it always sounded harsher, too, to tell someone off in Spanish."

"No one would expect it. A white girl like you swearing in Spanish?" Evan laughed, a back-of-the-throat laugh, two beats to it. They were about the same height and he looked over at her, sideways out of his eye as they walked. Absolutely flirting.

They'd been walking for a while now and Laurel hadn't pointed out anything else. "There's the new knives," she'd said. The butchers severed the cow's limbs at the ankle; at the knee; at the thigh; the tail. The bones cracked like tree branches beneath a saw.

"Why didn't they automate this whole thing?" Evan asked.

"That was one of Abuelo's terms. He says it's better to give people jobs than to fill this place with machines."

"I'm surprised they went for that. Three-quarters of the other slaughterhouses are automated."

"It's not even cheaper. It's around the same."

"For now. But that's where we're headed. Automated everything."

"They've been saying that for years. But lots of us still drive our own cars and clean our own houses and butcher our own meat."

"Would you want to be out there, doing that?"

"No, but people need jobs." She cleared her throat and held the door open for him. "That's the end of the line. Now the meat gets shipped out to the distribution center and goes to stores and restaurants. Here's the packaging room." Mechanical arms wrapped the cow's muscles in plastic cling-wrap, and then topped each package with a sticker and a blast of instant-freeze.

"Automated, huh?"

"Just the packaging part. We have people load it onto trucks."

Evan laughed over her as she said that. It wasn't a mean laugh; it was how friends laughed at each other. It was nice having someone around who was close to her age. Someone who spoke English. By this point Paloma was already in college and most of

Laurel's high school friends had moved away. Before Evan, the only person Laurel talked to at work was Abuelo, and Abuela, too, before she died. She used to visit a lot; sometimes she stayed for hours, and she helped Abuelo with paperwork. She brought him lunch—rice and beans and stacks of corn tortillas, still warm and rolled up in a cotton towel.

Laurel started work about six months before Abuela died. She hoped that she'd made the transition a little easier for Abuelo after she died; that her presence had helped counteract the silence of Abuelo's house, with all those windows and the sunlight beaming in from outside. She imagined him in his living room, folding his own bedsheets. In the kitchen, washing his dinner dishes by hand. He would take off his wedding ring and place it by the dishrack and dry his hands carefully before he put it back on.

Laurel's mom had invited Abuelo to live with them, but he'd said he was fine where he was. "Maybe when I'm older and I forget who I am, then I'll need looked after," he said. "And when I forget who you are, send me out to the *montañas* and tell me, '*vaya con dios*, Papá.' Then give me a good shove."

"Papá!" Laurel's mother shook her head.

"You'd survive, Abuelo," Laurel said. "Even if you lost your mind. You'd survive out there."

"I'd come back to you all like a lost *perrito*, wouldn't I?"

Laurel couldn't remember what happened after that. Maybe she'd given him a hug, or maybe she'd just laughed. It seemed impossible. All her life Abuelo had been old, but she could never imagine him getting any older. He was static. He was a mountain. Not one of the mountains here, with their ugly burnt-dry-grass, but one of the big mountains up north that used to have snow on them all year, like the picture in her parent's hallway.

Abuela used to show Laurel pictures of when she and Abuelo were young, back when they still lived in El Salvador. Some were printed out and some had been converted onto a USB drive. New computers didn't even use USB anymore so the only place she could look at them was on Abuelo's old laptop.

A lot of their photos were taken on the farm. Abuela, one of two girls, was all set to inherit the property from her parents, but when she left for the U.S. she told them to give it to her younger sister, Tía Roberta. When Laurel's *bisabuelos* died, Tía Roberta spruced up the farm—with chickens, and vegetables, and an orchard, and a few animals—and she still lived there today.

When they were first married, Abuelo and Abuela lived in a shed on the property. The pictures showed how small it was— basically just one room and a closet—and how much the farm had changed. Back then they only grew sugar cane. Just fields and fields of brown-green grass, tall, and sharp, and spotted with dew in the mornings. They had one cow that Abuela's mother milked, and a horse named Oswaldo who they loved as a pet. He did nothing around the farm and no one knew how to ride him, but he wandered freely and came when his name was called, and that was enough. There was a certain picture of Oswaldo and his spotty nose that Laurel had always remembered—she'd remarked that his fur was the color of carob powder, and Abuela had said, no, it was the color of *dulce de leche*, caramel, and the spots on his nose were the color of milk, of *leche*. She'd petted the photograph. "Oswaldo was a good horse," Abuela had said. "He was already old by the time we left. I worried he would die but he lived to be eighteen."

"He was a super-horse," Laurel said. She was young then. Probably in middle school. For a long time she and Paloma went to Abuela's house after school. She always put old cartoons on for them, on her ancient flat-screen TV.

Every Saturday the whole family had dinner together. Abuela usually cooked. Laurel's favorite was *pupusas* with *curtido, chicharrones,* and *yuca frita.* And of course she also loved the *tamales* Abuela made for special occasions.

Every meal Abuela made was accompanied by fresh tortillas—Abuela kept giant sacks of *masa harina* in her pantry. "Enough to feed a one-man army," Abuelo liked to say, pointing to himself. For an after-school snack Abuela would make them scrambled eggs with tortillas, and they would each get their own little square of cheese on the side. She finely chopped some parsley and decorated the eggs with it, and gave them cloth napkins like they were at a restaurant. "*Gracias,* Abuela!" they would say.

"You're welcome, girls."

Laurel's mom still knew how to make *tamales.* Maybe she'd ask her to teach her. They could make a batch and wrap them in a towel for Abuelo. Maybe he would smell them, and wake up, and suddenly be okay. He'd eat a big plate of them, with each *tamal* wrapped in its own little corn husk and tied with its own piece of twine.

Laurel's phone rang. It was her father. "Hello?"

"Laurel, you need to come to the hospital."

"Why?"

"This might be it. That's what the doctors say."

"But the treatment?"

"He's awake, come down to meet us, okay?" He hung up. Laurel's hands felt numb. She stood slowly. One of her knees cracked. All at once the adrenaline hit her, and she ran to her car. It was a dusty day, so she held her breath and squinted through the gusts of beige powder. The sun hid in an orange veil of dust and dirt; a lump of firelight in the corner of the sky. She

sped as fast as she could into town. Traffic slowed outside the
city government building. A group of protestors held signs—

Expensive Water = Dehydration!
How Will We Feed Our Families?
Living Wages, Affordable Food & Water
We Can't Live Without Water!

People rarely protested in Terrysville. Why now? Their
chants burned through the windows. Some held religious signs,
You must repent your sins. You will go to hell. Jesus hates sinners.
Laurel wanted to scream at them, and at the cars in front of her
who had slowed down to watch.

Finally, she made it. She ran into the hospital. By now she
could easily find the way to Abuelo's room.

"Laurel." Her father grabbed her shoulders and pushed her
gently away from the door. "He's gone."

She shouldered past him. Abuelo looked worse than he had
just days ago. His skin was shrunken up like jerky, and his arms
looked like deer legs, bony and straight and more like sticks than
muscles. He would snap in half if you tried. Brittle and hollow.

"He's not—"

"He's gone, Laurel," her father said again. Then she noticed
her mother, sobbing into the chair, and Paloma, sitting on the
floor in the corner of the room, her eyes blank and unblinking.
How could any of them stand it? The smell of rubbing alcohol?
His purple lips and the breathing tube still stuck between them?
The little hairs around his mustache, white instead of gray? The
needles and the cords stuck up in his veins, the shiny skin around
them, the discoloration let loose like a venom, the undersides of
his wrists completely purple?

"He lived longer than anyone else has, with exitosus," her father said. "He gave it a good fight."

Laurel left the room. She walked to the restrooms and closed herself in a stall. Muffled stillness. The sharp smell of bleach. She couldn't cry, but, still, her face had grown puffy with grief. She moved her hands beneath the motion-activated sink, but nothing came out of the faucet. She tried another one. The faucet squeaked. One drop of water fell, and then—nothing.

For some reason she thought of the sea; of Blue Mar, a bruised puddle of land in the distance. It grew, breathing on its own, rising from the ocean, surprisingly mountainous, the peaks inexplicably covered in long hairs of dripping seaweed. She got off the boat and wandered inland. No birds, not even crows. A single beep, like a drum. She followed it. She ran beneath the cover of the trees. They fell limp with seaweed and toppled around her. She ducked and covered her head. A string of seaweed landed on her back. She tore it off. The air stunk like fish.

Abuelo was dead. She imagined him, tall and young again, like in the old photos. Abuelo, walking through a field, a herd of cows behind him. He walked, not like a shepherd, but like an adopted member of the cows, one of them, a cow-man. At any other time this image would have made her laugh, but, somehow, right now, it wasn't ridiculous. She replayed it in her mind. This was the only way she'd ever imagined the souls of cows, and it was now the only way she could imagine the soul of her abuelo. Abuela, for some reason, she'd imagined as a flurry of powder, flour or fairy dust, and Grandpa, her other grandfather, had become a sky creature, a cloud or something. All of this was made up, anyway, but she liked to think of them all in their imaginary afterlives, changed but eternal. Maybe that was how religions got started. And, hey, maybe that was how religions still were, if you believed in them. It was all just a way of imagining things.

She heard Abuelo's footsteps against the grass. Clomp. Clomp. And the weather coming in. The fog against the green mountains. Clomp. Clomp. Only Abuelo made noise. The cows' feet were silent. Air upon air. Grass upon grass.

CHAPTER SIX
PALOMA

THE FUNERAL WAS HELD AT THE CATHOLIC CHURCH IN TOWN, THE ONE WITH SPANISH MASSES ON SUNDAY EVENINGS. Once, when she was younger, Paloma had tagged along with Abuelo and Abuela. She'd thought maybe Spanish church would be livelier, but she ended up being bored and hungry. Her stomach growled throughout the second half of the service, once so loudly that the lady in the pew in front of them whipped her head back, startled and unsure what the noise had been. At that point Abuela pulled out a Ziploc baggie from her purse, and Paloma munched on crackers as quietly as she could.

It was an impressive looking church, with a towering steeple topped by a metal cross.

"Remember to start the slow cooker, Alma," Paloma's father said as they walked toward the entrance. "For after."

"Good. You remembered to remind me." Paloma's mom sent the start signal with her phone. "Everyone is going to be starving."

"How many people do you think will be coming over?" Laurel asked.

"We might have to stop and get more water. Maybe more chips, if they have them—"

Paloma stopped listening. This was all just a distraction. An attempt at normalcy. A desperate attempt to dull the intensity of the moment. Abuelo's dead body was in that church. She felt like it wasn't him anymore. It was just a thing, an artifact. And all of this, this slow wandering, these family members and old friends whose names she recognized but whose faces were unfamiliar, the white calla lilies tied to the pews, the smell of polished wood—all of it added to the dullness. She felt like she was not in her body. She felt like she was not there at all, just watching it all on TV.

The church reminded her of a cave, so dim and rounded, with stained glass windows filtering in only specks of colored light. The wind scraped through the open door, and, outside, cottonwoods glistened above the parking lot, their whistling mixed with the gurgle of the drainage ditch, the crunch of gravel, the feedback from the priest's microphone, some tía talking on her cell phone in, not Spanish, but Portuguese. She was probably the daughter of one of Abuelo's cousins. His parents had five siblings each so Paloma had a lot of second (third?) cousins who she'd never met. The children of these second cousins were, somehow, according to Abuelo, Paloma's cousins. Not third or fourth cousins, just cousins, because they were about her age. Abuelo's cousins—Paloma's second (third?) cousins—were then her tías and tíos. Sometimes they sent her Christmas money. At least one of the families was rich because they sent her a brand new, never-folded one hundred dollar bill every year. Who was that again? Tío Manuel and Tía Sarita?

It was a hot day and Paloma was surprised she wasn't sweating. This summer was supposed to be the hottest one yet. That's what they said last year, too, and the year before, and they were always right. One of these summers they'd all be burnt into pieces of charcoal. Maybe it would get so hot that the plastic island would melt and pollute the entire sea with a broth-like chemical magma. She could imagine the liquid-plastic trickling down—red, for some reason. Red like the plastic bucket she used to play with as a kid, the one she used to take to the park and fill with rocks from the riverbed. Her mom caught her doing that once and made her put them back. "Those rocks are dirty," she said. She said they were contaminated with chemicals and cow poop and that was why, even after it rained and the river filled up, they never went swimming.

Up in Oregon, the rocks were clean enough to collect, and, from her short visit to Washington for the interview it looked a lot like Oregon, all those evergreen trees—some dying, but some still beautiful—and mountains and meadows and rivers the color of seawater. She'd heard that the big cities like Seattle were dirty and crowded, but they tried to make up for it by planting gardens on the roofs of skyscrapers. It didn't matter much, anyway, because her school was a few hours from Seattle, out in the sprawl between suburb and country.

Paloma leaned against one of the stained-glass walls. She listened to the abstract chatter, how it echoed and jumbled together. From this distance words meant absolutely nothing. She knew she should greet some relatives, or at least sit solemnly in the pew, but she couldn't. Not yet.

A woman grabbed Paloma around the shoulders. "Is that you, Paloma? Look at you! I haven't seen you in years! You're looking like a woman, now. Marco, come over here!" She waved at Tío Marco, who was wearing a tropical-print shirt.

"*Mi sobrina! Como estás?*" He hugged her. She remembered him smelling like cigarette smoke, but today he smelled like fresh-cut fruit, mangos or something. "You remember Odeta?"

She nodded. Odeta looked both older and younger than him. Her eyes seemed stretched-back, and her lips looked a little too full. Maybe she'd had plastic surgery or something. Apparently she was from a rich Albanian family. Her mom thought that was the main reason Tío Marco dated her. They traveled the world together and she bought him nice things.

"What's the story behind this shirt, Tío?" Paloma asked.

"Your abuelo got it for me a long, long time ago. I got too fat for it and then, all these years later, since I've been on a diet, now I fit it again. Thought it would be a good way to honor him."

"That dress is darling on you, Paloma. Is it from El Salvador?" Odeta's Albanian accent translated well to Spanish words. She said El Salvador perfectly.

"Kind of. Abuela made it for me. She embroidered it."

Tío Marco's face drooped from its smile. He looked like he was about to cry. Maybe it dawned on him, in that very moment, that both his parents were dead.

"You and I are the colorful ones here, huh?" he said. "I think your abuelo would've liked that. Who wants a boring funeral? Not me." He patted Paloma on the back. "Come on. We should go sit down."

CHAPTER SEVEN
LAUREL

ONE TIME—PROBABLY HALF-JOKINGLY—ABUELO HAD ASKED FOR ONE OF THOSE MUSH-ROOM-LINED CASKETS THAT DECAYED INTO THE SOIL. Laurel hated to think of that. Was it true that every time she touched the soil she was touching the remains of dead people? Dead animals and plants, too? Was the soil one vast burial pit? She'd decided to forget about the mushroom box comment and hadn't brought it up to her mom.

Laurel climbed the stage. She tightened her hands on the podium. The microphone squeaked as she adjusted it up for her height. "*Hola familia,*" she said. "Hello family. Thank you for being here today." Her throat felt dry. She glanced at Evan, in the front pew, one leg crossed over his knee. He always sat like that. So sprawling. She wished he would sit normally. He smiled at her.

Laurel exhaled and the microphone caught it, a great booming wind. "Sorry," she said, and she cleared her throat. "For the past few months, Abuelo was giving me Spanish lessons. So I decided to use what I've learned. To honor him." She lapsed into Spanish, reading off her phone. She'd written the tribute in English, and then her mom had helped her translate it. The pronunciation came easily to her even though she'd forgotten what some of the words meant. They had become like music, beautiful but meaningless. She'd practiced this fifty times in front of the mirror. She'd even recorded herself on her phone to make sure she sounded all right. And her practice had paid off.

"*Vaya con dios*, Abuelo," she said, hearkening back to Abuelo's old joke, the one where he told them to push him off into the wilderness if he ever lost his mind. Abuelo never got the chance to become senile.

The crowd clapped. Were people supposed to clap at funerals? Laurel couldn't remember. It was a somber clap, appreciative but muted.

Then Paloma trudged up to the stage, her head down. "Good job," she whispered to Laurel, and she gently freed the microphone from her hand.

"Hi everyone," Paloma said. Her voice sounded thin. "I wanted to come up here and say a few words about my grandfather. I have no idea what my sister just said because I never learned Spanish. And, I just, I had a few things I wanted to say myself." She paused. Waiting for a reaction? Gathering her thoughts? The audience rustled.

Paloma told a story about how Abuelo took them camping, out to the old reservoir at the base of the mountains. Laurel remembered that too.

"Why did you take us here, Abuelo?" Laurel had asked him. "Why didn't we go up higher where it's wilderness?"

"Because here we can swim. The rivers are too fast and too shallow in the mountains."

Laurel had been a little disappointed because she'd wanted to see what the wilderness was like, but she had loved swimming, and going camping for the first time. They stayed in a small tent with a built-in barbecue next to it and a picnic table. Abuelo bought some brand new floaties, one shaped like a flamingo and one shaped like a flower.

"What about you, Abuelo? What will you float on?"

"My back, Laurita," he said, and he did. He floated right on his back, like a log in the water, his head dipped back and his short gray hairs wild like seaweed. Laurel tried to do the same, but she sunk down. "How do you do it, Abuelo?"

"I puff up the air in my chest and I let the water hold on to me. It's much easier when you're in the ocean. Someday we will go to the ocean where it's warm and I'll teach you."

"Like in El Salvador?"

"Yes, like El Salvador. We'll go someday."

Of course Paloma tried to float and did it right away, instinctually.

"You're doing it wrong. You're dipping down too much!" Laurel had said, but that was a lie. Paloma was doing it perfectly. Abuelo didn't see. He had his back turned, wading into shore.

"Abuelo, look at me!" Paloma yelled, but even back then Abuelo was old and he didn't hear her.

That night they spread blankets out on the sand. They stretched on their backs and waited for the stars to surface. It was uncomfortable—Laurel could feel the pebbles underneath the blanket pushing into her back—but she wished she could stay there forever. She loved the stars. She loved how they scared her.

"Abuelo, what's that one called?" Laurel pointed to a bright star just above the tree-line.

"That one, it has no name. It is a brand new *estrella*."

"No it's not!"

"I know what it is," Paloma said. How old was she back then? Nine? "It's the moon!"

Abuelo chuckled. "No, Palomita, that is not the moon."

"And it's not a new star, either," Laurel said.

"It is for me. *Sabes qué?* We have a whole different sky in El Salvador. A whole different sky. *Las estrellas* are so different, some of them. Some are the same. In El Salvador you have half the constellations of the south, and half of the north." He looked over at Laurel. "So, you see, that one, that is the *escorpión*. And that one, up there, he is Ursa Major. *Oso*. Bear."

"That doesn't look like a bear," Laurel said.

Paloma sat up. "Yes, it does! I see it!"

"No, you don't."

"Right there!"

"You can only see part of the bear here. The lights from the city are still too strong. In El Salvador you can see all of him. You can see all of his arms. Here he is a cup. A dipper."

"The big dipper?"

"*Eso*, you got it."

"I see it now," Laurel said. She tried to imagine the sky in El Salvador.

They left the next morning. "Say *adios* to the lake," Abuelo said, and they waved to the water.

"*Adios!*" Laurel had yelled out the window.

"*Adios!*" Paloma copied her, and they yelped together like coyotes, their voices caught up in the wet, morning air that hung just above the water.

They were supposed to go back every year, but then the drought hit, and the reservoir got blocked off and used as drinking water. Abuelo said they'd go camping at the coast sometime, but he could never take off work long enough. That was their one and only camping trip.

"Abuelo taught us so many things." Paloma's eyes fell. Her mouth opened and closed like a fish. Laurel could tell that she didn't know what to say. The audience watched in silence. "He taught us so much. And we'll miss him." Paloma nodded, a definitive, single nod that meant she was finished. Now the audience clapped, just as they had for Laurel. Paloma dismounted the stage and sat beside her.

Laurel knew she should try to comfort her in some way, but there was no comfort in this situation, no good to be found, no "Abuelo has gone to heaven," no "He's in a better place," no "He's watching over us." She would save that for their Catholic relatives. Laurel liked to imagine spirits but she didn't believe in them. Did Paloma? Did Paloma believe in Gods or ghosts? Laurel had no idea. She probably had some complicated philosophy about it all.

Evan curled his arm around her shoulders. "You did good, babe," he said into her ear. "Everyone's impressed."

"Everyone?"

"Ramon would be proud of you."

"He'll never see me learn Spanish."

Laurel's mom gave them a sharp glance because the priest had started talking and they needed to shut up.

The burial bothered Laurel more than anything else. What if Abuelo wasn't completely dead? What if he was still in a coma? There was an old *telenovela* that Abuela used to watch where the main character was buried alive on his wedding day and his evil twin married his fiancé. Of course Laurel didn't understand a word of it but sometimes she would sit and watch the pictures, and make up a new story to go with the actions. She did that with other telenovelas too. Back in high school she fell asleep watching them because she hoped the Spanish would seep into her brain. She did that with Spanish music, too. She remembered curling up in her bed, listening desperately to a Latin-Pop playlist on YouTube, wishing she was fully, one hundred percent, confidently Latina, and knowing that she never would be.

Laurel felt guilty for even thinking about these things. These stupid high school memories while, look—her abuelo. In a casket. The dry, deep soil, and Abuela already in it, right next to Abuelo in the deep, deep, dusty soil. It hadn't rained in so long. Abuelo solidified into stone and then crumbled. He stopped wandering and collapsed at the cows' feet. They sniffed him with their fat pink noses. They grunted at his absence, pig-like and nasally, and they kicked loose grass over him until he was covered. One cow raised his nose to the air and everything turned black with water. Abuelo floated skyward, part of the sea, lost in the tumult of the tsunami. The cows could swim and they paddled, and paddled, and paddled, until they made it to Blue Mar Island. They shook off their fur and let the sun dry the salt from their backs.

"I'm so sorry, babe," Evan said, and he was crying, too. Laurel hugged him.

"I'm going back in to work tomorrow," she said into his chest. "I'm so behind." She would be in charge now. The slaughterhouse, in a sense, was hers, at least the management of it.

"Well I'll be right beside you," he said. "It'll be weird without him."

"It already has been."

"I haven't gotten used to it yet," Evan said.

"Me neither. I never will. I'm still not even used to *Abuela* being dead. Now Abuelo—" She forced herself not to cry. Enough with crying. It didn't help anything. "It doesn't seem real."

A woman came up to them. Laurel didn't recognize her, exactly, but she looked familiar.

"Laurel, let me give you a hug, *cariña.*" The woman was pretty but older, with gray hair tied back in a bun, and worn skin that had seen the sun. "You don't remember me? Roberta, your tía! You haven't seen me since you were this high." She held her hand just above the ground. "I came to visit you and your family when you were young."

Laurel did remember now, but just barely. "You had long hair, down to your waist, right?"

"Still do. I tied it up today."

"You're Abuela's—"

"Sister. Her little sister. Don't you remember me visiting? We went to the movie theater. And we had a big party, remember?" She spoke with only the slightest tinge of an accent. Most likely she'd learned English at a young age, probably in school. "Ah, don't worry, you were pretty young. That's a long time ago to remember."

"It's good to see you. Does my mom know you're here? Are you staying at the house?"

"No, I haven't talked to her yet. I walked in late, I couldn't find the church. I flew in this morning, my plane landed at five, and then I gave the taxi the wrong address. It was a last-minute decision, the whole thing. But I had to say goodbye to Ramon. He was a friend to me, you know. He was like an older brother, all that time he stayed at the farm. I was just a girl, then. He used to run around with me in the fields, play tag. We made crowns out of the sugarcane and my parents would get mad at us." She laughed through the chest and the throat all at once. There was a roundness to her cheeks that made her look too young to have gray hair. No—silver; silver hair. Laurel wondered how old she was. Ten years younger than Abuela? So she must've been in her sixties?

"Oh, and is that your sister over there?" Tía Roberta waved Paloma over. By the blankness of her face, she also didn't know who this was. Paloma whispered to their mother and the two of them walked over.

"Tía Roberta! So good to see you," Laurel's mother said. "What a surprise!" They hugged each other.

"A surprise to me too. A little last minute but I made it. I'm so sorry for the loss of your papá." She held Laurel's mother's hands, sandwiched them between her own. "Ah, Paloma, look at you. Look at these girls. They are both so beautiful. So grown-up."

Laurel was almost thirty. Of course she looked grown-up.

"Paloma, you look so much like your grandmother when she was your age. Doesn't she? You've seen the pictures, Alma. That same small forehead. And you got the lips." Paloma smiled and nodded. "I've heard you're going to be a doctor," Tía Roberta continued. "That's very impressive." She looked at Laurel. "And you, missy? What have you been up to? Taking over the family business, I hear?"

Laurel burst into tears. What was happening? She wasn't a burst-into-tears kind of person. She usually only cried when she was alone, in bed with the covers over her head, or in the shower where the water could wipe her tears away. But now Laurel couldn't stop crying. These were powerful tears, too. She hiccupped and gasped and couldn't catch her breath. Evan, who she'd almost forgotten about, had been silently standing next to her this whole time. He hugged her around the shoulders.

"He's gone," Laurel mumbled into Evan's chest. "He's never coming back."

"I'm sorry, *querida*." Tía Roberta patted Laurel on the back. Her palm felt hot through Laurel's t-shirt. "Yes, of course you're taking over the business. Of course. Is this the *novio*?"

"Evan," he said, and he stuck out one hand, the other still wrapped around Laurel's shoulders.

"Pleasure to meet you, Evan. What's your line of work?"

"I work in the slaughterhouse too. In finance."

"Oh, great. That's a good industry. Finances will always be needed. Teaching, too, and doctors. All the other industries are dying out, it seems."

"How's the farm, Tía?" Laurel's mother asked.

"I just replanted after the last storm. The crops are doing well now."

"Are you a farmer?" Paloma asked. Laurel had forgotten she was even there. Her arms were crossed over her white dress, like a little girl.

"No, no," Tía Roberta laughed. "It's just a big garden, something to do, extra food. I still go to the *mercado* in town."

"What do you grow?"

"All kinds of things. The old classics—corn, squash, beans. The new classics—kale, spinach, lettuce. I have one cow, one horse, and one old burro. And chickens."

"That's awesome," Paloma said.

"It's a big old property. Right up against the ocean."

"It sounds beautiful."

"Come visit anytime, Paloma. You too, Laurel."

"I think it's a little too dangerous," Laurel's mother said. "That's what I've heard."

"There's been a break lately. The new president is popular so far. Riots have stayed in the city, mostly. The gangs are around, but you just have to be smart about it. And things have been quiet lately. Everyone is distracted by that boat. That plastic boat."

"What plastic boat?" Laurel's mother asked.

"The one going to the island?" Laurel asked.

"That's it, yes. The pirate boat."

"It's coming to El Salvador?"

"It's sailing down the Central American coast. It's in Guatemala right now, headed to El Salvador. They say it's headed down to Chile and then to the South Pacific. They're like—what is it? Peter Pan."

"Peter Pan?"

"They steal from the rich and give to the poor."

"That's Robin Hood, not Peter Pan," Paloma said.

"Yes, that's it. I haven't seen those movies in a long time. They steal from the rich and give to the poor."

"What are they stealing?" Laurel's mother asked.

"Have you not been watching the news?" Laurel said.

"I've been a little busy," her mother said quickly, and Laurel knew she'd upset her. "Sorry, Tía, but I'll talk with you later. We have guests." She stepped forward. Her dress rustled at her feet, like a curtain with wind through it, and she left.

Tía Roberta patted Laurel's shoulder again. "Your mom's focus has been elsewhere."

Laurel wanted to shout at her. Yes! She knew that already!

The four of them stood in silence for a moment, their faces turned to the ground. Tía Roberta readjusted her turquoise, beaded necklace and then folded her hands in front of her stomach. "All right, my girls," she said. "I'm going to talk with your father. I'll see you later."

She walked away in what seemed like slow motion, like a feather falling through the air. Another moment of stillness and silence. Paloma's eyes met hers. She stepped toward Laurel and opened her arms for a hug.

"I've never seen you cry this much," Paloma said into her shoulder.

"I'm not crying anymore."

"Still."

Laurel pulled away. "We're at a funeral."

"Just saying. I've never seen you cry this much. Ever."

"I cried when Abuela died."

"You did?"

"Paloma, I can't deal with this right now."

Laurel was mad at Paloma, sure, but she was also mad at everyone, everything, even Evan's heavy arm, the way it pressed into the bones on top of her shoulders.

"I might pop into work today," Laurel said suddenly, her voice flat. "Check up on things."

"Isn't it closed?" Paloma said. "It's Saturday."

"I need to get organized."

"Laurel," Evan said, pulling his arm tighter around her. "I'll help you on Monday."

"No, I'll go now. I need some time alone."

"Ditching our grandfather's funeral to work?" Paloma said.

"Our grandfather? Why do you try to act so white?"

"Abuelo, grandfather, same thing."

"He wasn't Grandpa, he was Abuelo."

"Abuelo, grandfather, same—"

"He was our abuelo."

"So he was our grandfather, what does it matter what language it's in?"

"We're Latina, that's why it matters," Laurel said.

"We grew up going to the English-speaking high school. Neither of us is fluent in Spanish. We've never even been to El

Salvador. And you, especially—have you looked in the mirror lately? What right do we have to call ourselves 'Latin?' We're white girls."

"Have *you* looked in the mirror lately?" Laurel said. "No one would ever call you white."

"Some people do." Paloma stared at her feet. Her hands moved into the pockets of her dress. "And we are white. We're mostly European."

"Why are you so afraid of our heritage? We're half *Salvadoreña*. Half!"

"We have Salvadorian heritage. We have a Salvadorian-American mother. But it doesn't count. Yeah, I may look not-white, but I don't look Latina, either. No one knows what I am by looking at me. And we were raised here. We're American."

"We're Salvadorian-American," Laurel said.

"So what? We're not special or different or anything at all."

"You've got some real issues, Paloma. You know that?"

"Me?" Paloma laughed. "You're the white girl who calls herself a person of color."

"I've never said that. All I know is we're half Latina and no one can ever take that away from us."

Paloma smiled. Her white, even teeth suddenly seemed shark-like. "You know, this isn't the place for this, is it?" she said.

"You brought it up."

"No, I think you did—"

Evan cleared his throat. "Maybe we should all get a drink?"

Laurel nodded and walked as quickly as she could toward the bar.

*   *   *   *   *

That night, after everything, Laurel sat on the edge of Evan's bed and watched the video messages on her phone. One was from her apartment's landlord, the pre-recorded monthly rent reminder. Another was from Tío Marco, from after the funeral, asking for directions to Laurel's parents' house. And the last was from Paloma. It was only an audio message.

"Hey. It's—Paloma. Obviously. I just wanted to apologize. For earlier. That wasn't—it wasn't what I meant to say. Not like that." A brief silence. Paloma's breath pulsed against the speaker. "The funny thing is that I've been wanting to go to El Salvador. Despite everything. Abuelo told me he wants me, or you, or both of us to go there. And all the old stories. I don't know. It would be nice. Anyway. Just wanted to say sorry. Goodnight."

The long beep reverberated in her ear like the prick of a needle. Paloma had called at 6:30 PM. Laurel had still been at their parents' house, then, and so was Paloma. She'd probably seen Laurel's phone, abandoned on the kitchen counter. She'd probably hid in her bedroom, just a wall away, and called knowing she would get Laurel's voicemail, instead of talking to her in person.

Laurel leaned back into the pillows of Evan's bed, and she tried desperately to sleep.

CHAPTER EIGHT
PALOMA

PALOMA SAT BY THE WINDOW AND LOOKED OUT AT THE WORLD. A field of smoke covered the sky, a stagnant blanket of white and gray. The smell seeped through the walls. For the first few hours, it had smelled good—like campfires, and cedar. It smelled familiar. But then it built. It began to scathe. Her throat itched. Her eyes watered, even inside the house.

The fires themselves were fifty miles to the south. Lightning fires, as usual. The drought had allowed them to build, and build, until they stretched the lengths of entire cities. These were the biggest fires in a decade, and they were still growing. Paloma imagined the fires as living beings, reaching their arms outward and dancing in broad circles, igniting everything in their path.

Paloma missed running outside. The treadmill wasn't the same—her mind needed something to focus on, something more than just a screen. It would be months before the air was clean enough to run again.

Her phone buzzed. Kara had sent her a video. She was on a graduation trip to New York. "Look at this; from the storm last night," Kara was saying. She laughed and pointed the camera at her feet, which were buried to the ankles in water. "This is just a sidewalk, not a stream." She pointed the camera back at her face. "This, my friend, is the apocalypse." She smiled, and the message ended.

Paloma held her phone to the window and filmed the smoke. "No, Kara, *this* is the apocalypse."

She sent the message, then stretched back on the couch, her folded her hands over her stomach. Was it true? Was this the apocalypse? Things got worse every year; more intense, longer-lasting, heavier, deeper, wilder.

Paloma's mother stepped through the front door. She took off her filtration mask and hung it on the doorknob.

"Paloma, have you been sitting there all day?"

"Most of it."

"Aren't any of your friends in town?"

"No. Most of them are gone."

Paloma's mother said nothing. She sat next to her on the couch and sorted through her purse.

"Almost everyone's on trips to celebrate graduation," Paloma went on. "Kara's in New York."

Her mother nodded. "Good for her. Even with the flooding."

"I was thinking maybe I could go somewhere," Paloma said. "I have so much time. And I have the money Abuelo left me."

"You can't go off by yourself."

"I could stay with family."

Her mother set her purse aside. "Not in El Salvador."

"You heard Tía Roberta. It's not that bad."

"Not bad for El Salvador is still bad for everywhere else."

"It can't be much worse than here."

"What's going on here? Just the smoke. And the shootings."

"The smoke, the shootings, the food shortages, the drought. I'm sure the water's not shut off at Tía Roberta's house."

"If she even had running water to begin with. I don't think she even has electricity."

"It can't be that much worse there. Everywhere's bad."

"You're an adult now. You can do what you want. But I want you to know that you may be disappointed. You have this picture in your head of what El Salvador will be like, and it's not like that. Even thirty years ago it was dirty. We couldn't go out after dark. It had changed so much from when my parents were young. There was this tree I wanted to see. Your abuelo told me about it; this big ceiba tree on the side of the road. He said the trunk was as wide as two cars stacked next to each other; it was the biggest ceiba tree he'd ever seen. Every spring, just before Easter, thousands of *chicharras*—cicadas—absolutely covered the tree, every inch of it. They were beautiful bugs, with blue, green, purple bodies. He used to take one and put it on his shirt collar, and it would stay there all day, completely calm, completely happy, like a little pet. It would stay on his shirt until nightfall, and then it would fly off. For some reason the *chicharras* loved this ceiba tree, and only this one. As soon as they hatched from their nests in the ground, they flew up to the tree, so many of them that the cars driving under it were dusted with what looked like rain. Only it wasn't rain." She laughed, softly, to herself. "It was pee from the *chicharras*."

"Wait, cicada pee? That's kind of gross."

"Well. But everyone in town knew that tree, and those bugs. And they loved them. I wanted so badly to see it when I visited, but the tree had died and been cut down, and the highway had been replaced with a freeway." Her mother frowned. "You're going to be disappointed."

"Maybe. But I need to see it for myself. And now's the best time. The only time, maybe; I have nothing to do all summer."

"You could get a job."

"Here? What, work in the slaughterhouse with Laurel?"

"You can do whatever you want, *cariña*. Just be wise about it."

Paloma nodded.

"And make sure Tía Roberta can pick you up at the airport. It's a long way to her house."

CHAPTER NINE
LAUREL

EVAN STAYED BY LAUREL'S SIDE ALL WEEK. He was quieter than usual, somber, and she appreciated it. Laurel couldn't handle jokes right now. Distractions, yes; jokes, no. She slept over at Evan's place every night. He left music on as they fell asleep, and he snored, just a little bit, just through his nose, like a sick person breathing through stuffed-up nostrils. That was exactly what she needed. Noise. Filled-up spaces. Body heat. She wanted to retreat into the dull, gray part of her brain where there were no memories. Empty, that's what she wanted. She wanted to be empty.

Despite his own somberness, Evan kept trying to cheer her up. He made pancakes for her one morning—from a boxed mix, sure, but still homemade. Every afternoon he brought her a cup of coffee in his own mug, the white one with "LIFE." written on its side. He suddenly seemed older. In certain lighting she could see creases forming on the outer edges of his eyes. Three prongs on each side, like forks. And, after he smiled, his cheeks moved slowly back to neutral, half-parenthesis smile-lines lingering for much longer than they used to.

"I'm here for you," he said at night as he rubbed her back. He sounded stupid when he said that. Too stiff. I'm here for you. Well yes, obviously, thank you, but that was something one should show rather than tell. It would be like her saying, "I appreciate you." Who were they, robots? Greeting cards?

"You'll never guess who's going to El Salvador," she said into the pillow.

"Your mom?"

"Guess again."

"You?"

"No. Paloma," Laurel said.

"Why aren't you going?"

"I don't know. I have stuff to take care of here."

"If you want to go, I can manage—"

"No. No, that's okay."

"Why not? You have the money. I'm telling you I'll cover for you at work. It would be good to reconnect with Paloma."

"I don't think this is the right time for me to go. Abuelo left me with a big responsibility."

She was scared. Scared of being called a *gringa*. Scared of no one realizing she was half *them*, half Latina, half El Salvadorian. She wasn't fluent enough in Spanish to make up for how she looked. She would be seen as a tourist, a vacationer, an outsider. And maybe she was.

Besides, she had to concentrate. A few days later, they had a meeting with Bradley & Bradley. They'd asked to sit down with her and Evan to discuss "what things would look like moving forward." So, essentially, they wanted to tell her they were sorry for her loss, and officially designate her as the new manager.

The day of the meeting, she wore professional-looking slacks and a flowery blouse that suddenly felt a little too tight around her neck. "Do I look okay?" she asked Evan.

"Yeah. It's just Bradley & Bradley. No need to get dressed up."

"I just want them to see me as someone who can take things over."

"Honestly they're probably not going to notice how you're dressed."

Maybe he was right, but Laurel felt better anyway. She felt ready. Ready to take on anything.

The guys from Bradley & Bradley always dressed in one of two ways; slacks with dress shirts, or dark jeans with blazers and ties. Today they were wearing the latter, both of them, and she wondered if they'd planned it.

"Ms. Monti. Nice to see you again."

"You too."

"Of course, not so wonderful under the circumstances," the other one said. "We're so sorry for your loss."

She hadn't figured out what to say to that yet. Thank you? I'm sorry too? Yes? "Everything's all set up in here," she said. She took them into the break room, where Evan was waiting at one of the long dining tables.

"Evan. How's it going?"

He stood up and shook their hands. "It's good. Things are good."

The two men sat down. She always forgot their first names. Their last names were Brentwood and Gamache, but she could never remember which was which. One had a square face and one had a chubby face but a slim body. Evan was usually the one who dealt with them.

"We know that these last few weeks haven't been easy for you and your family. Your grandfather did an excellent job of managing this property. He was organized and prompt."

Organized? Abuelo was diligent, but he wasn't incredibly organized.

"When he signed on with us, he agreed to a step-by-step growth process. Originally he was doing it all; sourcing the livestock and distributing it after processing. First we helped him streamline by taking on the sourcing, and expanding to larger markets. We branched out from California to some of the cheaper feedlots in the Midwest. But the reason we bought this company is because we liked the branding. People like their local food. And as long as the slaughtering process is being done here, we can tell Californians that this is a local product. The stores and restaurants who pay to use this slaughterhouse pay a little bit more to have that label. There's bigger and cheaper slaughterhouses in, say, North Carolina, in Iowa, in Texas. But for a time people were willing to pay extra for local."

The square-faced guy took over. "But then, Ms. Monti, you know all about the drought here in the west, and the economic impacts of it. Running this place—the cleaning, the steaming, the rinsing—it's getting more expensive."

The other guy again: "The bottom line here is that we need to make some changes financially. This has been a downward trend and it doesn't show any signs of letting up. Given the managerial circumstances, we think this would be a good time to execute those changes."

"What changes?" Laurel asked.

"We need to do an update of the machinery here. We know your grandfather didn't like the idea of an automated disassembly line, but that's the way things are going in the industry. This property is the last in our holdings to make the transition to a robotic workforce."

Square-faced guy cut in: "And, let's be fair, this will lead to a better situation for the workers as well. They can find better jobs elsewhere."

"Will you help them find other jobs?"

"Unfortunately no, we can't do that, but surely they'll find something. They'll all get good references from us."

"The other big change is our sourcing. We're using genetically enriched cattle now, from a lab-farm in Kansas. We've signed an exclusive contract with them. The cattle require half the amount of water and a third the amount of food as standard cattle."

"Now, to help these changes along, we need a new manager. We'd like to ask you, Evan, to take over for Ramon. Ms. Monti, we would be honored if you would stay on with us in your current position."

"My abuelo wanted me to take over."

"Your abuelo?"

"My grandfather. Ramon. He wanted to hand off the position to me. I'm supposed to be the new manager. Didn't he tell you? That's always been the plan."

"When your grandfather sold the slaughterhouse to us, he gave up some of the decision-making to us as well. We understand your position, but we have to do what's best for this property."

"Tell them, Evan. You know Abuelo wanted me to be manager."

"Laurel," Evan said. "Should we step outside for a second?"

"Sure. Fine."

Evan grabbed her hand. Sweaty. They huddled outside the break room. "Babe, you know how much your grandad meant to me? I thought of him as family."

"Exactly. And you're going to respect his wishes."

"If I don't accept this job, they're going to pull in someone from the outside."

"Or maybe they'll let me—"

"They don't trust you to do what needs to be done. You're too sentimentally attached to all of this."

"What does that mean?"

"You're too much like Abuelo. You care about more than just the money. You'd resist the automation, and the GMO's. Honestly, I'm surprised they're not closing the place completely. They want someone who's going to make this place more profitable." He grabbed Laurel's shoulders. "But if I take the job, you'll still have a say in things. It's me, you know? You can be my co-manager even if you don't have the title."

"We can't automate this place. We have hundreds of workers here who will be out of a job. And the animals—what if something goes wrong with the automation? What if they suffer?"

"I mean, they're going to die anyway. And it's unlikely anything will go wrong. Robots are more reliable than humans. That's why it's called *human error.*"

"This whole place is unraveling."

"They're here to help. They're experts." He smiled weakly. "And you have to acknowledge that this is a big step for me in my career. You can't ask me to give that up."

She said nothing. Her eyes fell to the floor, to Evan's leather dress shoes.

"You want me to go back in there? Insist that you should be the manager? The honest truth, Laurel, is that I want to do this. Okay? I said it. I want to be the manager. Wouldn't it be—can't we make some sort of a compromise?"

"You would put that many people out of a job?"

"I have to do what they tell me to do. They know what's best for the company."

"And how exactly do they know that if they're hardly ever here?"

"You're being childish."

That was it, that was enough. She shoved her way back into the break room. "If you can't make me manager I can't work here anymore."

One of the men stood up. "Ms. Monti, we'd love to have you stay on."

"Stay on?"

"Ms. Monti, we have to do what's best for the company."

"It's what your grandfather would want," the other guy said. "To grow and keep this property alive."

That's when Laurel left. Evan grabbed her wrist but she didn't stop. "Laurel!" he yelled. "Come on, wait!" He hurried behind her. "I know you don't understand, but I'm trying to do what's right. At least call me. Call me later when you calm down."

She didn't call him. There was nothing more he could say. Nothing would make up for this. She hoped that ghosts and the afterlife weren't real, that Abuelo, wherever in the dark universe he might be, couldn't sense the collapse of his life's work, the belittling of it, this slow crumbling of sand into the sea. She couldn't stand to see it spiral away from her. She couldn't bear to watch Evan betray her; to watch the slaughterhouse turn over to automation and genetically modified cows.

Laurel drove through the smoke to her rat-infested apartment. She sat on the bed, on top of the neatly tucked sheets. For a half-hour or so she listened to the scatter of rat-feet against the walls and the ceiling. Then she called her sister. "What flight did you book?" she asked. "I'm going with you."

CHAPTER TEN
PALOMA

PALOMA WATCHED THE PATCHWORK DANCE BENEATH HER. Dark green hills faded into bone-white expanses, and then back again; green, white, green, white, white. She saw *los volcanes*, all of them, towering, hollow, primeval. She saw, too, the thin line of the ocean, leaning in toward sunset. As the plane lowered, she felt the humidity seep through the walls of the plane. The air became liquid. Through the window she saw a distant hill, rimmed in fog. This was the only green visible amidst the concrete.

"Finally," Laurel said, leaning over to look out the window. "We made it."

Tía Roberta was waiting for them by the baggage claim. She looked older than Paloma remembered, even though she'd just seen her weeks ago. Maybe it was the lighting coming in from the sides, bringing out her sunspots and the delicate lines around her mouth. Maybe it was because her hair was down, long and healthy, but graying.

"Welcome, girls." She hugged each of them. "So good to see you. I have some little presents waiting for you at home."

They stepped outside. The humidity deepened. Sweat rose on Paloma's forehead and her chin. A filmy grayness coated the sky, but it wasn't thick enough to block the sun.

"Come, this way," Tía Roberta said. "Stay close." She led them down the sidewalk. Hundreds of people milled around them, dragging suitcases and plastic shopping bags and children's clothes still on hangers. A man shoved Paloma's elbow. Another held up an old milk carton with the top cut off. Inside was a collection of ancient-looking cell phones. *"Diez dólares para la señorita,"* he said, shaking the tub at her face. "Ten dollars for you."

"No, *gracias,*" Paloma said.

"No," Tía Roberta said. She grabbed Paloma's hand. "Don't talk to him. Don't talk to anyone. There are lots of *malos* in the city."

"You think he's a gang member?"

"Him? No, probably not. Every time I come into the city he's selling the same cheap things. *Salvadoreños* don't buy them. It used to be the tourists, and we don't get many anymore."

"How does he make a living, then?"

"That's why you have to be careful. A lot of the vendors are not there to sell, they're there to steal. It's sad because a lot of them are talented; they used to sell nice things, hand-made things, homegrown things. They used to have big markets on the weekends here and everyone from the country would come to sell. Not anymore. Everything's too expensive now."

The air smelled like gasoline and something riper, sweeter— mangos. They passed a fruit stand and Tía Roberta said, "Who would buy mangos when the trees are everywhere?" She pointed at a tall, dark tree a few blocks away, in a grassy area next to a steeple. "Those mangos are ripening as we speak."

They made it to her car, which she'd parked a half-mile away. "It's cheaper here," Tía Roberta said. "At the airport, they charge you fifty dollars." She helped them throw their suitcases into the trunk.

Paloma climbed into the backseat and rolled down her window. San Salvador looked a lot like Terrysville. It had the same stores, only darker, plastic-crusted, worn. McDonalds, Burger King, KFC, Lustro-Mart, Target, Nike, Starbucks, Amazon, Walmart, their logos garish against the heavy sky. Most of them looked empty.

If it hadn't been for the voices, the Spanish words rising and falling, the masses of people crowding the sidewalks, the men in their collared shirts, the women in their jeans and *chancletas* and long-sleeved blouses, she could easily have never left home.

They drove into the suburbs, the outskirts, and things became more interesting. There was so much to see—a brightly painted wooden cart pulled by two horses; a rusted truck with no tires, abandoned on the side of the road; a fruit stand selling imported apples; two little girls—blonde, surprisingly—playing with sticks on a front lawn; a billboard advertising Coca-Cola with real *azúcar*; an old man riding his bicycle along the highway; a dog with white spots sniffing through a recycling bin.

The sky opened up as they drove farther from the city. They passed sugar cane fields, blue-green, the same color as the mountains in Oregon. Clouds circled over them, dark and light, the shades moving fast, ethereal, manipulating the sun into long, thin bands. White birds plucked through the fields. They were tall and elegant, with snake-like necks, and they danced slowly in the afternoon light.

"Roll up the window, Paloma," Tía Roberta said. "We're going to pass the trash pile."

There had been trash along the side of the road the whole way—plastic cups, chip bags, water bottles—but nothing compared to the trash pile. Out of nowhere it rose up from the sugar cane, a great black-brown hill stretching endlessly toward the sun. TV's, laptops, tires, couches, cars, everything imaginable, interwoven with plump, leaking darkness, brown things, filthy things, dirt and muck and rotting food and used tissues and toilet paper. Even through the car she could smell its denseness; its damp, rotting odor.

"We used to have a dump," Tía Roberta said. "A real dump, far away from where anyone lived."

"What happened to it?" Laurel asked.

Tía Roberta laughed. "It got full. Now people put their trash wherever. Most of them put it here. *Es una lástima.*"

Paloma looked down at her lap instead of out the window. She waited until they passed the trash pile, until the smell had dissipated.

Laurel broke the silence. "What's going on with the boat, Tía Roberta?" she asked. "Have you heard anything?"

"Which boat?"

"The one going to the island."

"Ah, yes. People are excited about it. They think it might bring tourism into the town." She laughed, deep in her throat. "I don't think many people are traveling, these days."

"We have to see it," Laurel said, her eyes, too, aimed out the window, at the trees, off, behind the fields, behind what seemed to be miles of dead, bleached sugar cane.

They passed a parked car with its trunk open. A woman leaned against the passenger door. She waved them down, both hands above her head, her eyes calm, unworried. Tía Roberta didn't stop.

"Tía Roberta, I think that lady needed help," Paloma said.

"We don't know her. She might be up to something. You have to be careful around here, Paloma. People are crazy. We might stop to help her and men will pop out of the car. With guns. It happened to my neighbor's nephew. They shot him and took his phone and his money. You never know what the gangs will do. Sometimes they stop the car, stand in front of it, and they point a gun at your head."

"What?"

"I keep the doors locked and I don't stop for anyone."

"I thought you said it was safer here, now?" Paloma said.

"It is if you're smart about it. You just have to be careful, that's all."

After another hour of driving, they made it to the *finca*. Tía Roberta's cow waited at the fence. She was creamy white, with wrinkly skin and a string of twine tied around its neck. She stared at Paloma with big brown eyes. Black, but a faint, balmy black, like coffee grounds.

"We're here!" Tía Roberta said. "Welcome to the *finca*."

Paloma stepped outside, onto the gravel. The wind smelled like fallen leaves, like still pond water, and, distantly, like salt.

"Are all these fields yours?" Paloma asked.

"Out to the beach."

"Those trees, too? The forest?"

"All of it."

"This must be worth so much money," Laurel said.

"Maybe. Maybe not."

The house was small and clay-colored, with a row of shrubby trees along the walkway. "These are the *flores de mayo*. Some of the girls around here put the flowers in their hair. Makes them look Hawaiian. By now the flowers are gone already. Earlier every year. See the dead ones on the ground?"

"Plumerias?"

"Yes, I think that's what they are in English."

The tile in Tía Roberta's living room cooled her feet. Framed pictures sat on every surface—were those her great-grandparents, standing next to an old truck? Was that Abuela—a scrawny but big-chested teenager, wearing a one-piece bathing suit on the sand, her hair wet from the ocean? And—pictures of Paloma and Laurel? A dual frame held both of their senior pictures. They looked slightly grainy, like they'd been printed out from an email. Next to it was their cousin Victor in a private school uniform.

A wooden cross hung on the wall, next to a bookshelf full of shells. Some looked like snail shells, but others were enormous and spiky, spotted like leopards. One was dark blue, almost black. Another was a bleached, salmon-pink, smooth and skin-like. They seemed store-bought, polished, like they'd never seen the sand.

"Where did you get all these?"

"The shells? I found them."

"Right out here?"

She laughed. "No. Some of them. Some are from Honduras. Some are from Nicaragua. One is from Chile." She picked up the bleached-pink shell and rolled it over in her hands.

"I didn't realize you'd traveled so much."

"I went on a lot of road trips when I was young. Once I drove up to Mexico and then down to Argentina, then back up here again."

Paloma had never heard of anyone driving that much.

"I thought I would collect shells to remember my travels," Tía Roberta said. "Instead of trinkets and little things that are not so pretty over time. Although I have some of those too. Speaking of which." She disappeared into the bedroom and returned with two bundles of tissue paper. "These are for you. A little something to remember."

It was heavy. A shell? Paloma unwrapped it carefully. It was a wooden bird, tall and slender, with a long beak. The dark wood was carved with the details of each feather, and the bird's wings were outstretched in flight.

"A young man in town, Eugenio, he makes them. He and his sister. They go up into the *selva* and use the mahogany trees. Only the ones that have fallen down."

"They're beautiful," Laurel said.

"A trinket but a nice trinket, I think," Tía Roberta said.

Paloma turned it over in her hands. It was smooth, and so dark it was almost purple.

"*Gracias*, Tía Roberta," Laurel said.

"Yeah, thank you," said Paloma.

"You should meet Eugenio one of these days. He's interested in medicine, just like you, Paloma."

Paloma's chest tightened. Medicine. Medical school. She'd almost forgotten. "Yeah, that would be great."

They unpacked. Paloma and Laurel each got their own rooms. One had been Abuela's when she was young, and the other had been Tía Roberta's. Paloma chose Abuela's. There was nothing of hers in there, not anymore. It was generic; a guest room. The furniture was dark and old, but clean. Each drawer was lined with flowery paper, and smelled vaguely like wet wood. A black and white painting hung on the wall—it showed a straw-roofed house and a woman walking with a clay pot on her head. A chicken pecked at her feet. The volcano towered behind her. Paloma tried to turn the light on, to see better, but nothing happened. Maybe there was only electricity at night.

In the hallway she heard Laurel ask to see the beach. She poked her head out. "I want to go too," Paloma said. Tía Roberta nodded and moved slowly to her bedroom to change into sandals.

They walked through the trees, the understory completely bare except for a few twigs and a carpet of brown, rotting leaves. Every brown speck seemed like it could be a snake, but Tía Roberta assured her that they didn't see many.

The ocean blurred through the tree trunks. How long had it been since she'd seen the ocean? She'd visited the Oregon coast her first year of college, but it looked nothing like these tropical waters. Pockets of sun made the waves sparkle. Close to shore it was almost turquoise, and farther out it became a color she had no name for—a blue that was both dark and brilliantly transparent. It didn't smell like the Oregon coast, either. There was no fishy smell, and the wind wasn't as strong.

They emerged from the forest and the water scooped onto their feet, as warm as water from the sink.

"What happened to the sand? Is it high tide?" Paloma asked.

"This is the low tide."

"What about the beach?"

"It used to be here. The water has risen a lot in the last few years. We used to sit out here and have picnics. We would read in the sun and then swim for hours."

"Why has the water risen so much?" Laurel asked.

"Sea level rise," Paloma said. Was her sister that uneducated? "From the melting at the poles. You learned that in school, right?"

"It's been a while," Laurel said without looking at her. "It hasn't been in the news for a while, either."

"It has been here," Tía Roberta said. "All the time. If the ocean rises much more, the whole town will eventually be washed away. But not for a while."

"Can you still swim here?"

"Sure. It's shallow until you go out farther."

Paloma had never swum in the ocean. In Northern California and Oregon the ocean was far too cold.

She waded in slowly, holding her arms out at her sides until the ocean was up to her waist. Her feet wrapped over sticks, and slimy rocks, and sharp, small pebbles. She pressed herself underwater, and then popped up, saltwater stinging her eyes. She took a long breath, then went under again. She swam, absolutely weightless, surrounded by color and shifting light. She could feel it; how the light pierced the water, how it spread quietly over her skin. The ocean was warm, and unbelievably soft, and she felt that she was moving with it, not against it, that her limbs were extensions of the water, in constant movement that took no effort. This was exactly what Abuelo had told them about. She floated on her back and let the sun dry her face, and then she dove down again.

CHAPTER ELEVEN
LAUREL

LAUREL COUNTED TO TEN, AND THEN SHE FLIPPED AROUND TO RINSE OFF HER BACK. Another ten, and then she shut the water off. How had Tía Roberta done this, not once, but *twice* every day, for her entire lifetime? Even in hot, humid weather, a cold shower just didn't feel good.

Laurel wrapped herself in a scratchy towel and waited for the warm air to seep over her. She closed her eyes for a moment. Evan popped into her head. His face, as she'd last seen it—his jaw tight, his eyes just barely beginning to water. No one else would have noticed that. No one else would have seen the purple beneath his eyes, either, or the pink tinge along the side of his nose. He hadn't slept well. He'd known what was going to happen. Maybe it had always been the plan, even before Abuelo had died.

Laurel stepped silently into her room. Tía Roberta and Paloma were still sleeping. The sun had barely risen. Maybe she would go for a walk. She put on a sundress, sandals, and sunglasses, and she tucked her phone into her pocket.

The *finca* was quiet, and dusted with dew. Papaya trees grew in a line against the fence. Behind the house, more fruit trees rimmed the patio—guava, lemon, orange, and mango—and a hammock was strung between two thick-trunked avocado trees. Next to them was a vegetable garden—right now a square of black earth, between plantings—and a tiny, wooden house for the chickens, who had yet to wake up. Tía Roberta's cow, donkey, and horse lived in a fenced-in field of yellow-green grass on the other side of the yard. Laurel could smell them from here. It wasn't a bad smell—just unfamiliar; hay, and fur, and warmth.

She started along the road into town, enjoying the feeling of the sun on her shoulders, and the freshness of the ocean air. Her feet crunched against the gravel, but otherwise it was a quiet morning. She was surprised; she'd expected the birds to be loud. Abuelo had told her stories of the motmot, and the quetzal, and the macaw, all bright and unbelievably colorful, iridescent in the sunlight. He'd told her that their songs—their whoops and high, long whistles—shifted with the weather, and the time of day. "They were so loud, Laurita. All those birds in the forest. They were always singing. I wish you could hear them. And at night, it's the frogs who sing. Someone is always singing."

The ocean peeked through the trees, turquoise and enormous. For some reason it spoke of loneliness—the water, and the dim, curving rainforest trees, with hairy vines hanging from their branches, and the sharp stones, there, beneath her feet, and the emptiness of the road, and the scattering of cardboard and chip wrappers in the drainage ditch.

She passed a circle of houses, their walls made of clay, and their roofs made of what looked like old wooden fences, and sheets of aluminum. A half-folded tarp, a plastic bin, and several drinking glasses were spread out on the grass. Laurel remembered Abuela telling her that, in El Salvador, the poor were unbelievably poor, and the rich were unbelievably rich, and, besides a small middle-class, there wasn't much in-between. That was part of the reason why they'd fought the civil war, but evidently not much had come from it.

A woman—young, round-faced, maybe a teenager—stepped out from one of the houses. She wore what looked like a men's Nike t-shirt paired with a long, flowing skirt. Wet hair dripped down her back in two tightly-wound braids. After a few steps she paused, her eyes on Laurel.

"Good morning," she sad slowly, and then she waved and smiled.

Laurel waved back. "*Buenos días,*" she said, surprised by how far her voice carried, how loud it sounded against the openness of the field. The woman smiled again and bent to tend a campfire. Laurel continued walking.

At last she made it to the big, white church at the center of town. Its stained-glass windows slept darkly in the morning shade, and a flock of birds napped on its stone steps. They looked like pigeons, or doves, with blue-rimmed eyes and gentle, white feathers. Birds—birds at last.

Laurel took a picture with her phone and continued on. She passed a *panadería* and a *carnecería*, a *farmacia* and a *pastelería*, their walls beige and peeling, their windows dark; she passed several multi-story buildings that looked like they'd once been hotels or apartment buildings; and she passed a brand new Lustro-Mart, whose shopping carts were chained to a streetlamp. All this time she'd seen only one other person, an old man walking a fluffy white dog.

At the edge of town, a stone wall overlooked the sea. There, a walking path intersected a grassy park, dotted with palm trees and benches, and bordered by a parking lot. Laurel gazed out at the ocean. That's all it was; ocean, straight up to the wall. Where was the sand? Where was the beach? And the dock, and the fishing boats? Wasn't this where Abuelo used to spend his summers?

Laurel leaned over the railing. The only way to get down to the water was a set of concrete steps. Where did the stairs lead? Straight into the ocean. The last step was completely submerged.

Wind carved toward her in warm sheets. A storm was coming in. It felt good. Even when it was sunny, the humidity reminded her of storm clouds—of the air right above the sea, the full width of the ocean carried in each gust and unfurled onto sand, and concrete, and coconut palms. This was the air of her ancestors. Some of them, at least.

The sky darkened at the horizon. Laurel took off her sandals and wandered down the steps. One, then another. The salt intensified. The wind pressed against her body. Another step. The water splashed at her ankles.

She breathed deeply. This wind had traveled the world, across the empty middle ocean where no one could feel it—across, and across, over Blue Mar and the boat coming down the coast.

Laurel kicked one foot against the water. If only Abuelo was there with her. It was still hard to believe that he was gone. She hated to imagine the slaughterhouse without him; to imagine Evan in Abuelo's chair, at his desk; Evan, overlooking the concrete floor, the line, as it was pounded with water at the end of each day by a machinated hose; his shadow against the shallow liquid, the blood and water pooling together like sunset clouds, blushing, burning, diluting, and then receding into darkness. They could have protested and quit together and started something new. He could've been next to her, right now, on these steps, as the warm and cold mixed together in the water and the air. But he wasn't.

Laurel made her way back to the house. She found Tía Roberta kneeling next to the garden plot, wearing a floppy hat and gloves, her hands poised delicately above the soil.

"*Buenos días*, Tía Roberta," Laurel said, but Tía Roberta's eyes remained on the dirt. She tried it louder: "*Buenos días!*"

Tía Roberta's head whipped up, startled. "*Por dios*, there you are, Laurel. Where did you go?"

"I took a walk into town."

"All that way? It's not good to go alone."

"It was fine. Quiet."

"Go with your sister next time. Or tell one of us, at least."

"It didn't seem dangerous at all."

"It never does, until it is. You just have to be smart about things."

"I passed some houses, on the way. Made of clay. Who lives there?"

"It's the *pobres* who live like that. They have almost nothing. I take them extra *tomates*, when I grow enough. And *huevos*." She stood and dusted off her hands. "Did you have breakfast? Let's heat you something while the electricity's still on."

Paloma sat at the small, wooden kitchen table, eating scrambled eggs, beans, and a corn tortilla.

"Morning," Paloma said.

"Morning. It smells good in here," Laurel said. "Like coffee. Are you making some?"

"*Casi.*" Tía Roberta lifted the lid off a metal pot on the stove. "This is made from the *diente de león*."

"Lion's tooth?"

"That's just the name. It's a yellow flower, very small. It looks like a little sun, and it gets puffy in the summer. The seeds fly all over."

"Dandelions?" Paloma said.

"What's a dandelion again?" Laurel asked.

"It's one of those wishing flowers. You blow off the seeds and make a wish."

"Oh."

"They grow everywhere," Paloma said. "And they're good for you, medicinally, especially for your liver."

"Good," Tía Roberta said, nodding. She turned to Laurel. "Your sister is smart. The *diente de león* is good for you. I grew some in the garden and collected the roots. You grind them and it makes something like *café*. It's much cheaper."

"Is it traditional here?" Laurel asked.

"No," Tía Roberta laughed. "Not at all. But it's popular now."

"You probably won't like it, Laurel," Paloma said. "It's bitter."

"I'll give it a try."

Tía Roberta poured some of the brown liquid into a paper Starbucks cup, which was stained amber on the inside. "Don't worry, I washed it. I always reuse these," Tía Roberta said. "They work for a few more times, at least. Here."

Laurel sipped at it. She'd never tasted anything so bitter. "Do you have any sugar?" she asked.

"Sugar, no. But I do have honey." She handed Laurel a wooden spoon and a glass jar with chunks of honeycomb inside it. "It's fresh from the bees. There might be some wings in there, or some pollen."

"What?" Laurel stared into the jar. "There's wings in here?"

"Eat it, Laurel," Paloma said. "That stuff's good for you. It builds your immune system."

"Yes," Tía Roberta laughed. She patted Paloma's shoulder. "Listen to the doctor."

"Are you serious?"

"Don't worry, Laurita. I have yet to find any wings in my honey. But, pollen—yes."

"People pay good money for pollen at home," Paloma said.

"Your kind of people, maybe," Laurel said. "Not mine." She plopped a large spoonful into her cup. It still tasted bitter, but slightly less so.

Laurel drank dandelion coffee every day after that. It never tasted any sweeter, but the bitterness grew on her, and it gave her energy. Each morning she awoke inexplicably early, just before dawn. She knew she should sleep in—she *was* on vacation—but she couldn't. She awoke naturally, and suddenly, stirred by unremembered dreams, the shadows of which lingered in her tired muscles, and in the heaviness of her eyes.

"Bad dreams? It's because we ate that chicken last night," Tía Roberta said. "Because we had dinner so late." She told Laurel not to eat meat right before bed, because otherwise she would be bothered by the thoughts of the animal. Its energy would be absorbed into her body, into her heart and her brain, and then it would be strung out into her dreams.

Each morning Laurel spent time outside in the garden, where mosquitos and ants and other, lesser-known bugs bit her legs. By the end of the first week her skin was covered in red bumps. Tía Roberta told her to eat raw garlic, and then her sweat would keep the bugs away. Apparently, when you'd lived there long enough, the mosquitos didn't bite you anymore; they grew used to your blood—got bored of it—and they focused on tourists and newcomers instead. Laurel did as she was told, popping a clove of raw garlic after dinner. She was desperate enough; sometimes the mosquitos even bit her inside the house, when she was sleeping, or when she first stepped out of the shower.

El Salvador was stickier, buggier, and more humid than she'd ever imagined. Most days she and Paloma just wandered Tía Roberta's property. This wasn't what she'd expected; she'd envisioned herself lying on the beach, in the sun, diving into the ocean to cool off; heading into town to buy ice-cold mangos on a stick, and carved wooden bracelets to take home as souvenirs; she'd imagined herself going to the fishermen's market to buy giant lobsters, still salty from the sea, and cooking them over a bonfire in the sand.

But it was fine. She'd arrived at a state of mind where everything was neutral; where the world passed through her like a ghost or a cloud. Sometimes she stood where the beach used to be and let the water rise to her knees. She tried to imagine the sand, ivory and clean, and the turquoise line where the water met the beach.

One day a dead bird washed up next to her, its feathers splayed out like thorns. She ran away then, like a child, and she leaped over fallen branches and mountains of ants to get back to the house. Tía Roberta said that birds washed up all the time. This one had a cut in its belly, and she could see the plastic inside, all dark and bloody. Tía Roberta said that was how most of the sea birds died.

One afternoon, when the sun began to cool, just slightly, Laurel and Paloma sat on the hammock beneath the avocado trees, upright, their feet pressed against the soil, their arms sticky with sweat. For a long while they sat in silence. Then Laurel asked: "What do you think?"

"Hm?"

"What do you think of El Salvador? Is it what you expected?"

Paloma leaned forward and rested her elbows on her knees. "I don't know. I guess I thought it would be different. I thought there'd be something left; I thought we'd recognize more from Abuelo's stories."

"We haven't looked, though."

"Looked for what?"

Laurel stood up. "For the things Abuelo told us about. It can't all be gone. Like—the beach. There has to be a strip of sand left somewhere around here. A place where we can tan. Doesn't that sound so good? To lay on towels and let the sun make us hot, and then dive in the water?"

"We've done that. We got to swim. Right over there." She pointed toward the old rainforest trees.

"But that was different. There's no sand."

"Technically there is. Underneath the water."

Laurel exhaled.

"Don't get mad," Paloma said.

"I'm not mad." It would be easy to; in a way she was always mad at her sister. But she remembered the phone call; the message Paloma had left her after the funeral.

That night, when Laurel and Evan had gone back to Evan's apartment, she'd sat on his bed, drinking beet-beer and staring at the rim of beige lipstick on her cup while he took a shower. She'd left without saying good-bye, and she never called Paloma back.

"I just think we should explore," Laurel said. "Let's walk around a little. Look around. We've barely seen anything."

Paloma smiled. "Aren't you the one who's always telling me I'll die if I walk around town by myself?"

"At home."

"Not here, where it's even more dangerous?"

"We probably won't come back. To El Salvador. You know? This is it."

"Maybe." Paloma stood up from the hammock. She dusted off her backside.

Laurel smiled. "This is our one shot," she said.

Paloma laughed. "Okay," she said. "Here, I'll look it up on my phone. 'Beaches, nearby.'"

"You might have to do it in Spanish," Laurel said. "'*Playas.*'"

Paloma's phone dinged. "Okay. Looks like there's one five miles down the road?"

"Why don't you have this on talk mode?" Laurel grabbed the phone from her. "No, that's in town. There's nothing there. Just a wall."

"Well that's the only one that's showing up."

"No. There has to be at least one. A real beach." Laurel spoke into the phone: "*Busca playas con arena, cerca.*"

Her phone responded: "Sorry, I didn't catch that. Could you please say that again?"

Paloma grinned. "Wow, your accent is just too good for my phone."

Laurel handed the phone back to her. "Let's go for a walk," she said. "Who knows what we'll find. Forests, birds, horses, fish. Who knows."

"Lead the way."

Laurel took them away from town, on the dirt road. For a long while they walked through the dust. Sweat clung to Laurel's forehead, her back, her underarms. She brushed a cloud of mosquitos away from her ankles. Next to her, Paloma walked heavily, her eyes cast down.

"God," Laurel laughed. "Abuelo never mentioned all the bugs. Maybe Abuela did. I don't remember."

Paloma smiled. "Me neither."

"I do remember that one story, though, about the family of monkeys who lived in the forest. And the bird that visited them every day, on the fence post; the one with the long tail."

Paloma nodded. Her eyes looked ahead, now, toward a grove of trees that guarded the ocean. "I loved that story."

They were silent for a moment. For many moments. Hours, maybe. They continued walking.

Laurel counted her breaths. Her footsteps. She looked ahead, trying to see beyond the next bend in the road, beyond the wall of trees on either side. Most likely they wouldn't find a beach on this road.

"So. Has anything been how you thought?" Laurel asked again.

"We already talked about this."

"I'm just trying to make conversation."

Paloma's shoulders softened. "The world's going to shit."

"Well yeah. Okay, let's talk about something else, then," Laurel said. They rounded the bend and the trees opened into yellowed grass fields.

"Look at that." Paloma pointed to a building, far down the road. It looked a lot like the huts Laurel had seen near town. The sides were made of flimsy scraps of metal, and the roof was made of what looked like flattened cardboard boxes.

"Tía Roberta told me that the *finca* used to be bigger," Paloma said. "Way back in the day, it was an *hacienda*. All of this would've been our family's land. Whoever lives there, their ancestors were probably our family's servants."

"I've never heard that."

Paloma nodded. "That's what she told me."

Laurel felt a wave of guilt, which was silly. Their ancestors had been rich, so what? "Well that must be why Tía Roberta takes eggs to *los pobres*, down the road, then."

"Yeah. It's a peace offering. She's well-off compared to most people around here. Bigger house, more land. I bet she's afraid the neighbors will cause a mutiny; that they'll rebel after all these centuries of guilt and inequality."

Laurel shook her head. She could tell Paloma was about to get into her academic mode. "Well, like you said, the world's going to shit. Nothing we can do about it."

"Yeah." Paloma laughed, strangely, highly, like a trickle of water. "And what's the point, then?"

"Don't go all moody teenager on me."

Paloma glared. Her eyes seemed darker beneath the cloudy sky. "You never want to hear what I have to say."

"Yeah I do. Tell me."

"Just the future. That's all."

"The future? In ten years or whatever you'll be Doctor Paloma Monti. You'll live in a big house in the suburbs of some big, ugly city, and you'll send a little money home to mom and dad. Probably Tía Roberta, too. And every summer you can travel to Canada or Iceland or Russia or wherever for a nice cool little break. Or Blue Mar. Wherever you want."

Paloma smiled at the ground.

"Come on, you know I'm right," Laurel said.

"I don't know. It's weird. I'm going to be 23 soon."

"Hey, that's nothing. Try turning 30."

"Don't round up. You've still got a few more years," Paloma said.

Laurel nodded. Those few more years lingered in front of her, dark and empty. She didn't like to think about it.

They walked for another hour or so. The air pushed down on Laurel's shoulders. Her footsteps sounded like two damp sponges against the dirt. She looked desperately for a path to the beach, for faded wooden signs, for one single fisherman along the shore. Instead it was only dust, and the thick, hot sun.

"Let's turn around," Laurel finally said, and they began the slow trek back.

They made it to the *finca* by early evening. Suddenly tires crunched, and Tía Roberta pulled up next to them. She rolled down the window.

"Girls," she called. "A certain boat has arrived. Let's go have a look."

*   *   *   *   *

They drove into town. The roads were just as quiet and desolate in that direction, too. For a moment, Laurel worried that maybe the boat wasn't going to be there. But then she saw it—a flag with Planet's logo—the Earth with one of the continents shaped like a heart—high above the palm trees. The harbor's parking lot was completely full. Tía Roberta parked along the street and they walked down to the docks.

"Look how small this boat is," Tía Roberta said. "This isn't going anywhere in the open ocean." She laughed. "*Qué locura.*"

It was a tiny sailing boat. The people on board wore clean, white outfits, and all of them were young. Their skin was unblemished, unwrinkled, not at all sunburnt or windblown. All of them appeared to be white, although Laurel knew better than to judge a person's heritage by their looks. One—a boy who hardly looked eighteen—stepped down onto the dock. He spoke in fast Spanish with a Spain-Spanish lisp.

"What's he saying?" Laurel whispered to Tía Roberta.

"I thought you spoke Spanish now?" Paloma said.

"Not with that accent."

Tía Roberta smiled. "He's talking about the boat. About how hard it was to line it up with the dock here because of the tide. He says that they are here to pick up people who have lost their homes or who are going to lose their homes within the next decade. He says that he is from Planet and they are using donations to give people new homes on the plastic island. They already have houses built. They're looking to become more self-sufficient. They'll give free passage to farmers because they want to improve the agriculture there. Come up there if you have questions."

The guy finished talking, and the crowd pressed against him.

"Where did all these people come from?" Paloma asked.

"In town, and the next town over. We've all been waiting for this. Everyone will be talking about it for a long time."

Laurel smiled. The island itself—that had been revolutionary enough. But taking people there? That was like taking people to Mars.

"I'm surprised everyone felt safe enough to come out here today," Paloma said.

"It's a big deal," Tía Roberta said.

Just then, a woman wearing jeans and a long-sleeve shirt walked over. She hugged Tía Roberta.

"*Mira, tu familia ya está aquí*," she said, looking at Paloma.

"*Sí. Paloma, y esta es Laurel. Las nietas de mi hermana.*"

"*Son de California, verdad?*"

"*Sí*," Laurel said.

"*Habla español! Qué bueno.* It is nice to meet you. You are very pretty."

"Thank you," Laurel said. She hadn't heard that in a long time. "*Gracias.*"

Tía Roberta talked to the woman in fast Spanish. Laurel understood the words *barco* and *isla*, but otherwise she couldn't concentrate. She watched Planet's flag willow back and forth in the wind. What would it be like to go to Blue Mar? To be one of the first to walk on the island?

"I think I'm going to talk to that guy," she whispered to Paloma.

"What guy?"

"The main guy. The one who was talking. I just want to ask him some questions," Laurel said. "I'll be right back."

The line of people extended to the edge of the parking lot. Another crew member—a girl with red hair in dreadlocks—came out, and the line sped up and split in two. Laurel stayed in the guy's line. The sun beat against her forehead. She felt like she was going to get burnt, even in the waning afternoon light.

After ten minutes or so, she made it to the blonde guy. His eyes widened, and he smiled.

"You look like you speak English," he said. "Are you a visitor?"

"Sort of. I'm visiting my great-aunt. She lives here."

"In this town?" His voice was calm, and warm, and devoid of any accent.

"Yeah."

"Is she interested in going?"

"To the island?"

"Unless she lives on the edge of town."

"No, she lives by the ocean," Laurel said. "The water's risen over the years, but it's not that bad—"

"Half this town will be underwater soon. Almost all the residents qualify for a free transferal."

"To the island?"

"Yes, to Blue Mar. That's why we're here."

"How could this boat make it to the island?" she asked.

He glanced behind him, as though he'd forgotten that the boat was there. "This isn't the boat we take to the island. This is just for going up and down the coast. There's another boat that's going to come in and meet us and pick up the passengers. Then they'll take the passengers to one of the big boats that go to the island itself."

Laurel wondered how Planet could afford so many boats when they ran on donations. And these crew members looked so well-paid, or at least well-taken-care-of. Even this guy's fingernails were spotless. The island itself must be a marble sheet of perfection, everything clean, and fresh, and in its place.

"If your aunt wants more information, she can come to our meeting tomorrow night." He handed her a slip of paper.

"You guys still use paper? Isn't that bad for the environment?"

"In this case we're trying not to have too much information online, in case of dissenters." He looked especially young when he smiled, with his cheeks all scrunched up. "But let your aunt know. Maybe she'll be interested. It's a great opportunity."

"I will. I'll tell her."

CHAPTER TWELVE
PALOMA

"WHAT'S THIS WHOLE MEETING ABOUT?" Paloma
asked.

"It's just informative," Laurel said. She handed Tía Roberta
the paper.

"*Free Passage to Blue Mar.* That's the plastic island, *verdad?*"
Tía Roberta said. She held the paper at arm's length, squinting at
the small type. "*A New Community for Climate Refugees. Create a
Better World with Us.*"

"What are you going to do when the sea level rises even more?"
Laurel asked. "You said it flooded last summer, right? What if it
does again? What if the water never goes back down?"

"I can't control the ocean," Tía Roberta said.

"But where would you go? The whole *finca* will be underwater
eventually."

"I will leave when I have to leave, but not before."

"Your job will be gone, too. The whole town."

"If there's nothing we can do about it, then why worry?"

"It's not worrying, it's planning."

Paloma noticed the hardness in Tía Roberta's eyes, like she was trying not to cry.

"Everything will be fine," Tía Roberta said. "*Dios* will take care of things."

Other than the cross on her living room wall, Tía Roberta had never given any hint of being religious. Did she believe in God? For some reason Paloma didn't think so. *Dios will take care of things.* It seemed empty. Tía Roberta's eyes didn't soften at all. There was no comfort in them; no relief.

"You can't trust God with this sort of thing," Laurel said. "You have to do it yourself."

Laurel had seemed a little off since they'd arrived in El Salvador; her hair was un-combed and frizzy, and she walked around with her shoulders curved and drooping, like she was always cold, even in the heat. Paloma didn't know what exactly was bothering her—was she worried about not having a job to go back to? Was this still grief over Abuelo? Over Evan? Paloma wanted to help, to try talking to her, but she didn't know how.

Paloma grabbed the paper from Tía Roberta. "What is it that you want Tía to do?" she asked Laurel.

"Just go to the meeting, that's all. See what these guys have to say. That guy was telling me that Tía Roberta qualifies to go to the island."

"How would he know that?" Paloma asked.

"Everyone in the town qualifies."

"That's ridiculous. They can't be taking entire towns of people out to the middle of the ocean."

"Maybe they don't expect everyone to go," Laurel said. "They know some people will be skeptical. But everyone they approve gets to go for free. It's a pretty low-risk situation."

"What would happen to the *finca* in the meantime? What if the island didn't work out and Tía Roberta wanted to come back?"

"She wouldn't have to sell it or anything," Laurel said. "Just leave it for a while and see how it goes. It's either that or wait here for the whole place to go underwater."

"This land has been in the family for as long as we know," Tía Roberta said. "It goes back to my abuelo's abuelo, and maybe even farther, maybe to the *Pipil*, who knows. I told my parents that I would look after this land and pass it on. I'm not leaving it until I have to."

"Who are you going to pass it on to?" Paloma asked. She had always wondered why Tía Roberta had never married and had kids.

"It doesn't matter," Laurel said. "It's going to be underwater."

"Laurel. Really?"

"I'm serious. There will be no passing on of any of this."

Laurel had a point, but she didn't have to say it like that, so harshly and clinically, not when Tía Roberta was upset.

"There's a little piece of the property that starts up into the hills," Tía Roberta said, her voice heavy. "There's a chance that part will be okay."

"Where?"

"Behind the Sanchez's yard. It curves up and goes behind their property, behind the fence."

Laurel seemed to have no response to this. Her eyes blinked between the two of them.

"I'm sure it'll be fine," Paloma said. "You can live in a little house on top of the hill, or you can come live with us in the U.S."

"It'll be hard to get citizenship," Laurel said.

"How do you know?"

"She's right," Tía Roberta said. "It's hard to get citizenship there. Much harder than it used to be. Everyone wants to go to the United States."

"Things will work out. It'll be fine. I'm sure of it." Paloma hugged Tía Roberta.

"Yes. It's all fine," Tía Roberta said.

Paloma smiled weakly. "I think I'll go outside for little bit," she said.

She escaped the heaviness of the room. The sun had gone down but it wasn't completely dark yet. Light lingered on the tree trunks, a reddish, deep, sunset glow, how she imagined Mars might look. She slid through the grass wearing only flip-flops. They had such strange grass here. It was thick and papery. Tropical grass. She knew the ants would probably bite her, but she didn't want to go back inside and change into closed-toe shoes.

She made it to the fence where Tía Roberta's horse, Galleta, stood. Her fur was reddish-brown, with a white spot between her eyes. So far Galleta had been waiting there every night. Tía Roberta said she'd never done that before—"She's waiting for *you*, Paloma. She likes you." Paloma hoped that was true.

"Galleta, how are you today?" She stroked her nose. "How are you, *muchachita*?"

Her breath warmed Paloma's palm. For a while they breathed together in silence. The chickens quieted. A scant chorus of night-frogs chirped gently, metallically. Tía Roberta told her that they used to be louder; their sound came from every blade of grass, every bush, every tree. They still sounded impressive to Paloma.

Dusk calmed her. The breeze coming in from the ocean; the rustling of the chickens; the honks of Ballena, the donkey; the rumbling bellows of Marisol, the cow. The air smelled green, somehow, like leaves and the gathering of rain, and the sweet, open wildflowers pollinated at night by bats and moths.

She loved this farm already. She couldn't imagine how Tía Roberta must feel, with her whole lifetime of memories here, and, on top of that, the memories of her parents and grandparents and great-grandparents passed on as stories. Who were the first ones here? Her Spanish ancestors? Her *Pipil* ancestors? The first mingling of the two, the first *mestizos*, somewhere back in foggy, ancient time? Nothing seemed real that far in the past. Nothing in the future seemed real, either. This whole place underwater? Her, and Galleta, and a flush of seawater drifting in, higher and higher, murky from the mud between grasses, inching up to her calves. She imagined Galleta trying to kick it away, her feet slicing through the water, the water slicing through her feet, the slithering of muck and fish and seaweed. She imagined them paddling higher, higher up, her and Galleta, until they were at the feet of the mountains. She imagined how the wind might sculpt its way around her face. Her head would be an island. It would bob on the surface, curved, light brown. A bird would land on her scalp and dig its talons into her hair. Then, all at once, everything would run out from under her, the water cycloning down a drain somewhere, and the bird would let go, and she and Galleta would fall.

"Don't worry, Galletita," Paloma whispered, still stroking her nose. "Don't worry."

Mosquitos bit her arms, but Paloma didn't want to go inside. Another gust of wind. The smells changed. Manure. Smoke from a wood fire. Salt. The old wooden barn where Galleta and Marisol slept. Mold. Soil. The tinny, plastic-seated, gasoline smell of Tía Roberta's car. The popcorn scent of rice cooking.

Paloma's hair flew up. She let it pulse across her face. The wind curved in from every direction. It felt like it might storm, but the sky was clear.

"What do you think, Galleta? Can you hear it? Can you hear if the rain's coming?"

Galleta's ears twitched. Maybe she understood. Maybe it was just mosquitos.

"*Palomita, vamos a comer,*" Tía Roberta yelled out the back door. That was the first time she'd spoken a full Spanish sentence to her. Usually it was just smaller bits, a word here and there, kind of like at home. Tía Roberta's English was so good that sometimes Paloma forgot it was her second language.

They ate their *arroz con frijoles* quietly. The news played softly on the bulky TV in the living room. Newscasters always spoke such fast Spanish; Paloma couldn't understand a word they said, but it was nice, having it there, like background music. It eased the mood a little bit. Paloma tried to help, too.

"You know, you actually look tan, Laurel," she said. She held out her arm so they could compare, but Laurel shrugged hers beneath the table.

"I'm tan for me, I guess," she said. "I'll never be as tan as you two."

"Yes. *Chele.* Still *chele,*" Tía Roberta said.

That night, as she tried to sleep, Paloma heard Tía Roberta's slow, sliding footsteps in the kitchen. The water ran in short bursts. The window creaked open, and then the door. What was she doing? Paloma lifted herself to the window and peered out. Tía Roberta stood in the now-calm wind, her eyes toward the bright half-moon. Her hands were tilted up like plates, like offerings, drawn together, and she pulled them higher, until her hands stretched above her head. Paloma opened the window a crack. Tía Roberta's mouth moved, but the frogs drowned out her voice. Maybe she wasn't saying anything. Maybe she was smiling. The moonlight flickered as a cloud passed by. Tía Roberta didn't move. The light spiraled down her arms and onto her hair, her nose, her neck.

"*La luz de la luna*," she heard Abuela's voice. "It will heal you. If you stand out under the moon and let the light touch your skin, it will take away *el dolor*." She pointed to her chest whenever she said this, and Paloma wasn't sure if she meant physical pain or the other kind of pain—emotional pain, inner pain, whatever it was called. Maybe both. "The moon heals you, Palomita. Our bodies are mostly water. If you listen closely you can hear the tides."

Paloma couldn't tell if Tía Roberta's eyes were open. Darkness and distance faded them out, so her face was mostly moonlight. Her hands lowered and separated, and out of them fell a heap of something, flour, or water, or sand, something heavy that gravity brought down fast. And then she left. Paloma jumped back into her bed. Tía Roberta's footsteps returned to the kitchen. A chair dragged. Footsteps slid past Paloma's door, and then Tía Roberta's bedroom door shut, as quietly as she could.

Paloma watched the clock on her phone for half an hour. Then she crept through the dark hallway. Her feet cracked against the tile floor, but she made it outside without Tía Roberta or Laurel rising to see what she was doing. Maybe they heard her, maybe not.

Outside, the night pushed in on her—the tall rainforest trees, leftover from the time before the *finca*; gray, absolutely gray, their tops fragmented and moth-like. The edges, the open spaces between grass and forest, trembled. She looked at the sky. Relief. Absolute relief. Everything around her continued to push and sway, except the sky, with its small, yellow suns and galaxies. The stars—this many of them, at least—were a new concept. They scared her. She loved them immediately. For some reason she wanted to run, just as she had wanted to jump in the ocean that first day. She felt like she was made of air. Maybe it was the water in her body. Maybe that was what she felt; the pull of the tide.

She held out her arms so the moonlight could paint them. Wind passed through, heavy, humid, straight off the ocean. It was a warm wind, but goosebumps rose beneath her arm hairs. The longer she stared at the moon, the more it began to look like a rock. She could see the curve of it, the perimeter that held it there in the darkness. After a while she felt the moon, too, begin to press down on her. She felt like she should sit, and so she did. The grass had already dampened with morning dew. What time was it? How early did dew form on each blade of grass?

Her breathing deepened. In, out, with the distant waves. She stretched long on the grass. Her back grew damp, but she didn't care.

Tía Roberta's laugh cut through the stillness. "Paloma?" More laughter.

The sun shone down behind her, through the thick, wild strands of hair draped over Tía Roberta's shoulders. Paloma sat up. "I guess I fell asleep," she said.

"You're lucky it was windy. Otherwise the mosquitos would've eaten you alive." She looked like she wanted to say more, like she wanted to ask why Paloma was out there in the first place, but she only laughed again. Maybe she had done the same thing before, slept out on the grass beneath the wind-pulled stars, out in the humid moonlight.

CHAPTER THIRTEEN
LAUREL

LAUREL RUSHED TO THE FRONT OF THE OLD HOTEL LOBBY. It was less crowded than she'd expected; about half the seats were filled, mostly by older people. Laurel looked for the guy she'd talked to at the boat dock, the one with the Spain-Spanish accent and the blonde hair. There he was—at a table off to the side, his hands folded in front of him.

"How are you?" he asked. "Did your aunt decide to come?"

"No. Not exactly. I'm the interested who's interested, actually."

"And what did you think of the meeting?"

She'd hardly understood any of it in that fast Spanish, except for the basic tone of it, the audience's reactions—shaking their heads, whispering to their neighbors, laughing under their breath. "It was a lot," Laurel said. "The idea of starting something completely new—"

"Not completely. We have a lot of infrastructure set up already. We're getting solar panels in next week. We have refrigeration and a whole range of housing units. The big thing is getting the agricultural plans going. That's the only way we're ever going to be self-sufficient. And the desalination facility. That will take a few more months, but once those two things are done, we'll hardly have any shipments coming in."

"Who did you say is paying for all of this?"

"We have quite a few donors funding this project, but most of them want to remain anonymous. Legal issues."

"Have any of them been there? Has the Planet guy been there? The director?"

"Shreifer? Not yet, but he plans to visit soon."

"How many people are there right now?"

He half-smiled and glanced at the floor. "Are you thinking about going?"

"I think the whole thing is fascinating, and I would love to see it. I don't live here, though."

"You're part of your aunt's family. You're living with her for the time being. You qualify."

Laurel suppressed a smile. She suddenly felt ecstatic. "Are you sure?"

"Absolutely."

"Where would we meet? If I wanted to go?"

"There's another meeting next Monday. Same place. We'll discuss the details and get the paperwork sorted out."

Did he want her to go? Were they desperate for people, for citizens?

"I'll talk it over with my family," she said.

"Great. Let us know." He seemed older than he had last time; at least twenty. Maybe he was Paloma's age.

"How old are you, by the way?" she asked him.

"Guess."

"Twenty-one?"

"That's what people always say. But I'm twenty-seven."

"Twenty-seven?"

"I have that baby face thing. I've always looked younger than I am." He smiled. It was a nice smile; real, reactionary, not placed. "How old are you?"

She thought about making him guess, but she was afraid his answer would be older than she was. "Twenty-seven. Almost twenty-eight."

"And remind me of your name again?"

"Laurel."

"Laurel. From the United States, right?"

"Yeah. From California. What about you? Where are you from?"

"It's complicated. Believe it or not, I was born in Mexico. We moved to Spain when I was four, and I grew up there, near Barcelona. That's where my grandparents were from, and my parents wanted to be close to them. After that we moved to the United States when I was thirteen."

"Why did you move?"

"We lived by the ocean. We were there when the sea wall broke."

"Oh my god. I remember hearing about that. Was your family okay?"

"We were fine, but our house was flooded."

"Well that's good you were able to get to the U.S."

"It was Planet that helped us with that. They paid for us to come over."

"And now you're paying them back?"

"In a way. I wanted to pass it on. Pass on the good. They do a lot for the displaced." There was a sadness in his eyes. Something about him reminded her of an old man looking back on his life. Nostalgia, that's what it was. Nostalgia for the present. Like he knew everything was about to change.

"Do you think this whole thing is going to work?" she asked.

"What do you mean?"

"The island. Do you think it'll be successful?"

"It already is. This is our time to start fresh, you know? It's out there, waiting for us. We're going to do things right this time."

She believed everything he said. He seemed incapable of lying; incapable, even, of sarcasm.

"We? Are you going, too?" she asked.

"I signed on as a recruitment volunteer down through Panama. Then I'm heading out to the island."

"Do you get paid for any of this?"

"No, but Planet takes care of all my expenses; travel, food, everything. That's how it'll be on the island, too."

"So if I go, I'll see you there—you never told me your name."

"Oh. Mauricio." He shook her hand. "Nice to meet you. Officially."

"Nice to meet you, too."

She looked at him more closely; at the down-turned curve to his nose; the brown, wet-earth color of his eyelashes, so much darker than his hair; the delicacy of his fingers, which he bunched together into his pockets. Something about him reminded her of the white-caps on waves, fleeting and always newly formed, but reliable; you knew the waves would be there but you also knew they would be different—a new current, a new capsule of water-cycle time pulled and stirred by the moon. She wanted to talk with him a while longer.

"And you're sure it's okay for me to go instead of my aunt?"

"As long as you're a family member, you're good. At this stage, Planet is handling things pretty loosely, on the honor system. If someone says they need help, and they're from a designated area, we believe them. Peter, one of the guys in administration, he says that the only people crazy enough to do this are desperate people; displaced people. That's our insurance policy right there. If you're crazy and desperate, we'll take you." He laughed. "I think he heard that in an interview of something. Probably from Shreifer."

"I guess I'm crazy, then."

"Maybe. But crazy in a good way."

"And why are we going to the island by boat? Because planes aren't environmentally friendly enough?"

"No, it's not that. Planet has access to some great electric planes. But they're small, and expensive to run, and hybrid, so it would cost too much. Almost everyone will be on the boat. It's comfortable, I've heard. And it's fast. It can get you halfway across the Pacific in a day."

"The island's not very big. How are you going to fit everyone on it?"

"To start, we're just bringing people over from the Americas. Once that's settled, we'll incorporate people from other continents. We're doing outreach and screenings in Asia and Africa right now so the process will be smoother. Once everyone sees how well the island is doing, more people will want to come over, and we'll have to be more selective. But it's estimated that Blue Mar can hold a population of 700,000 people."

"That's impossible."

"It's called density. And smart city planning. Shreifer gave a great talk about it a few months ago. You should watch it; it's on Planet's website."

"My aunt's wi-fi doesn't do videos very well. It's old."

"Then you can watch it on the boat. High-speed wi-fi throughout. And there's satellite phone service on the island."

"Mauricio!" a woman in a Planet t-shirt yelled across the room. She motioned for Mauricio to come to her.

"Come to that other meeting, okay? We'll sort everything out." He patted her shoulder as he walked past her. "I'm glad you're going. Get ready for the biggest adventure of your life."

CHAPTER FOURTEEN
PALOMA

PALOMA WANDERED INTO THE KITCHEN. Tía Roberta sat at the table, and Laurel stood next to it, her phone on speaker.

"Is everything okay?" asked their mom's voice. "The news said there was a shooting not far from you."

"Did you hear anything about a shooting?" Laurel asked Tía Roberta. She stood up and hovered behind Laurel's shoulder, but said nothing.

"Everything's fine here," Laurel said.

"No, it's not. Your daughter is planning to go to that plastic island," Tía Roberta said. She explained it to them, the whole thing.

"You can't be serious, Laurel," their father said. "This is a joke."

Paloma sat down at the table. She felt a shock, like cold water dripping down her throat. Was it true? Was Laurel actually going?

A long silence. Laurel switched the phone to her other hand and combed her fingers through her hair. "I'm going," she said. "I've made up my mind."

"But why?" their mom asked. Paloma couldn't tell over the phone if she was laughing or crying. "That's what I don't understand. Why would you want to go there?"

"I just have to see what it's like," Laurel said. "It's completely free, and completely safe. And if I don't like it, I can come home. I'd be helping make the world better—"

"There are other ways to do that," their mother said. "How much do you know about this island? It could be a concentration camp, for all we know. The government could be planning to bomb it. Those pirate people stole the island. Who knows what *they* want out of this."

"And what if it's not so easy to come back?" their father said. "How are you going to communicate with us? Do you think there's cell reception there? Internet? An airport?"

"Have you thought this through, Laurel?"

"Yes. And I think it's what's best for me."

"This is not something to take lightly."

"I know."

Another long silence.

"Tell us when you get there, if you can."

"There's internet on the boat. I'll call you on the way over. And there's phone service on the island." She told them she loved them, and she hung up. Her forehead shone with sweat.

Paloma stared hard at the floor, then she glanced at Laurel. "Maybe I can go with you."

"No," Tía Roberta said firmly.

Laurel echoed it: "No. You have school in the fall."

Paloma stared at her.

"The boat only takes half a day to get there," Laurel said. "It's as fast as a plane. I'll be able to come back and visit."

"This is all so sudden, Laurel," Tía Roberta said. "It doesn't feel right."

Laurel shook her head, about to say something, when Paloma interrupted. "It feels like you're going to Mars," she said.

Laurel laughed. "But look how great Mars has done. The new baby; the indoor farm thing. They're thriving. And if humans can thrive on another planet, Blue Mar should easy by comparison."

Paloma didn't think it would be that easy. Nothing was. Even Mars had its issues; because of the differences in gravity and oxygen, the settlers would likely have shorter lifespans, living only until their sixties. They were completely dependent on Earth for most goods and materials—including most of their food, since the indoor farm could only supply about a quarter of the settlement's needs. If anything interrupted a shipment, they would be condemned to months of vegetables and only vegetables, which, thanks to the stresses of Mars' atmosphere, contained only half the nutritional value of Earth crops. And, worst of all, the settlers were trapped. Sure, they could leave their bubble if they were wearing space suits, but that wasn't the same. What if they wanted to feel the wind on their face? What if they wanted to bask in the sunlight, to lay in the sun like the iguana that wandered onto Tía Roberta's patio the other day? And a world without life—a world of red dust, of ancient, dry riverbeds, of barren, untouchable, unknowable rock, devoid of the warmth of chickens and horses, the shy pips of birds, the darkened whisper of leaves, the velvet softness of ocean water— Paloma didn't think she could take it.

"Do you know why they settled Mars? So we'll have a place to go when the Earth can't support us anymore," Paloma said.

"If that's true, then that was smart."

"But it's not working. They still get most of their stuff from Earth."

"They're working on it, though. They're trying. It's better than sitting around and watching everything get worse."

"They're running away. They're not helping. Think about it; even if they figure things out, not everyone will get to go to Mars."

Laurel breathed in deeply. "That won't happen for a long time. And for now we have to do the best we can."

Paloma didn't know what to say.

Tía Roberta spoke: "Understand this, Laurita. That place is made of plastic. There's only so much that can be done."

Laurel nodded. Her lips curled up into a small, mean smile, and, at that point, Paloma knew she was gone.

CHAPTER FIFTEEN
LAUREL

L AUREL WOKE UP IN THE BLACK, REDDISH DARK-
NESS OF PRE-DAWN. Tía Roberta and Paloma hadn't
spoken to her the night before. She wasn't expecting them to say
good-bye that morning, but there they were, waiting for her at
the kitchen table, their eyes half-squinted with sleep.

"At least eat something before you go," Tía Roberta said. She
motioned to a bowl of cereal and Laurel sat down.

"When are we going to see you again?" Paloma asked. She
sounded like a little girl. Laurel felt a tug, a sharp sadness that
almost made her want to stay. She thought she might cry.

"I'll let you know when I get there." She didn't answer
Paloma's question because she didn't have an answer. She had no
idea when she would see her family again.

She felt, somewhat ridiculously, like she was about to head
off to her first day of school. Eating cereal. Off to catch the bus.
The nerves, the excitement, the dread and expectation of being

independent. It made her sad. She missed her parents. How her mom used to give her a bowl of cereal just like this every morning, with a glass of orange juice that was always, always called *jugo de naranja*. She set down her spoon.

"I should head out now," she said. Tía Roberta hugged her. She smelled like the lavender lotion she rubbed on her hands before bed.

Paloma stepped up next, her eyes stern and suddenly awake. "*Buen viaje*," she whispered in Laurel's ear, as though it was nothing, as though she had always spoken Spanish to her sister, when in fact it may have been the first time.

"*Gracias*," Laurel said, and she picked up her bag, and she left, out into the humid, wandering air, to the van that waited for her, its orange lights awash in mosquitos. She glanced back at the *finca*. Marisol, the cow, stood at the fence, her eyes brown and wet and reflecting back the first threads of sunlight.

Laurel handed her suitcase to the driver. He was a round, balding American man. He tried to talk to her about the wildfires in California, how over half the state was burning, but Laurel retreated into herself. She watched the smoke rise up from the clay houses of the *pobres*. She watched the old rainforest trees shudder in the wind. As they passed through town she scanned the church steps for birds, for gray-white feathers, but she saw none.

"Wait here a minute," the driver said, and he left her at the edge of the dock, where a yacht bobbed in the water. A family of five stood with her. She recognized them from the meeting—according to Mauricio, the father was once a fisherman, and he'd now been unemployed for five months. They'd survived, in part, off the fruits that grew feral on their property. Papaya, passionfruit, mango, guava. The mother also planted corn and other vegetables, but they died when the saltwater washed in during storms. Neighbors gave them food, too—leftovers from dinner, batches of cookies, bags of masa, cartons of eggs—but it wasn't enough.

There was no work in town. They didn't have enough money to move. They had no other family members still alive. The two children seemed like young teenagers, maybe twelve and fourteen. Their skin was sun-darkened. The dad was like this, too, but the mother was a lighter olive-tone, close to Laurel's own skin color. Like the woman at the *pobre* village, she wore a faded t-shirt—Puma brand this time.

Laurel smiled at her. "*Ustedes van en el barco?*"

"*Sí.*" The woman laughed shakily. "*Hablas español?*"

"*Un poquito.*"

"*Y como se llama?*" the woman asked.

She said her name the Spanish way, La-u-rel. "*Y usted?*"

"Matilde." The woman asked her something that she didn't understand. But then it was time to go. They were helped onto the yacht, which carried them to the port where the boat was docked. It was as big as a cruise ship, but thinner; sleeker. Inside, every surface was stainless steel—sparse, but clean, and somehow comfortable in its bareness.

Twenty or so *Salvadoreños* waited in stiff plastic chairs below deck. The captain's voice welcomed them in Spanish. Then the boat jolted forward. Slowly, everyone scattered, either above deck or further into the cool interior. Laurel wandered down a level, to a small room with two plush chairs, a charging port, and an underwater window looking out into the sea. At first she saw nothing but water. Then—a cloud of jellyfish, gathered in a translucent, purple colony. They writhed, like organs come to life, raw, and veined, and formless. Trash, too, bobbed against the side of the ship. Baby dolls. Tupperware. Ziplock bags. She knew that deeper down there was more—tiny, broken-up pieces of plastic, old toys or fibers from clothing that were now microscopic or at least small enough to be unrecognizable. This was what the fish and birds ate. Humans, too. Anyone who had the money to eat wild fish had tiny pieces of plastic in their intestines. They'd done studies on it.

Laurel remembered seeing something on the news once about how there was more plastic in the ocean than fish. She'd found that hard to believe, especially after they'd picked up all that plastic to make Blue Mar. Now she believed it.

But if she looked past the trash, and the jellyfish, the water became pure again, a bright, flickering blue that reminded her of space, of the dark places between starlight. It was right there in front of her but still incomprehensible. No one could fully grasp the ocean with their minds—not its size, nor its depth, nor its ancientness. That was why people once thought the ocean was invincible. But humans were powerful. Humans could destroy anything; probably even space.

Laurel watched for a few hours, and then she went up to the deck for fresh air. The wind beat against her bare limbs. Goosebumps rose on her skin. Her eyes watered. She stood at the railing, gripping the cold metal tightly. The water kicked and curled against the side of the boat. Farther out, the water lapped more quietly; up, and down, like living shards of glass. The ocean as a whole seemed strangely fragmented. Like it was a photograph, or a ghost—misty and blue, but barren.

She went back below deck. She called her parents. She took a nap. Within a few hours, they announced that Blue Mar was close. Laurel ran back up to the open air. She expected to see the island from a distance, a great sheet on the horizon, with some sort of control tower on it, and lots of buildings, everything white or silver, like a cloud collapsed into the sea. But it was only a lump. It looked, not like plastic, but like concrete, scattered with small, colorful buildings, steeple-like light posts, enormous, metal bins—dumpsters?—and what looked like several porta-potties. A dense wall snaked along the perimeter, downslope from the buildings.

"Look at that. You could almost forget it was made out of trash," a man—probably in his early forties—said to her. He wore a polo shirt with "crew" written on the breast pocket.

"It doesn't look like plastic at all," Laurel said. "It looks like a parking lot."

He laughed. "And it certainly doesn't look like it should be called Blue Mar. Nothing is blue except those little houses."

"Are those what we'll be staying in?"

"I don't know. They didn't tell us much. All I know is that everyone will be matched with roommates."

"We don't get to choose?"

The man shrugged. "I don't know. I'm sure they'll keep families together." He looked at Laurel more closely. "You American?"

"Yeah."

"How did you wind up in El Salvador?"

"My family's from there. I was staying with my great-aunt."

"And why the island?"

"The newness of it, I guess. It seems better than anything we left behind. Or at least like it could be."

"That's noble of you. I'm here because I needed work and Planet was hiring."

"Did they tell you anything? What it's going to be like? What our lives will be like? I'm having trouble picturing it."

"All I know is that, right now, they mostly need people to grow food."

"Maybe they can get some fishermen involved," Laurel said, thinking of Matilde's husband. "There must be fish out here."

"We could feed one person with the amount of fish in this water. The fisheries collapsed a while back, world over," the guy said. "That's why everyone farms now. Trust me, my grandpa guided fishing tours in Washington. He saw it all go down."

Fisheries collapsing. It reminded her of lungs collapsing, and for some reason she pictured a woman falling on a dark street somewhere, clutching her neck and gasping for air.

"I better go make myself useful," the guy said. "We should be docking soon."

"What was your name?"

"Sam," he said.

"Laurel."

"Catch you later, Laurel."

Within moments, it seemed, they had anchored, and a smaller boat began to funnel passengers to the island. Laurel waited her turn in line. Her stomach hurt. It was a deep, aching pressure, like her heart was beating in the wrong part of her abdomen. She hugged her arms against her chest as she boarded the boat.

They rocked speedily through the waves. Laurel felt slightly nauseous. Beads of saltwater gathered on her nose, her forehead, her chin. She breathed in deeply.

"If you have to puke, do it over the side," the skiff's captain said into his microphone. "These tiny boats make a lot of people sick."

More deep breaths. And then the motor quieted. And then the land grew closer. And then, at last, they were there, really there, at the opening in the sea wall, at the edge of the dock. Laurel stepped out, onto a ground with no history. All at once she was freed from deep time, and from the future as well; from weathering, from erosion, from the cycles of nutrients, from the memories of animals. She was freed from nostalgia. Blue Mar was anything humans wanted it to be. It was in their complete control—a land of their creation, a land of their own right, a land without a history of war or conquest. A new beginning—a new ending, a place to go when everything crumbled.

"Dump your bags here," a polo-shirted woman said. She cupped her hands around her mouth. "Dump your bags here. We'll bring them to your housing areas."

"You will not be looking in our bags?" an older woman asked. She was wearing *chancletas*, and a long, fraying skirt.

"For safety reasons we're required to scan your bags. But we won't open them."

"Where is the scanner?"

"*Vamos,*" a man said. He placed a hand on the old woman's shoulder.

"It's a scanning wand. New technology. Hard to keep up with sometimes."

"I have in mine—they can break—"

"Don't worry, *Señora*, we'll be gentle with everyone's bags." She cupped her hands around her mouth again. "Everyone! Leave your bags here! *Dejen sus maletas aquí!*"

The older woman walked away, arm in arm with her husband. Laurel dropped her bag in the pile. She paused and looked around. Everyone moved busily, like ants. How were they not amazed by all of this?

The sky cracked open. Cloudless, like a mirror. There it was. Blue Mar, illuminated before her. The island wasn't as flat as Laurel had imagined; there was the hill in the middle, and the slope leading down to the sea.

The wind smelled brackish, and old, and undone. There were no roads, and no cars, only walking paths, outlined by teal-blue lights embedded in the ground—solar-powered, most likely; maybe leftover from the resort.

One path led to a large, pale building, which cast its shadow upon the rest of the island. Another led to a row of blue houses, the size of small apartments. White borders framed their tiny windows and cheerful blue doors. Each had its own porta-potty, and its own streetlight.

Beneath Laurel's feet there was no dirt, no grass, no shoe-smudges or mysterious brown stains, no weeds growing through cracks in the pavement. It reminded her of the floor of someone's kitchen or meticulously cleaned bathroom. It was an inside floor, unscathed by salt, sunlight, and wind. It seemed as though the island had been covered and kept safe all these months, and it was just now ready to be unveiled.

Laurel was assigned to a tiny house with a Honduran woman named Augusta. She was near thirty and traveling alone. There was a heaviness to her features. Dark circles rimmed her eyes, the color of bruises. She had dark, curly, cinnamon hair, and a mole just under her cheekbone. Augusta knew only a little bit of English. Laurel tried to speak Spanish with her, but she couldn't keep up with her fast-paced answers.

Augusta slept on a bed in the loft while Laurel used the pull-out bed in the main room. They had a kitchen with a minia-ture refrigerator and a gas-powered camp stove, and an outdoor shower that grew cold after fifteen minutes. Once a week, someone came by to collect the waste from their porta-potty, and it was turned into compost.

For the first few days, there was nothing to do. They were told to wait and to acclimate. In the mornings, the day's food was delivered in stainless steel containers labeled breakfast, lunch, and dinner. Laurel found them on the doorstep that first morning, and she quietly checked to make sure hers and Augusta's were all equal. Yes, they were. They'd been measured carefully. For lunch, each tin had exactly ten grapes, ten carrot sticks, five whole wheat crackers, and about one cup of rice and beans. It was a strange combination, but Laurel appreciated the cleanliness of it, how it was arranged so neatly in its little container, perfect and ready and fair.

Augusta slept most of the day. Laurel wasn't sure why she was so tired. All Laurel wanted to do was wander. She walked all morning, all afternoon. Outside of the tiny house village, and past the towering administrative building, Laurel found a giant wooden box filled with dirt, and three enormous, empty depressions that were probably supposed to swimming pools at some point. Beyond that she could see nothing but concrete and sky. One of the crew members on the boat had told her that there were four settlements on the island; East, West, North, and South. They were in the East Settlement. Eventually, once infrastructure was in place, they would build inland, and all the settlements would be connected.

Laurel continued on. The water danced against the sea wall. Next to the dock, where a beach might be, the concrete—how was it that plastic could look and feel so much like pavement?— sloped down gradually, catching the waves in its shallowness, the water neon and spectacular, before disappearing into a sudden drop-off. Laurel felt like she was on the edge of a cliff, staring down into a deep valley, so deep that the sun couldn't reach it. She felt small against the overcast sky, like someone lost in a desert. From a distance she would look like a speck, dangling there between the clouds and the water.

How did the sea not wash all of this away? She wondered this every time the wind picked up. It swept over the concrete barrens, growing so strong that it rocked the walls of their tiny house. The slithering, high-pitched, tea-whistle sounds woke her up at night. She'd never heard wind like that.

One night she stepped out into it. Everything lay still for a moment, and then a gust of wind poured over her. This was what it would be like to stand under a waterfall. Wind and water—it was all the same. She turned in a circle, closed her eyes, and listened. She realized then why the wind sounded weird; there were no trees, no grasses, even, to rustle and sway. The few bushes planted near the docks were the only green things to catch the wind. This was a desert, she realized. A pale, concrete desert, out in the blue middle of things.

CHAPTER SIXTEEN
PALOMA

PALOMA HIKED UP THE HILL TO THE CITRUS ORCHARD—lemons, limes, grapefruit-oranges, orange-lemons. She sat in the shade on a wool blanket. The trees swished, like feathers, or waves. If she stared at them long enough they vanished. The sky poured through, a shifting mess of clouds, and far-away rain, and peaks of sun-heated blue. Most days she could pick out the occasional seabird, too, a high, black speck disappearing into the sun, but not today.

She held her phone up to her face.

"Good afternoon, Paloma," her phone said. "Would you like to hear today's top stories?"

"No. Tell me—what's the weather in California?"

"Where in California?" her phone said.

"Terrysville."

"Terrysville, California. Weather advisory in effect. Wildfires in neighboring cities. Particulate matter at hazardous levels. Residents are advised to stay indoors. Temperature: 105 degrees Fahrenheit." Her phone paused. "Would you like me to contact your family members in Terrysville?"

"Yes. Text them and ask if they're okay."

"Texting completed. Would you like to know the weather in your current location, brought to you by World-King Cellular Latin America?"

"Let me guess—it's at least 100 degrees."

"Does that mean you would like to know the weather in your current location?"

"Okay."

"Playa Del Sol, El Salvador. Partly cloudy. Thunderstorms expected at 3 PM. Temperature: 100 degrees Fahrenheit."

"What's the humidity?"

"Humidity: 90 percent."

"Yep. It feels like it."

"Heatwave expected, with temperatures rising to 110 degrees Fahrenheit by 4 PM Friday evening."

"Great. And no air conditioning."

"Would you like me to switch to conversation mode?"

"No. Tell me—what's the weather on Blue Mar Island?"

"Blue Mar Island. I'm sorry. There is no weather data for Blue Mar Island. I see in the news that it is a new landmass. Would you like to submit a place request to World-King Cellular Latin America, weather division?"

"No," Paloma said.

"Would you like me to contact your family member on Blue Mar Island?"

"Laurel?" She flashed back to the morning Laurel left. The gray light of the kitchen. The dark windows, reflecting all three of them back as pale, lightless ghosts. The air outside, heavy, about to rain. Laurel's hug. Her half-eaten bowl of cereal. "Ask her how the island is," Paloma told her phone.

"Error. Blue Mar Island has been temporarily blacked out. Messages cannot be sent to that area."

"Then why did you ask?"

Paloma exited out of the voice control system and returned her gaze to the leaves and the sky. For some reason the air smelled more like pine needles than citrus. She closed her eyes. Why did the days have to move so fast? In just two weeks she would be flying back home.

Her phone vibrated. A text from her mother. *We're fine. It's just hot and smoky. All okay there?*

"Tell my mom that everything is fine here, too," she told her phone. "Just hot and humid."

"Texting completed."

A mosquito pestered her ear. She swished it away. Somewhere across the fence, Marisol grumbled. Paloma sat up to look for her, but she saw only grass. The heat hummed. Were those insects? Or just the air?

Another mosquito buzzed past her neck. It began to itch, just under her chin. Time to go inside.

She found Tía Roberta at the kitchen sink, washing dishes under a gentle stream of water. Her hair was tied up in a loose, gray bun.

"Tía Roberta, did you hear about the heatwave?" Paloma asked. "It's supposed to get to 110 degrees by the end of the week. What is that—43 in Celsius?"

"43? *Qué calor.*"

"Have you ever thought of getting air conditioning in here? I'm sure they sell cheap window ones at Lustro-Mart."

"It would only work at night when the electricity is on."

"That's better than nothing."

"You and I, we can get used to the heat. I'm more worried about the plants and the animals. They usually do good in the heat, but they still have their limits."

Paloma had her limits too. The 80's and 90's had been fine, but 100 plus humidity?

"Your face looks red, Palomita. You should drink some water. Here." Tía Roberta handed her a freshly washed glass. "But no ice. The generator for the *refri* is broken."

"When did that happen?"

"Before work. But it's okay. There wasn't much in there. I'm cooking the chicken tonight, and, the milk, and the cheese, and the *marmaon*, we'll just have to use by tomorrow. Good thing is I invited some friends to have dinner."

"Who?"

"The young man I told you about. The one who likes natural medicine."

Paloma had completely forgotten. The bird. The guy who gathered wood from already dead trees.

"His name is Eugenio, and his sister Isa is coming too. Their abuela, Doña Yolanda, owns the old *farmacia* in town."

"They're pharmacists?"

"No. We call it the *farmacia* but it's an herbal shop. Herbs and teas. Plant medicine. Doña Yolanda knows more than anyone about plants. The people who can't afford the clinic, they go to her."

"Did you invite her over, too?"

"No." Another roll of laughter. "She goes to sleep too early. She never goes anywhere for dinner. But you should go and talk to her in the shop sometime."

"Does she speak English?"

"No. But Eugenio and Isa do. They learned it in school. No accent, nothing."

"Same with you. You barely have an accent."

Tía Roberta smiled doubtfully. "No?"

"Just a little bit, maybe. *Un poquito.*"

Tía Roberta hit her playfully with the kitchen towel. "*Un poquito. Claro.*"

In a few hours, Eugenio and Isa knocked at the door. Tía Roberta hugged them both, and then introduced them to Paloma. She tried to shake their hands but Eugenio pulled in for a hug, and Isa did the same. Their skin was far darker than hers, a rich, deep brown. She felt pale in comparison. Isa's long, straight hair hung silkily down her back, all the way to her waist. She smelled like lavender essential oil, and Eugenio smelled like rosemary, or sage. She wondered if they made their own perfumes. Eugenio looked like he could be in a business office somewhere, with slacks and a collared shirt.

"It's so great to meet you," Eugenio said when they sat down at the table. "I hear you're going into medical school soon."

"Yeah. Soon." She tried her best to sound excited. "And I heard you work at the *farmacia?*"

"Yes. We brought you some gifts from there. From our grandmother to both of you." He handed her a cloth bundle tied at the top with string. Inside she found blue-green leaves, and twig-like branchlets. It smelled like earth and incense.

"It's an herbal tea," Isa said. "A mix. It helps relieve stress and can help you sleep. It's our best-seller."

"*Gracias,*" Tía Roberta said. "Tell your abuela thank you."

"What are the herbs?" Paloma asked, still sniffing the bag.

"Passionflower, lemon balm, hops, California poppy, valerian, and lavender."

"You can grow all of that here?"

"Some of it," Isa said. "The passionflower is native to Central America. That's where you get passionfruit from. Have you seen the flower? It looks like a little sun, with a bunch of rays and hairs sticking out. And it's purple."

"Is there any around here?"

"Not that I've seen. I've only seen it in the rainforest, up in the mountains."

"Roberta said you might want to go to the rainforest with us?" Eugenio said.

"I'd love to see what it's like up there."

"Lucky for you we're making a run on Friday. You should join us."

"You know the way, right? You take the good roads?" Tía Roberta asked.

"It's a safe route," Isa said. "I haven't heard of a car being stopped in a few months."

"Don't worry," Eugenio said quietly to Paloma, as Isa and Tía Roberta continued on about the roads. "We do this all the time. It's not dangerous if you know what you're doing." He smiled. It was a nice smile, even though his left front tooth had a chip on the corner. "Do you like dogs?" he asked.

She laughed. "I love dogs."

"Good. We'll bring Mosca along."

"*Mosca?* Like fly?"

"Hey, so you do speak Spanish."

"Just a little. Why did you name your dog Mosca?"

"She always used to bother us at night, when we were sleeping. She'd come up and nudge us until we woke up. She was like a little fly, always nipping at us. We'd say, do you know what time it is! Go away, *mosca!* And that became her name."

"Does she still do that?"

"Oh no. It was a puppy thing. Now she's gentle. You'll love her."

"You mean she wouldn't hurt a fly?" Isa jumped in.

"What—you want her to congratulate you on your English?" He shook his head. "They teach us all these sayings in school. Isa was the captain of the English club."

"I was the president, not the captain."

"She was the best at learning new languages. She also speaks French, Italian, and German."

"And I'm learning Portuguese."

Paloma laughed. "That's so impressive. I only speak one and a half languages."

"That's okay," Isa said. "You'll pick up more Spanish while you're here. The best way to learn is through immersion."

"I've been here for three weeks already. I think I'm just bad at languages."

"We'll speak Spanish all the way to the mountains tomorrow," Eugenio said. "We'll teach you some things. Car time is now the Spanish tutoring hour."

Paloma agreed, even though she didn't believe it would help. All her life she'd been exposed to Spanish and, somehow, she could barely get through a sentence without pausing to conjugate verbs in her head.

On Friday they picked her up in a gasoline car with ripped, plastic seats. The air conditioning didn't work, so they rolled down the windows. Mosca—who, it turned out, was a fluffy, young border collie—nudged her nose against Paloma's shoulder in the backseat.

"She wants you to pet her," Eugenio said. "See—she's a *mosca*, always there."

"She's sweet," Paloma said. She petted her soft, velvety head, and tossled her ears.

Isa put on a mix of flamenco and reggaetón. "Let's begin your Spanish lesson with some *música*," she said. "Listen to the lyrics and see if you can guess what they're saying."

Paloma guessed wrong for the first few songs. The only words she recognized were *amor* and *bailar*.

They'd only been driving for about twenty minutes when Isa pressed mute. "*Mira*. Roll up the windows, Eugenio." She turned around to face Paloma. "This is not a good area, but we have to pass through it."

"*Por dios*," Eugenio said, his voice unusually quiet. He leaned forward, into the steering wheel, as though he were trying to see the road better.

They passed empty, peeling buildings. McDonalds. Lustro-Mart. Scatterings of trash. A wrinkled woman selling something Paloma couldn't make out—lighters? Pocket knives?

"What are those?" she asked.

"Cell phones," Isa said. "Old cell phones that people up north didn't want. They keep sending them here and they go into a big pile. People go through and take out the phones that are still good."

"So they're sent here to be recycled?"

"No," Eugenio said. "They're sent here to be forgotten."

Paloma thought back to all the phones she'd owned throughout her life, all ten of them. When they'd died, she'd thrown them into the electronics recycling bin at the grocery store. Maybe they had never been recycled. Maybe they were out there now, on that old lady's table.

After passing through the city, Isa rolled down the windows again and turned the music back on. They drove past thickets of browned sugar cane, and fields of clumped, red dirt. Despite the vague manure-scent of the soil, Paloma was grateful for the open windows, and the wind. Even hot outside air was better than a closed-up car. Her thighs and back stuck sweatily to the plastic seats. Beside her, Mosca panted heavily. How could she stand it, with so much fur? Paloma hoped it would be cooler up in the hills, but she was doubtful. The closer they got, the browner it looked.

"There *are* forests up there, right?" Paloma asked.

"Yes. We're going to one of the last little pieces of forest," Isa said.

"It used to be green, all of it," Eugenio said. "Back when our grandparents were children."

"What happened?"

"They cut down the trees to try to grow more things."

Isa turned around to face Paloma. "And the crops failed because the soil didn't have enough nutrients. So they left the fields there, empty."

"Was coffee one of the crops? My abuelo grew up on a coffee farm in the hills. Would that have been around here?"

"Yes, it would have been near where we're going, most likely. Most of the coffee used to be. A lot of it was shade-grown coffee, though. Grown in the forest, between the trees."

"Well that sounds better than cutting the trees down. Why did they stop doing that?"

"People just don't grow as much coffee anymore. There was a big outbreak of a disease. It killed about ninety percent of the coffee plants in El Salvador. And what's left doesn't grow as well anymore."

"And a lot of those people, the ones who worked on the coffee farms, they were forced to move to San Salvador," Eugenio said. "But they couldn't find jobs."

"It was a big mess," Isa said.

"Still is," Eugenio said.

The car bounced over bumps and potholes. Dirt roads led them higher, away from the ocean and the trash-lined cities, past empty, wooden structures; houses, barns, and sheds, all of them rain-darkened, crumbling, rotting. Sunlight baked the bare dirt into cracked, rusty plains. Was this where Abuelo once rode horses bareback? Where he'd harvested coffee beans into woven baskets, the sun on his scalp, his mother telling him to put a hat and sunglasses on, and to drink more water and to take some time in the shade? Was this where he wandered with his brother, machetes in hand, as they chopped through vines and underbrush, in search of agoutis, peccaries, and the last of the pumas?

Any of these barren fields could once have been Abuelo's home. It was sad to think of it. The weedy underbrush weaving its way through old trellises, choking the corpses of coffee plants. The swaying, breathing forest, reduced to battered, runny dirt.

She wanted to see it, just once, just for a moment, how it was in memories—how it used to be. A thunderstorm on the greenest of all grasses. The great, watery upheaval of birds at dawn. The wind and sun mingling softly above the fields, and the tree branches—as old as light—as old as time itself.

Paloma felt tears draw into her eyes. Empty tears; hard, useless tears. She tried to focus on the thorned weeds and the newly unfurling palms growing quietly on the fringe of things.

"Will it grow back?" Paloma asked when she'd steadied herself. "The forest?"

"No one knows for sure," Isa said. "But if it does, it will never be the same as it was, not for a long time. You'll see. Where we're going, we pass through a second-growth forest. It used to be logged and it came back thick and dense. The trees are small.

And then you'll see how different the old forest looks. Here, we're about there. Around this corner."

Finally, some trees. They parked on the side of the road, and Isa led them down a hill, into a flurry of spiky leaves.

"This is the young forest," Isa said. They pushed through palms, and broad, leathery, lizard-like plants. They weren't sharp, just serrated, but Paloma still worried they would scratch her. The rainforest immediately felt untouchable. Ants at her feet; mosquitos on her arms; unknown plants at her hips; the foggy bellows of something—a bird? A monkey?—in the distance.

"Keep an eye out for snakes," Isa said.

"Mosca will let us know if she sees one," Eugenio said, laughing, his voice flat against the forest's denseness.

Silence, for a moment, and then—

"What's that sound?" Paloma asked. "That bellowing sound?"

"That's a spider monkey," Eugenio said. "Hopefully we'll see one up close."

Paloma felt relieved. There were still spider monkeys, and snakes. There were more plants than she'd ever seen.

This all made her feel a bit better about the oceans rising. The rainforest, up here in the hills, would be okay. It was unstoppable, a wild mess of weeds and damp, moving shadows. The rainforest would change and adapt, but it would never die. It was not a stoic monument, as some of the forests in Oregon had seemed—it was chaos, a bursting, rich, rain-soaked explosion of living beings. Even when it was cut down, it came back.

"Now we're getting into the old-growth forest."

Little by little, the underbrush lessened, and the space between trees grew.

"You hear that? You hear how our footsteps just got louder? How they sound different against the earth?" Isa said.

"I have no idea what you're talking about, Isa," Eugenio said.

"I do," Paloma said. "I hear it." It was hollower, or deeper, or maybe wetter than before. "What does it mean?"

"I don't know," Isa said. "But it always happens right here, in this spot. And this is where the old-growth starts. Like, look at this. Look at this tree." She ran to a giant trunk, of deep, reddish wood. "All the trees start to get bigger here. And look at this one." With Mosca at her heels, Isa ran over to a tree with textured, charcoal-colored bark. Vines clung to it, and on its lowest branch, a leafy plant like a pineapple grew next to bundles of moss.

"Watch this," Eugenio said. He slipped a pocket knife out from the back pocket of his jeans and scratched into the bark. Paloma knew that trees couldn't feel, but she felt bad for it anyway.

She held out her arm. "Wait—"

"Nope. Wait for it." Eugenio pulled the knife away. Dark red liquid seeped out of the tree.

"Is that—blood?" Paloma asked. Eugenio dabbed it with his finger and showed it to her up close.

"See for yourself." He motioned for her to touch it. Hesitantly, she dabbed her finger into the tree's incision. The blood coated her fingertip. It was soft and thick; slow-running like red paint.

"Is this sap?"

"Yes. The sap of the dragon blood tree," Isa said. "It's highly sought after as an antibacterial."

"You put blood on your blood," Eugenio said.

"It's true," Isa said. "It's good topically for cuts and scrapes. There used to be more of the trees around, but now there are hardly any. I think this is the last one in El Salvador."

"There's no way we could know that," Eugenio said.

"I just have a feeling about it."

"Very scientific."

Isa shook her head. "I'm serious. I think this is the last dragon's blood tree in the country. It's not like we have much forest left at all. Where would the other ones be hiding?"

Eugenio's smile faded. "You never know," he said.

"Right," said Isa. "Right. You never know."

They continued walking. Mosca sniffed along joyfully, her tail wagging. The rainforest was completely windless, and just as humid as the *finca*. Paloma felt sweat gather on the back of her neck. She was starting to get used to being hot all the time; to sweat sitting on her skin like a blanket. The air was water. She was water. It all worked.

The forest, above all, smelled like rain, and dampness, and crumbling earth. Paloma lingered at a tree with a braided trunk, taller than any building she'd ever seen. Moss dotted its branches, which spread out into a wide, sun-mottled crown.

"I love this tree," Isa said. "It must be at least a hundred years old."

"It's beautiful," Paloma said.

They continued wandering. The soil was soft, spongy, and peppered with decay. Paloma kept her eyes on the trees. Every so often branches rattled, and swung, and groups of long-beaked birds flashed through the canopy. All the while, spider monkeys continued to bellow, but, from where, Paloma couldn't tell. They sounded human but not human. She imagined them as hairy little prehistoric things running up in the trees.

As they walked, Isa pointed out more trees—mahogany, fig, cecropia—and shrubs—pipers, ferns, and fan-like palms desperate for sunlight.

"What kind of wood do you use for your projects?" Paloma asked.

"Whatever's down. We find bits of fallen trees here and there," Eugenio said. "Usually after storms."

"Are you going to pick some up on the way back?"

"No. We're not here to get wood today."

"I thought that was the reason we came?"

"We don't need to stock up again quite yet."

"Then why—"

"We wanted to show you around." He smiled.

"And we should also pick some wild yam for our grandmother," Isa said. "If there's any left."

"I'm telling you, we should just grow it in the garden," Eugenio said.

"With the heat it won't grow."

"You never know."

"Don't you remember? Doña Maria tried growing some last spring and they all died."

"But she needed to give them more water."

"You know it's better when it grows wild. It's different. Stronger."

"What's wild yam used for?" Paloma asked.

"It's used for a lot of different things. It eases pain. It can be used as a natural birth control, or, if you prepare it differently, it can be used to heal women's hormone imbalances. It's soothing. It eases the nerves. And it's good for allergies. Our grandmother sells it in the *farmacia*."

"Wow."

"You should stop by sometime," Eugenio said.

Isa nodded. "And if you're interested more in natural medicine, our grandmother has a lot of connections in the community. There are a lot of people here who are practicing natural medicine."

"Like naturopathy? Homeopathy?"

"Like that, but better," Eugenio said. "Like that but with a lot of innovations."

"I guess you could call it the new naturopathy. Traditional stuff combined with new and edgy science. One doctor, Señor Medina, he's looking at the ways that viruses evolve. Superbugs. He's trying to work with them instead of against them."

Superbugs. Did they know about Abuelo? How he died?

"They meet in a group about every other week," Isa went on. "Everyone who's doing natural medicine around here gets together, and they share their ideas."

"How do they afford to do research like that?" Paloma asked. "Do they have a grant?"

"No. There's this international organization that gets money from donors. They pay doctors and scientists and herbalists and naturopaths all around the world to work on this sort of thing. Not much, but it's something. There's a big movement behind it," Eugenio said. "I think the United States is one of the last to catch up with it."

"As usual," Paloma said.

"Yeah. But if you're interested, there's a meeting next weekend at the *farmacia*," Isa said.

"That sounds great," Paloma said. "I'll be there."

CHAPTER SEVENTEEN
LAUREL

L AUREL'S JOB WAS TO PLANT SEEDS IN LONG, STRAIGHT ROWS, AND TO SPRINKLE THEM WITH FERTILIZER. The gardens were packed into giant, metal-framed beds, filled with strange, woody dirt that had been frayed to a fine, fluffy consistency. She'd grown used to the soil in El Salvador, which smelled like crumbled leaves, and stream water; like shade and rotting fruit. Here, it smelled like paper. She'd asked Mauricio where they'd gotten the soil from, but he didn't know.

There were a lot of things he didn't know, even though he spent all his time writing things for one of Shreifer's assistants. Press memos. Sponsorship emails. Funding plans. He was basically Shreifer's assistant's long-distance assistant.

One evening, when they were both done with work, Laurel and Mauricio walked around the settlement. They followed the blue path-lights in a long, looping circle. Ahead, off the edge of things, the sun set into a curtain of silvery, purple water.

"So how was it today?" Mauricio asked. "Are you getting tired of garden work yet?"

"No. I like it. It's a good job."

"Are you sure? Because I can get you a job in the office," Mauricio said. "If you're interested."

"I don't know—"

"You're more than qualified. You said you worked in an office for your grandpa."

"Yeah—"

"You should do it. We need more people in the office. And why work outside if you don't have to?"

But Laurel liked being outside. Every afternoon a white bird flew overhead, way, high up at cloud level. It glided without flapping its wings. She thought it might be lost. It never landed; it let the wind guide it, and the wind had brought it here.

Laurel liked the feeling of the wind on her face—that big, empty, dragged-down wind, straight off the ocean. She was not a creature behind glass anymore. She was not in a dark building where animals died and became supermarket products. Instead it was her duty to create life. She whispered to each seed, just as she'd seen Tía Roberta do on the farm, in a small, tight whisper. *Please grow.*

"You could always try it out," Mauricio said. "And if you don't like it you can go back to the gardens."

"I don't know—I'd rather stay out here. If you think about it, this is one of the most important jobs on the island. The donated food will run out eventually. We'll need a way to support ourselves."

"Oh, Shreifer has plans for that."

"What, the fish farm? In the old swimming pools?"

"Yes. But there's more to it. I just saw the order for the kinds of fish he's bringing in."

"Are they GMO?"

"Of course they are. What isn't, these days?"

"The seeds."

"No, they are too."

"No!" Laurel frowned. "All of them?"

"Do you think regular seeds would grow in a place like this? With all this wind and salt?"

Laurel shook her head. "But GMO's? Part of the reason I left the slaughterhouse was because of the genetic modification that was going on there."

"Why?"

"My abuelo hated it so much. He said the animals weren't allowed to be themselves anymore. He said we had to draw the line somewhere, the line between right and wrong, and it seemed like adding, I don't know, frog DNA to a cow was taking things a bit too far."

"Did he look at any of the studies? I know they're funded by the GMO corporations, but that doesn't completely discount them," Mauricio said. "GMO's have been around for a while, and we've seen almost no negative health consequences."

"It's not the health consequences. It's the animals. It's not fair to them."

"But these are just fish."

"I guess."

"It's the only way we're going to grow food on this island. The wind is too strong. The soil's not rich enough or deep enough. We need things to be tailored to our surroundings. And we're eating the plants and the fish anyway. Why does it matter how they're grown?" Mauricio locked his gaze onto Laurel's. "Anyway. That's my take on it."

Laurel crossed her arms over her chest. The wind coaxed goosebumps onto her skin. "We might as well eat lab-grown meat," she said.

"That's part of the plan, too. A self-sustaining lab to grow chicken breasts."

"You're joking."

"Dead serious. Shreifer's thinking big, here. We're going to have it all."

"I've always found the idea of lab-grown meat just—disgusting."

"It's the same thing as a regular chicken. Just without the rest of the body. No life, no body, no cruelty, same nutrition."

"That's disgusting."

"Okay, how about this—the fish Shreifer bought They don't need to eat anything; they can photosynthesize."

"So they're plants."

"They have algal DNA added to them, or something like that. And they also produce no waste. So all we have to do is put them in the old swimming pools and let them be."

Laurel glanced down at her feet; at the sparkling blue lights. Her tennis-shoes clicked against the concrete. "It just doesn't feel right," she said.

Mauricio laughed. "Come on, how are photosynthetic fish a bad thing? It's good for the fish, too. If we weren't going to kill them, they'd live to be over a hundred."

Laurel smiled, not out of happiness, but out of exasperation. "I guess I shouldn't be the one to complain. I did work in a slaughterhouse. It's not like things were perfect there, either." She sighed. Waves rose and fell against the sea wall—one, two, one, two. Out farther, the sky dimmed to a deep, honey yellow. "The sun sets so quickly out here," she said. She felt homesick, but not for Terrysville. No—she felt homesick for something she'd never seen, or known. Something old. What was it—what? What was it that she wanted to know? What was it that she missed? Trust, maybe. That they were doing things the right way. That, even if they messed up, things would go on, cycling and circling, molding and changing, on like that forever.

Sometimes she felt like she was on a small boat in the middle of the ocean. She worried that it would sink; that she would be plunged into the cold-churned sea, down and down, until even the sun was extinguished.

That night she dreamed that the ocean evaporated, wisp by wisp, into a coarse, red desert. She stood out in it. Clouds of dust darkened the sky. Through the haze, she saw Augusta, Sam, and Mauricio, all still, and pale, and tired, and crouched on the ground like animals. She felt a buzz, a shift; something breaking in the air. Her face tightened. She tried to call out, but her voice was gone. Then, one by one, her friends evaporated into pockets of mist, and, at last, so did she.

She woke up to the wind on the side of the house. Sharp and moving, like water. She rolled onto her stomach. The blue pathlights glimmered through the window. She woke up her phone, and it spoke to her:

"Good evening, Laurel. Would you like to hear today's top stories?"

"Yes." She turned down the volume.

"Based on your location, the international bulletin is the only source available. Would you like to watch the international news?"

Just then, Augusta marched sleepily down the stairs.

"Oh no. Did I wake you up?" Laurel asked.

"No. *Solo quiero un poquito de agua*," Augusta said, and she pointed at the sink.

"Would you like to watch the international news?" Laurel's phone said again.

"Yes."

"Your phone lady." Augusta filled a plastic glass with water.

"Yeah, it's my phone."

"It talks with you. My phone doesn't talk with me."

"Welcome to the international headline round-up. I'm Maria Gervais. Today's top headline—protests grow during record-breaking food shortages in central Asia, eastern Europe, and many cities around the world—"

Augusta shook her head. "Mine can only make the calls."

"Seriously? It must be old."

"*Sí. Pero funciona.*" Augusta sat at the end of Laurel's cot. She drank her water in long, loud gulps as they listened to Maria Gervais's lofty voice.

When the newscast ended. Augusta asked: "*Por qué despertaste tan temprano?*"

"*Porque tuve una—como se dice*—nightmare?"

"Nightmare?"

"*Como un sueño, pero mal,*" Laurel said.

"*Una pesadilla?*"

"*Sí. Una pesadilla,*" Laurel said.

Augusta sat up straighter. She pointed to her chest. "Me too. Nightmare."

"And what was it?" Laurel asked.

"Home. It goes down, beneath the ocean."

"Flooding?"

"*Sí.* The ocean, it comes up and it covers everything. My parents, that's how they die."

"In the dream?"

"No. *En realidad. Murieron hace dos años.*"

"Augusta, I'm so sorry. *Lo siento.*"

Augusta ran her fingers along the edge of the cup. "It's why I'm here. I have no family. *Solo me quedan los recuerdos.*"

"Records?"

"*Recuerdos.*" She pointed to her eyes, and then to her forehead. "*Memoria.*"

"Memory. *Lo siento, Augusta. Qué triste.*"

She smiled emptily. "I think—Blue Mar, how beautiful. I will go. But it's not. It's gray. No color. And no money. We don't get nothing. *Comida y esta casita, es todo.*"

"That's because it's new. I'm sure it'll get better."

"Something is not here. Something missing."

"What do you mean?"

"*Esta tierra no está viva.*"

"The earth isn't alive?"

"Here, no."

She knew what Augusta meant. There was something about the cardboard soil and the concrete-plastic earth that felt incomplete. But it also felt clean, and purposeful. In the sun it almost seemed to sparkle. "Look at what humans have done! Look at their great achievement!" the island pronounced to the sea, and to the plastic still floating within it. "Look at us!"

*   *   *   *   *

The next morning, just after sunrise, Laurel arrived early for her shift at the gardens. Usually, at dawn, she felt like she was the only person on the island, and the garden seemed bigger, grander—like a *finca*. But not today. Today she found a rope encircling the beds, arranged purposefully in a large circle. The dirt inside was wild and tussled.

"No," Laurel said. She stepped inside the rope. "No, no, no."

The new seedlings lay sideways, their pale roots unearthed and exposed to the sun. Dead. They were all dead. She held one in her palms. Its leaflets trembled beneath the wind.

"What the hell happened here?" a voice said.

Laurel turned. Sam hovered at the edge of the rope holding a bin of stainless steel containers. That was his job; to help deliver the meals.

"Look at this," Laurel shouted. "Someone dug them up. All of them."

Sam joined her in the dirt. "Could've been the wind," he said. "It was strong last night."

"Then what's this rope? And look at the way the dirt's crumpled. Someone ripped these out."

"But—look. They'll grow back. Stick the roots back in the ground. My parents had a garden, back in the day. They taught me some of this stuff. Look." He took the plant from her palm. Delicately, he loosened the roots, combed a spot for them in the soil, and patted the plant into place. "See. Good as new. Now you just have to water it."

"It's still—all the rows are ruined. Who knows what plants these are even supposed to be. They all look the same when they're young." Laurel picked up another one and gently brushed the dirt off. But there were no roots; they'd been severed. She felt a great jolt in her chest. These were her plants. Hers. And now they were dead.

"Someone knew what they were doing," Sam said.

"I told you."

"Might be the first taste of mutiny."

"Mutiny?"

"Your friend didn't tell you about the automation?"

"What automation?"

"They're bringing in a team of drones to do all the deliveries," Sam said.

"Why would they do that? What are you guys going to do for work?"

"They'll think of something else for us."

"What's the benefit of bringing drones in, though? I don't get it."

"That's what makes people uneasy," Sam said. "None of us have any say in it. None of us have a say in anything. We just do our work and keep our heads down, and all the big decisions are made by Shreifer." He lumbered back to the meal bin and picked it up again. "Doesn't bother me, though," he said. "They're letting us live here for free. And someone's got to take charge of this place. If any of us don't like it, we can leave."

But Laurel knew that wasn't completely true. Most of the settlers were there out of desperation. They had nothing to go back to.

When the other gardeners arrived, Laurel showed them the damage. Most spoke English as well as Spanish, but there were a few who only spoke Spanish, so she tried to explain as best she could. She held up the severed roots and gestured to them as she spoke. There wasn't much to explain, anyway. They could see it. It was all right there.

Laurel felt guilty. Like it was her fault. She'd been the one to discover it, so she should take charge.

She walked quickly to the administrative building to find Mauricio. She pulled him away, back to the site. The other gardeners had left, and it was just the two of them, there, with the sun burning against the dirt.

"I'll have to report it," Mauricio said flatly.

"Report it to who?"

"Shreifer."

"You think Shreifer's going to care about something like this?"

"Of course. This is a big deal. And it's going to take a lot of planning, going forward. We're going to need to replant and take security measures to make sure this doesn't happen again. This sets us way back. We were supposed to be getting more beds in, not re-doing these ones."

"What about the person who did it? There's someone out there sabotaging us."

"There's not much we can do to find them."

"I just want to know why they did it."

"They're probably making a statement. Maybe they're like you and they hate that we use GMO's."

"Could be. Or maybe they hate that they're not getting paid."

"None of us are getting paid. We're an egalitarian society. It's like—it's like we're on Mars. You think the settlers there are getting paychecks every Earth-month?"

"No. But people weren't expecting this. People are mad about it."

"None of us knew what to expect going into this," Mauricio said. "It's all a big experiment."

"Maybe whoever did it was sent here to keep an eye on things. A spy. All of this is illegal, after all."

"If the American government wasn't okay with this, none of us would be here. Trust me. It's called looking the other way. Partially because they support our mission, and partially because Planet has some friends in high places, if you know what I mean." He looked out at the dead, flaky soil. "And other countries— their governments aren't going to mess with ours."

"What are we, then? Are we part of the United States? Are we a country, a state, a territory, a colony?"

"We're something new. We're the future."

Laurel laughed. "Right. That means you have no idea."

"Honestly, no one knows. Not even Shreifer." Mauricio half-smiled and took a deep breath. "I have to get back to work. But don't worry, we'll take care of this."

"Mauricio, why didn't you tell me about the automation?"

He stared at her. "How did you hear about that?"

"Sam told me."

He nodded. "Well—it's all new. The initiative just got approved yesterday morning. And it's going to make things a lot more efficient around here. The drones are solar powered. They charge as they go. And they even have these pockets where they can keep the food warm." He smiled again. "It's going to be great. In a few months we're going to have everything we had at home, only cleaner, and greener."

"Okay," Laurel said, because she didn't know what else to say.

Mauricio went back to work and Laurel walked down to the docks. She sat at the edge. Her legs dangled over, out above the sea. Every so often a wave crashed against the pillars beneath. Maybe this was all absurd—this bare scrap of plastic in the middle of the ocean. She'd always pictured it as an escape from everything at home, from the crumbling world, but maybe it wasn't. If the world was dying, well—they were still on it, weren't they? Blue Mar was supposed to be independent, and fresh, and new, but, no—it was still on the world, and of it; still affected by the wind and the sun and the rising waters. If Blue Mar was only going to be a cleaner and greener version of the rest of the world—was that enough? Was any of this enough?

That night, Laurel took her dinner outside, to the front step. Augusta joined her. The wind, always stronger at night, slipped past them in great sheets. Luckily they had sandwiches in their containers today, and not something like salad that would blow away.

"Did you hear about the garden?" Laurel asked.

Augusta took another bite and nodded. Her eyes seemed sleepier than usual.

"They think someone did it on purpose."

Augusta shrugged. "I know who."

"You know?"

Augusta nodded. "I know."

"It wasn't—"

"Some of my friends. And me. We want to change things."

"Augusta!"

"It's the beginning. We want control. To do things in good ways."

"What are you talking about?"

"*Está bien.*" Augusta packed up her sandwich. "*Está bien.*" She went back inside.

Why did she tell her that? Did she want Laurel to get involved?

Laurel followed her. "Augusta," she called. "You know I need to tell Mauricio what you said."

"Is okay." Augusta popped her head out of the kitchen.

"You're not making sense, Augusta."

"Don't turn them in. Turn me in. Say I did it. Only me."

"Why?"

"Because I don't care if I go home. I want to go home more than my friends do." Her dark eyes—amber dark, honey dark—rested on Laurel's.

"But do you *want* to leave?"

"I do. They say I can't go."

"You asked them? They said that?"

She nodded.

Laurel swallowed hard. Could that be true? "Well, what about—you just said you wanted to change things?"

"It doesn't work. They will put the plants back. Again and again. We need bigger. More. All of us need to go together."

"You mean like an uprising?"

"*Cómo?*"

Laurel had no idea how to say that in Spanish. "All together? *Todos—juntos?*"

Augusta nodded. She stepped closer to Laurel. "You help?"

"I'm confused."

"*Preguntale a Mauricio. Preguntale si nos va a ayudar. Porque el sabe mucho sobre los jefes.*"

"*Los jefes?* Chiefs? Bosses? Like Schreifer?"

"*Sí, el Schreifer.*" Augusta scrunched her face.

"*Es cierto,*" Laurel said. Mauricio did know a lot about Schreifer. But what good would that do?

"*Todos juntos,*" Augusta said. She pointed to herself, to her own chest, and then to Laurel's.

Laurel felt like she was at the edge of a precipice. She could stay up here, where it was safe, wearing her plastic gardening gloves, tilling the paper-laced soil. Day after day. Wind after wind. Bird after bird. Safe. Separate. Empty. But she couldn't ignore it. There, over the edge, lay the dark and crumbling world. Everything. All of time. Every cave painting. Every car. Every birthday, and space shuttle, and calendar, and trampoline. Every vacation, and funeral, and pumpkin patch, and movie premiere. The nuzzling of deer against soil. The low, long exhales of cows against grass. Every animal and plant and bacterium that had ever lived. She felt the weight of all this pull her down, down to where she could not see anything, not the dirt beneath her fingernails, not even the shade of her own skin. All of it would be lost. All of it. She wasn't sure if there was anything she could do. Probably not. But she looked up for the precipice again, the top of the mountain's edge, and it was gone.

CHAPTER EIGHTEEN
PALOMA

"TÍA ROBERTA, WHAT ARE YOU DOING?" PALOMA CALLED.

She was crouched on the back patio, with a chicken's neck between her hands. It was the chicken with the white spots on its wings—soft, white spots, like snowflakes. Paloma had secretly given all of the chickens names; this one was, of course, Spot.

"We're running out of food, Palomita. The market has been understocked for a week now."

"It has?"

"Yes."

"Even Lustro-Mart?"

"Yes."

"That's been happening at home, too. For the past few months."

"It's been happening here for years. Every so often, the market won't have much to sell. And what they do have is too expensive.

189

So at times like this, I kill a chicken and make a good *sopa* to last the week."

Paloma leaped forward. "No, Tía. Not this chicken. One of the other ones, maybe." She crouched down, too, and stroked Spot's back. "Feel how soft her feathers are. How sweet she is."

"The others are still giving eggs. This one hasn't given any for a while."

"She's young. Give her a chance."

"Paloma, this is the reality of living on a farm."

"I'd rather not eat."

"You won't be saying that in a few days."

"We can eat the plants. The vegetables."

"It's not enough, Palomita." Tía Roberta re-adjusted her grip higher up Spot's neck, just under the beak.

"There's eggs," Paloma said desperately. "Eggs and vegetables. And *masa*. We don't need to kill her."

"Go in the house. You don't have to see it."

"I'm not eating her. You'll have to eat her by yourself."

"Go inside, Palomita."

Paloma backed away and walked heavily toward the orchard. Her muscles stiffened with adrenaline, or dread, and her whole body slumped along like it was filled with a dense fluid. Down on the grass. On her back. She pressed her fingers to her mouth. It didn't seem real. Maybe it wasn't. She thought of all the cows that had died in the slaughterhouse. Their ghosts. Their spirits, lost somewhere between the sky and the earth. She thought of Spot fading away and joining them.

Why was it so horrifying to think of Tía Roberta wringing a chicken's neck? It was certainly more horrifying than imagining a cougar or a coyote tearing one to pieces. Why was that? What was the difference?

Paloma laid outside for hours. She knew she was being childish; Tía Roberta was kind enough to be hosting her, to be feeding her, even when she didn't have much to give. Still, Paloma couldn't bring herself to move. Sweat puddled on her lower back, and under her arms. She listened to the great silence, the distant burning of waves, and, beneath it, her own breathing. The sun fell. Mosquitos surfaced. Finally, just before dark, Tía Roberta climbed the hill and sat with her back against a lemon tree.

"Come here," she said. She took Paloma's head into her lap and stroked her forehead. "It's alright. It's done."

Paloma focused her eyes on the lemon leaves; the dark pattern they made against the sky. "Sorry, Tía," she said. "I didn't mean to act like that."

"It's alright."

"Things are just different here."

"I acted the same way the first time I saw a chicken killed. I was much younger than you, much, much younger, but I remember being scared. I didn't want the chicken to die. And my mama said, 'you like the chicken we buy at the *mercado*? This is the same thing, *mija*. The exact same thing, only fresher. You eat that, you eat this.' I remember it so well. Your abuelo was here that day. He lived here from the time I was a little girl, you know that? And he took my hand and walked with me on the beach, just over there, and he talked to me about the *tiburones* and the *ballenas* out there, and the way they were all hunting each other, how that's just the way things were between animals."

"I miss him," Paloma said.

Tía Roberta continued to stroke her forehead. "*Ay, sí*. Me too."

Paloma sighed. "I always wondered—why did Abuelo live here when he first got married?"

"Here on the *finca*?"

"Yeah. Why didn't Abuela move in with him on the coffee farm?"

"His parents didn't approve of Mariana, or our family. We weren't in their class. We were, not poor, but poorer than them. But Ramon was a brave man. He gave up everything for Mariana. His inheritance; everything."

Paloma sat up. "I never knew that."

"Neither of them liked to talk about it. I think it made both of them feel guilty, both in different ways.

Paloma smiled into the darkness. "I can't believe no one ever told me that. It's like a *telenovela*."

They sat for a while. The heat hung over them softly, like a cloud. Marisol began her night rumblings, a dense, low, mmm. Behind the old rainforest trees, the sunset blossomed a dark purple-red above the ocean.

Paloma broke the silence: "I remember from the stories—you used to grow sugar cane here," she said.

"We used to."

"What happened?"

"It got too expensive. And I wanted to grow food for myself. You know, it took a lot of work to get anything to grow here. When I took the sugar cane out, the soil was bad. No nutrients at all. So I made compost for months and months, from the scraps of my food. And, over time, I made the soil healthy again."

"And now it's all going underwater."

"Someday. But not today."

"Doesn't it make you sad, Tía? How everything's changed?"

"That's just the way things are."

"All of this is going to be gone."

"A lot has been gone for a long time. This is a different El Salvador. The one we all grew up in? The one we all knew? It's gone. Long, long gone. And—you know what? We'll never get it back. Things change."

"They're changing too fast, now. No one can keep up. Not even the *mercado*."

"But you see, we have to keep up. We have no other choice." Tía Roberta pointed to the lemon leaves. "You see those branches? The *limón*? See how they sway in the wind? They bend. They move with it. That's why they don't snap off. That's why they don't break." Tía Roberta leaned forward onto her knees, and she inched out from underneath the tree, out beneath the open sky. "And you know what else? Come here. Look." The first stars had surfaced. They glowed a rich, cold, pale blue, the color of a shallow ocean. They were at once vacant and comforting, the remnants of cooled fires, reminders of warmth and closeness, and of distance, and passed time.

"You see those stars up there? Long, long ago, when things were good, when our first ancestors sat here like us, and listened to the warm waves at night, those same stars were up there."

A bat flew in front of them, quickly, with sideways flight. It reminded Paloma of a piece of cloth caught in the wind.

"*Mira*—there are still some *murciélagos* left," Tía Roberta said.

Paloma laughed. "They're so fast."

"Yes, they're fast. They need to be to catch mice."

"They eat mice?"

"Yes. Some do. Even better, some eat mosquitos."

Another one flew by. "They're pretty," Paloma said. "Like ghosts."

They sat out for another half hour or so. The stars brightened, and filled in, and by the time they wandered back to the house, the sky was full of them.

    *   *   *   *   *

The next day, Eugenio picked her up for the meeting. She told him about Spot, and he laughed at her.

"Why aren't you a vegetarian?" he asked.

She'd thought about it before. But she didn't want to label herself, and, honestly, maybe there was something else stopping her; a fear of separation. A fear that, perhaps, these same questions had troubled people for all time. A fear that it was a part of being human, that there were no answers, that those ghostly cave paintings of bison and mammoths in Europe, and all the indigenous rituals and songs about hunting, and all the myths and legends about animals from around the world—these were questions, and feelings, and they represented the tragedy and beauty of being an animal, the sadness of killing, the carnal, sinuous motion of hunting, the quiet relationships of farm life. She was afraid that if she stepped away from that she would step away from something deeper, and older, something she didn't understand, that hid inside her like a dense, volcanic rock, right in the middle of her stomach, shimmering, and black; a piece of the moon without the sunlight's glow.

Eugenio parked outside the *farmacia,* a small, wooden building with bright windows. Inside, it smelled like the center of a daisy, musky and a little bitter. Shelves lined the walls, holding glass jars and bundles of dried herbs tied with string.

Eugenio walked ahead of her. He swung himself behind the counter. "We got in something unusual," he said. "You will never guess what it is." He pulled an unlabeled jar from the shelf.

"Ambergris?" Paloma guessed.

"What?"

"Is it ambergris? That whale vomit stuff?"

"Guess again."

"Some rare orchid?"

"No. You'll never guess."

"What is it?"

"Close your eyes and hold out your hand."

"Is it going to be something gross?"

"You don't trust me, Paloma?"

"Okay." She closed her eyes. She waited for the pressure on her hand. Would it be furry? Alive? No. It was smooth, like wood.

"*Abra los ojos.*"

A tiny wooden horse sat on her palm. "Did you make this?"

"I did. You know who it is?"

"Galleta!" The horse's head bowed gracefully, and one hoof was raised and ready to trot. "Eugenio! I already have that wooden bird, you didn't need to make me anything else."

"You don't like it?"

"No, of course I like it, it's so sweet. *Gracias*, Eugenio." She hugged him tightly. They were about the same height, so she rested her head on his shoulder. "It looks just like her."

"You can take it with you. To remember."

"I'm not leaving yet. I have a few more weeks."

"I know. I wish it would never come."

"So do I." They looked at each other, then, perhaps for a little bit too long. With anyone else this would've been uncomfortable, and Paloma would've looked at the floor and changed the subject. But she never felt uncomfortable around Eugenio. She felt like she'd known him her whole life, like they'd grown up staring at each other and giving each other handmade gifts. Everything felt normal around him. Everything felt okay.

The door opened. Spanish voices fell in. By now Paloma could understand it well enough. The speaking part was still hard, but she could usually understand the gist of what was being said. She was, as Isa liked to say, "competent."

Every week the meeting's attendees changed slightly, but there were always some regulars. Doña Yolanda; Doctor Max and Doctora Lupe, who worked at the medical clinic; Penelope, a red-headed woman originally from Honduras who used to be a nurse; and Señora Rodriguez, who lived alone on the fringes of town and sold herbs from her home

They began each meeting by discussing the state of things; what was happening in town. Just days ago Tienda Sandoval, the family-owned store down the street, had gone out of business. All their customers had switched to Lustro-Mart, not because they wanted to, but because their food was less expensive, and because they had fewer shortages. But even Lustro-Mart couldn't keep up sometimes.

"There's been talk," Doña Yolanda said in Spanish, "of starting a community farming cooperative. Eugenio will explain."

Eugenio glanced around the table, smiling. "When she says there's been talk, she means we've been the ones talking, Isa and I, and Paloma, too. Because—as we all know, food shortages are becoming more common. We need to feed ourselves. And we need more space to grow herbs, too."

"The people here, they won't work together," Doctora Lupe said. "They don't trust each other. They don't like to be out of their houses."

"That's what we need to change," Isa said.

"Maybe we could start it between us," Penelope said. "Make our own farm. And then everyone will see how well it does—"

Doctor Max shook his head. "But you don't understand. The problem is not this. The problem is that food is not growing well here. Just look at the decline in our herb stocks. The decline in wild plants. The decline in crops. It's not all monetary."

"He's right," Señora Rodriguez said. "Just look at the Castillo farm. After the last flood nothing will grow."

"This has never been great land for farming," Doña Yolanda said. "It used to be a fishing town, long ago."

"What do we do, then? Leave?" Penelope said. "We have what we have. If we can get food to grow, I say we grow it."

"Even if we know the next storm might destroy it?" Doctor Max said. "And the dry season is getting drier."

"What, then?" Penelope said. "You think we should leave?"

"None of us have the money to move out of here," Señora Rodriguez said. "And the grant money is not for that."

"See, we have no options," Penelope said. "We should grow what we can."

"On what land?" Doctor Max said.

"Well the grant money could help with that."

"Why don't we ask Medicina Mas Allá for money to help us move to another town?"

"Wait," Paloma said. She could understand pretty well, but speaking Spanish was still hard. She spoke quietly to Isa in English, who translated for her to the group.

"Paloma says that Doña Roberta might lend parts of her land to us," Isa said. "And most likely she'd do it for free."

"Roberta Cañas? No. Too close to the ocean," Doctor Max said.

"It will certainly flood," Doctora Lupe said.

"Well?" Penelope said. "It would be our cheapest option."

"And Paloma says Doña Roberta has made lots of compost there."

"I don't see how this is going to help our mission," Doctora Lupe said. "The herbs, yes. But what else will this bring us?"

"Food, Doctora Lupe," Eugenio said. "We're all people. We need to eat to do our work. You know that. And we need healthy food. Not the shit they sell at Lustro-Mart."

There was a moving sort of silence, filled with short, hot breaths, and the rustling of sweaty arms against the table. Doña Yolanda stood and poured herself a glass of water from the pitcher. A fly swam on the top edges of it. She picked it out with her fingertips and flicked it onto the floor. After a long sip, she said: "I think we should do it. There's little risk. It's only time we'd be putting into it."

"And the seeds?" Doctor Max said. "They're expensive these days."

"Not the kinds we want," Doña Yolanda said. "I have them here. I've had some saved for a long time."

"See," Penelope said. "It's all coming together. I think this is a great idea, Eugenio. And smart on your part, too, Paloma."

"*Gracias*," Paloma said. She wished she knew how to say more.

Isa turned to her and spoke in English. "You think there's a good chance Doña Roberta will say yes?"

"I don't see why she'd say no."

That night, when Tía Roberta got home from work, she took the pot of chicken soup from the fridge—which, thankfully, had been working flawlessly for days—and she placed it gently on the stove. "Will you eat some?" Tía Roberta clicked the burner on to high heat.

"Maybe. I don't know."

It seemed like normal chicken soup, fragrant with the warmth of cumin, bay leaves, and black pepper. It was easy to forget where the cubed, white meat inside came from. Paloma's stomach churned with hunger.

Tía Roberta sat at the kitchen table. "How was the meeting today?" she asked.

Paloma told her the plan. The wooden horse was still in the pocket of her dress, and she ran her fingers over it as she talked.

"But why would they want to do it here?" Tía Roberta asked. "It floods more and more—didn't you see the trees?"

"Which ones?"

"The old ones. Down by the ocean," Tía Roberta said. "The water's up to them."

"Since when?"

"Since this morning, I think."

"It's done that before though, right?" Paloma said. "It'll go back down."

"It might. It might not. It might keep rising." The lid of the pot rattled. "Is that boiling over?"

Paloma opened it up to find pale yellow broth, just like regular chicken soup. The carrots and sweet potatoes inside smelled bright and vaguely earthy. "I'll turn down the heat a little," Paloma said.

"I don't think this farm is a good idea," Tía Roberta said. "You'll be leaving."

Paloma sat next to her at the table. "I don't want to go."

"You have a great opportunity there. All that schoolwork will get you a good job. And good jobs are hard to come by."

That was true. Completely true. But she didn't want it anymore. She hadn't for a long time.

"You can come back and visit all the time when you have the money."

Besides her parents, nothing tied Paloma to home. All she thought of were those great pools of wildfire smoke, and the dust-heavy cow fields, and the dying forests that surrounded the medical school in Washington. What was the point of going back and pretending that everything was normal? That everything would be the same in eight or nine years, after she graduated, took her exams, and finished her residencies?

"Medical school. That's important, Palomita. And I know you can do it."

She felt like she wouldn't be helping anyone. Not in time. She would just be sitting in a classroom for years, pretending everything was fine while, all around her, the earth was burnt, and dry, and barren, and above her, the sky was a woolen blanket of smoke and poison, so dense as to smother the stars.

"I still have some time," Paloma said. She folded her hands on the table. "So what are we going to do about the farm?"

Tía Roberta sighed. "Is it worth the time? We know it will be destroyed someday."

"We want to show people it's possible. When they see what a success this one is, maybe someone else will offer their land, and we can build another one."

"What people? *Por dios*, are strangers going to be coming here?"

"At first it will just be us, everyone in the group. But later we might get others involved. Other people in town."

"Did I not tell you how crazy people are here? This is not *los Estados Unidos*."

"A few people are crazy, yes, but most people are good. Most people are just trying to survive."

"How do you know that, Paloma? You've only been here a few months. I've lived here my entire life. I know how people are."

"It's just a garden. No one's going to come shoot us over it."

"If it gets good enough, they might. If we grow enough food, they'll want it." Tía Roberta shook her head. "You know I keep a gun next to my bed? You know that? You've got to be smart around here. Smart and careful. And inviting strange people to the house—no."

"Okay, what if it's just the Medicina Mas Allá group, and no one else? And we keep it small?"

Tía Roberta got up and stirred the soup. "I don't see the issue there. As long as they know that something will kill their crops someday, either storms or the flood."

"That doesn't stop you from planting yours."

"Yes. That's true." Tía Roberta turned back to Paloma. "Okay. Está bien."

"Let's do it?"

"Let's do it."

CHAPTER NINETEEN
LAUREL

AUREL CROUCHED AT THE EDGE OF THE POOL. She picked out one fish and kept her gaze on him. He flicked through the dark water, one side to the other, one side to the other, in a zig-zag pattern. The rest flowed like shadows, a mass of muscle and movement that turned and paced as though they had no choice, no other option; as though these were robotic bodies, things controlled by some outside force. She imagined their little fish brains. Dark. Primal. Sparks of emotion that glowed like lightning. Maybe they were afraid. Or, worst of all, maybe they weren't.

She continued on her way to the garden. The greens had sprouted again, light green blades pushing up through the dirt. A tall, wire fence rimmed the planter box. She typed in the code to open the gate—28554.

"Laurel."

She turned to find Mauricio coming through the gate behind her. The sunlight rested on his hair, making it seem even blonder than usual. He smiled broadly.

"What are you doing here?" Laurel asked.

"I just—"

"Watch out," Laurel said. "Don't step on this row, it's just planted."

He glanced down at his feet. "I just got news—Schreifer's coming."

"He is? When?"

"Tomorrow morning."

"I have to tell Augusta!"

"Wait—did she tell you what their plan is yet?"

A breeze blew through, lined with unusual chilliness. Laurel crossed her arms. Last night, Augusta had introduced her to her friends, a group of Hondurans and Guatemalans who met once a week, in a different house each time. As they talked, they'd drank hot water with nothing in it, and pretended it was tea. Laurel spoke Spanish as best she could, slowly and simply. They'd laughed a little, but they understood. She was getting better at it.

"I don't think they know what their plan is," Laurel said. "We all just want to have a say in things, for once."

"I just don't see why they wanted to know so much about Schreifer."

"I bet Schreifer knows a lot about us."

Mauricio laughed. "His aids do. Schreifer doesn't know much of anything."

"That's the first bad thing I've heard you say about him."

"Yeah. Don't tell anyone." He stared at his feet for a moment. "But, none of them—Augusta or anyone—none of them have guns or anything, right?"

"No one could've gotten one past the scanners."

Mauricio looked down again. "But if they took one from the inside. From the administration—"

"No. They don't need guns. They're not like that. We're not like that."

A drone buzzed overhead, its helicopter wings a tightly wound blur.

"I hate those things," Laurel said.

"But look how fast everything gets delivered."

"Delivered to who? A quarter of the island wants to leave."

"Not that many."

"Everyone I've talked to, everyone in the gardens, at least, if they're not talking about changing the government here, they're talking about going home. We're all getting tired of this already."

"It's not perfect," Mauricio said, "but we've accomplished a lot. Just look at this." He gestured to the darkly planted soil, and beyond to the still-empty fields, newly filled with compost and humanure.

"Oh, I know," Laurel said. "I helped plant it."

"We're on our way to self-sufficiency."

"You think we can get everything we need from this little strip of plastic?"

"Eventually—"

"You think we can separate ourselves from everything else?" Laurel said. "What happens when the sea levels rise more?"

"The island will rise with it."

"What do you mean?"

"That's how the Blue Mar people designed it," Mauricio said.

"What if the rest of the world was gone? What if it was just Blue Mar? Could we survive?"

He pressed his lips together. "Eventually, maybe," he said.

"Who knows?"

Laurel nodded. "Yeah. Who knows." She tried to smile.

"Anyway. Tell your friend about Schreifer."

"I will. Thanks, Mauricio."

According to the gossip she'd heard, the majority of the island hated Blue Mar. Laurel didn't hate it, not completely, but something was missing; something that remained gray on even the sunniest of afternoons.

Just off the edge, the ocean sparkled in lines of turquoise and indigo, always moving, shifting, running, coiling. She'd begun to think of it as a living thing, as a being that could not rest, whose moods shifted with the wind and the sun. On dark nights the moon rested on the waves in bent, silver streaks.

Once, she saw a fish leap out of the water. He glided for a moment, his fins splayed out like sails. She had never seen a wild fish before, besides jellyfish. His dark eyes seemed more alive than those of the genetically modified fish. Sometimes she imagined him, down there in the deep pockets of the ocean, weaving between forests of jellyfish and shopping bags. She imagined him as the last fish; as the only being on Earth, in flooded ocean water, spilled over a parking lot, shallow, coated in oil, or in a dried-up riverbed, or a swimming pool plastered with sunscreen residue, or even on Mars, swimming circles in a pressure-controlled tank that overlooked all the dead, orange fields, and the beige light, and the far, cold sun, his muscles aching for movement, and fear, and the mossy mineral-taste of the sea.

That night, Augusta brought her to another meeting, an emergency one to discuss Schreifer. They walked along the blue-lit walkway, down a new path that Laurel had never taken. The night had grown unusually warm. Somehow there was no wind. Laurel couldn't stand the silence.

"So, what are we going to do?" she asked Augusta in Spanish. Augusta's eyebrows lowered. "When? At the meeting?" she answered.

"With Schreifer."

Augusta cleared her throat. "Everyone here who has power is rich, and white. But most of us are not." Her Guatemalan Spanish sounded mumbled to Laurel, at least compared to Salvadorian Spanish. "We came here so things would be different," Augusta went on, still speaking Spanish. "Because we wanted a little power. Do you understand what I'm saying?"

Laurel nodded. She coughed and glanced away, out toward the darkened ocean.

"How we were raised. How we see things. You understand? That's what we want power for. So our culture is represented. So it's important. You understand?"

Laurel nodded. "I understand," she said. "I understand every word."

They made it to the house, where the door was propped slightly open. Augusta pushed her way in. They followed voices towards the loft.

"*Aquí están!*" someone yelled as they climbed the stairs. At the top, they found three familiar faces. One by one, each of them hugged her and Augusta. Silvana, an older woman who always wore bright pink lipstick, offered Laurel a cup of hot water.

"*Gracias,*" Laurel said. She leaned against the wall and sipped at it quietly.

Marta, a heavy-set woman with short black hair, started the meeting. "Here's my idea," she said, her accent quick and strung-together, like Augusta's. "El Shreifer needs to hear us. We can get a big crowd together—"

"No," said Jacinto, a young man with green, faded tattoos on his hands. "We won't be able to say anything that will make

El Shreifer care. We need to take action. Something big. Show them we know what we want."

Laurel wanted to suggest a strike, but she had no idea how to say that in Spanish. Still, she attempted it: "Why not—let's all stop work," she said. "Everyone, at the same time."

"We don't have time to coordinate that," Jacinto said.

"A strike would be perfect," Silvana said. "I heard that El Shreifer is bringing cameras here. To show people what a success we are."

Jacinto laughed. "No—for real?"

"Where did you hear that?" Laurel asked.

"I know someone in the administration," Silvana said.

"It doesn't matter. El Shreifer is filming us all the time," Augusta said. "The drones have cameras on them."

"What?" Laurel said. "Are you sure?"

"Your friend, he didn't tell you?" Augusta said.

"Either way," Silvana continued, "tomorrow El Shreifer is bringing people from the news. It's different."

"The news? And why didn't they warn everyone?" Marta asked. "Don't they want us to look perfect? Comb our hair?"

"He probably won't be filming us," Augusta said. "We're not perfect enough."

Jacinto laughed again. "Where's Oscar? Man, he needs to hear this."

"But don't you see why we need to be on camera?" Silvana said.

"I do," Laurel said. "They should interview us, not him. We're here. He's not."

"Exactly," Yolanda said. "She gets it."

"Well she can do it, then," Jacinto said. "I don't see the point."

"No, that's right, she should do it," Marta said. "She speaks English."

"I speak English too," Jacinto said.

"I can do it," Laurel said. "My friend Mauricio, he'll help me."

"Are you sure? But what will you say?" Augusta asked.

"She can't be the one to do it," Jacinto said. "She's white. People will see her, and they still won't know we're here."

Laurel's cheeks grew hot. Her gaze fell to the dusty, plastic floor. "I'm not completely white," she said. "I'm half *Salvadoreña.*"

"But you look like a *gringa.*"

"No," Augusta said. "She's *güera*, white-skinned, sure, but she's not a *gringa.*" She turned to Laurel. "It's in you, you know? In your eyes. I see it there. They are *chinitos*, like the *indígenas*. You'd have to be stupid not to see it."

"Really?"

"Of course. You are *Salvadoreña*. You are Latina."

"But no one else knows it," Jacinto said. "What kind of statement is that going to make? A white girl from the United States."

But maybe that was exactly what they needed. All the ugly racist people out there would listen to Laurel before they would listen to anyone else sitting there in the loft with her. She could amplify their voices. She could draw the attention in, and then they could speak. "I can do it," Laurel said. She wished she could explain herself better in Spanish. "I want to."

"What should she say?" Augusta asked.

"That we aren't allowed to leave," Marta said. "That we don't get paid. That we didn't get to choose our jobs."

"That we're treated like slaves," Jacinto said.

"That's not true, Jacinto," Silvana said. "But we will be eventually. When they build the resort."

"What resort?" Laurel asked.

"Your friend doesn't tell you anything, does he?" Augusta said. "The middle of Blue Mar is going to be a resort. We will be the local people. The ones who grow the food and wait on the tables."

"No, that was before," Laurel said, slipping into English.

"But this time it will be a, how you say, eco-resort," Augusta said in English.

"By Planet? Planet's building it?"

"*Sí.*"

"That's insane," Laurel said. "The world's going to shit and that's what they're doing?"

Augusta stared back at her blankly. She'd spoken too fast. Everyone else waited in silence.

"Shit," Laurel said. "*Mierda.* Shit."

"It's like we never left, huh?" Augusta said.

*   *   *   *   *

Later that night, after Laurel and Augusta had returned to their house, the wind began to pick up. Laurel couldn't sleep as the wind built up against the walls, coughing and slicing against the windows. By morning the rain kicked in. An announcement slip was taped to the door. It read:

According to meteorological predictions, we are due for a series of storms that could possibly coalesce into a hurricane. Please be advised to stay indoors as much as possible until the high winds have subsided. Please let us know of any questions or concerns. Thank you.

A hurricane? Their crops would be destroyed. Their houses would be flattened. And what about the plan? Was Shreifer still coming? She slipped on a raincoat and ventured out to find Mauricio.

The rain fell hard already. It stung her skin, like needles. She turned her face to the sky and let the water run down her eyelids, her nose, her mouth. Like ants. She had ants all over her. She opened her mouth. She ate them. She bit them. Take that, rain. She quickened her pace to a jog. The water sloshed at her ankles. Where was she going? Where did Mauricio live, again? The sun had never risen, it seemed.

"Mauricio!" she called out stupidly as she wandered the neighborhood. Why not? She was the only one on the street. All these people in their tiny little houses. All these people everywhere, everywhere on Earth, with their meaningless jobs and their meaningless lives and the sea about to suffocate them like a heavy blanket.

She knocked on his door. One of his roommates answered.

"Where's Mauricio?"

"He's right here. Come inside."

There he was, sitting at the tiny kitchen table. The house smelled like fresh wood, like it was somehow newer than hers. Maybe they just kept it cleaner.

"Laurel? What are you doing here? The storm—"

"Is Shreifer still coming?"

"Tomorrow, most likely. Depends how the storm goes."

"How stupid can he be? Why did he plan this trip—" Laurel coughed into her arm. Rain bled from her jacket and onto the floor—drip, drip. "Why did he plan this trip if there was a hurricane in the forecast?"

"They're not even sure it's going to be a full-out hurricane. It could just be a storm. The weather radar here isn't good."

"Do you want some tea or anything?" the roommate interrupted. Laurel had met him once, but she'd forgotten his name. He was prematurely balding around his forehead and he reminded her of one of her high school friend's dads.

"No thanks, I'm good." She sat down across from Mauricio.

"I think we'll be fine," Mauricio said.

"Why didn't anyone tell us earlier? What if it *is* a real hurricane? What do we do then? Evacuate?"

"How?"

"Call a plane in. Call the government. Get some emergency help here."

"That might be over-reacting," Mauricio said.

"You know we're going to lose our crops? They can't take all this wind. They'll be ripped apart."

"We'll just replant again. The donations are still coming in."

"You mean donations for the big eco-resort?"

"How did you hear about that?"

"Nothing's changed. Nothing at all."

"There's nothing wrong with a little business. This is all just the beginning. We have time."

She knew that wasn't true. She could feel it. She could smell it in the wind. Everything was at its peak, a great hill of flames, and ready to cool to ash.

She stood up.

"You're not going back out there?"

She stepped toward the door. "It's not a hurricane or anything. Why not go out in it?"

"Laurel—"

Back into the rain. It fell even harder now, and in certain dips in the concrete the water pooled up to her calves. She ran through it. Slosh. Her hood blew back off her head, and the rain soon tangled through her hair, stringing it out into long, heavy, frizzy tendrils. Her jeans soaked through. She moved without thought, an animal being. Where was she going? Where was the land, and where was the sea?

A voice yelled through the wind. It sounded like a bird, but she knew it was human. Another voice yelled. The lights in someone's house shut off, all at once, and then it happened in the other houses, too. Every window she passed was bathed in the quiet, black darkness of sleeping people. It was day. They shouldn't be sleeping. She wanted to yell at them but she was out of breath. Another voice. A flashlight beam. Where was she going?

The fish. What would the fish do? She'd been running to them without even realizing it. She knelt at the edge of the pool. They swam side to side, completely calm beneath the rain and the wind. She dipped one hand into the water.

Why did it matter? The fish would die anyway. They only had a few weeks to live.

She heard her own voice, her younger voice, echo in her ears. "And what would it matter? He's dead now." It was the day Abuelo took them on a tour of the slaughterhouse. He wanted them to see where their food came from. He wanted them to know the reality of things.

Laurel let Paloma keep her hand on her wrist. The grip tightened as the cows were rounded up. The men herded them into the holding room and shut the door. One by one they forced the cows through a plastic flap.

"This is the worst part, my little warriors. You have to be brave, okay?" Abuelo gave them plastic suits and made them stand far off to the side. "This is the *vaca* we will follow, okay?"

Paloma began to cry, silently enough that Abuelo didn't notice, or maybe he did and he just wanted to make her stronger.

"You don't have to do this," Laurel said to her.

"I know."

Laurel counted in her head, one-two-three-four, again and again like that. The cow was not a cow. It was beef.

This was the truth of the world. This was an old thing. Animals ate other animals. She was brave enough to face this.

She'd expected Paloma to turn her head, or to run away, but she faced it too. Luckily they couldn't see the cow's eyes when it happened. First, a stake was shot through the skull and through the brain. Then the throat was cut with a large knife. Spanish voices; they yelled at each other as they hoisted up the cow. The machine kicked in. It grumbled like the trash disposal in the sink at home.

"The worst part's over," Laurel whispered.

"It's still happening," Paloma said. "It's still there."

It was. The dark-purple puddle. The enormous pressure of blood streaming from the cow's neck.

"Do you think his life flashed before his eyes?" Paloma asked.

"Cows don't have memories," Laurel said. "And what would it matter? He's dead now."

"What does anything matter, then?"

Laurel wanted to free her sister, to take her outside and calm her and then walk home together with the sun on their faces. But she turned back to the action, to the disassembly line, spread like a slideshow against the white-tile walls. Paloma would become a vegetarian now, Laurel thought. There was no way she'd make it out of this unscathed.

And Laurel? All this was shocking but it was also the truth. She could handle it. She would remain an omnivore.

Cows among cows. Even back then the trucks brought in thousands at a time. One and then another, so many cows strung up that she lost track of the one Abuelo wanted them to trace. They transformed into lumps. They were no longer shocking. They were no longer anything at all. Like a word repeated too many times they became incoherent, just parts, just the letters of the words and the absurdity of language.

They watched from the spectator hallway, with windows protecting them. Laurel was glad she couldn't smell anything, just the acidity of whatever cleaners they used, part bleach, part vinegar, maybe, and some unknown chemical that burned and lingered in the back of her throat.

By the end of the line the cows became blobs. Laurel tried not to think of them as muscles, but that's what they were; fat-laced muscles, gelatinous, removed from their bodies. The insides were scooped into a great tin and wheeled away by two men. It was so full that the organs sloshed over the sides. At the time Laurel had wondered what they would do with all of that—was there a pile of rotting flesh in the landfill? Would they dump it at sea?—but now she knew that it would be condensed into a protein additive for other livestock. Sometimes even for other cows. Abuelo used to make sure that his cows didn't eat it, but after the Bradley & Bradley deal he had no idea what the cows were fed.

Abuelo would have hated these genetically modified fish, revolving like suns in their cramped little swimming pool. This is not a life, Abuelo would say. These *peces* do not have a good life.

Or did they? Did they have a better life than that wild fish, out there, who survived by eating plastic and avoiding the stingers of jellyfish? At least that fish had space. At least he was free.

"What do you think, fish?" she asked them. "What do you think we should do?" Her arms and abdominal muscles shivered. They seemed separate from her. "What do you think, fish?" She clenched her teeth. The cold didn't matter. She took off her raincoat and doubled it over, like a basket. "I'm going to help you out, here." She lifted one fish out of the pool. It wriggled in her palms, muscular and snake-like. She screamed and dropped it back in. Terrifying. It felt slimy, and, for some reason, it stunk like soil, like the earth. "I'm sorry," she said. She tried it again and this time dropped two fish in her jacket. The wind blew in even stronger. Her shirt soaked through in only seconds. Her body was water. She was water.

Down to the ocean. Laurel had never run faster. She felt wild. She felt like she wasn't a person anymore. The waves burst over the docks in great, crashing drum beats. Boom. Like rocks falling. What was that noise? An alarm? A siren? The wind hurt her cheeks and her nose. She ran out onto the docks. "You're free, fish," she yelled. They slopped out into the gray expanses, and dissolved into the waves. All at once it was over; they were gone, and she stood hunched in the wind, all alone as the blackness poured forth. Her eyes watered. Her hands stunk of fish. She watched for a moment. Another wave crashed over the docks in front of her. Time to go. She hurried back along the blue-lit pathways. Back to the house.

"Augusta!" she yelled up the stairs. "Augusta, *El Shreifer ya no viene.*"

She waited for an answer. The wind cracked against the walls. "Augusta! Where are you? *Estás aquí?*"

A knock at the front door. Laurel opened it to find Mauricio, his hair dampened over his forehead, his cheeks pale but flushed. He stepped forward and gripped Laurel's arms.

"You were right," he said. "It is going to be a hurricane." His thumbs dug in too hard. Laurel backed away.

"You changed your mind that quickly?"

"They're doing evacuations. On the other side of the island. I can get you out."

"A half an hour ago you thought I was crazy." She sniffed. When had her nose started running? She retreated into the kitchen-area for a tissue.

"Laurel, we don't have time. We have to go." Mauricio followed her.

"What about everyone else? Can Augusta come? And Marta? And Silvana? And Jacinto?"

"What—who are they?"

"Augusta, my roommate. And that group I told you about. And what about everyone else from the garden?"

"It's a small plane. Only a few people on the inside were even told about it."

Laurel shook her head. She laughed bitterly, though her teeth. "Paloma was right. It is just like Mars."

"What are you talking about? Laurel, do you want to go or not? Because we have to get going. The plane leaves in half an hour and there's a helicopter meeting at the administration—"

"No."

"What?"

"I'm not going."

"We can't save everyone, Laurel. And they're saying this is going to be a bad one."

Laurel swallowed hard. "If they're not going, neither am I."

"Why would you put yourself in danger if you don't have to? We have a way out."

"I don't want special treatment. I'm one of them. I'm not special just because I'm your friend."

"That's not—"

"And does it matter? Hurricanes here, wildfires at home." Laurel crossed her arms. "No. I'm not going unless everyone can go."

"Well then neither am I," Mauricio said. "You stay, I stay."

"No—wait. Go, Mauricio. You can go."

"Not if you don't."

"A second ago you were telling me how dangerous it is to stay here."

"You stay, I stay."

"Mauricio."

"I'm not leaving without you."

"Mauricio, you don't have to—"

"It might not be as bad as they say. It's all just predictions, right? Those things are wrong all the time."

Laurel stepped forward, and she hugged him.

CHAPTER TWENTY
PALOMA

AFTER THE STORM, THE SHORE WAS COVERED IN DEBRIS. Some of it was natural—sticks, kelp, a few dead fish—but mostly it was plastic—unidentifiable red and yellow chunks that almost looked like pebbles from a distance. Some of it was still in-tact, including a net of some sort and a popped balloon. Paloma tried to clean up at low tide, but the water brushed in and swept some of the debris back into the ocean.

"*Déjalo*," Tía Roberta told her. "Leave it. There will always be more. All those little pieces. You'll never get rid of them."

Still, Paloma paced barefoot at the edge of the old rainforest trees. She picked up whatever she could. Slivers. Chunks. Pieces. Dense, hard plastic. Floppy plastic. Wrappers.

The sun beat against her scalp. She crouched down. The ocean lapped at her ankles, and at the roots of the trees. She dipped her hands in and poured water over her face and her arms. It didn't cool her down at all. The water was sun-warmed; tepid. Her toes sunk into the mud.

At noon Tía Roberta called her up to the house for lunch. Paloma paused to look at Tía Roberta's garden. Kale stems and smashed avocados were strewn across the grass like severed limbs. The garden soil was barren, emptied of its lettuce, its squash, its onions, its chicory, its tiny, stunted strawberries. The fruit trees stood haggard, and wind-scattered, their branches gnarled and naked.

Alongside the house, a pile of glass glittered in the sunlight. A branch had swung through Tía Roberta's bedroom window. Otherwise, the house remained whole, but messy, with globs of white chicken scat on the floors. Tía Roberta had brought them inside during the storm. Meanwhile, Galleta, Ballena, and Marisol stayed huddled in their shed. If the storm had been worse, Tía Roberta would have brought them inside, too.

"There you are," Tía Roberta said. She handed Paloma a bowl of black beans, topped with the last of the cilantro, harvested before the storm. "Don't stay out there much longer. You'll get sick if you stand in that water too long."

"It's hot."

"Doesn't matter. Be careful. And don't step on anything."

Paloma took a bite. Tía Roberta had topped the beans with lemon, too. Lemon and a small drizzle of olive oil.

"Tía, do you think the Mas Allá bed is fine? I'm afraid to look. Just look what the storm did to your garden."

"It didn't flood up that high, but all the rain probably washed the seeds out. Go look at it after lunch. Dig down and see if they're there."

"What if there's another storm?"

"There will be. I told you. This is what happens. The storms come. Sometimes they're not too bad. Sometimes they are, and that's when I replant."

"That will be a lot to replant. It took us a whole weekend."

"That's why I kept mine small."

"I hope Doña Yolanda has more seeds."

"I'm sure she does."

After lunch, Paloma climbed the hill, back behind the citrus grove, to the Medicina Mas Allá garden. They'd spent days removing the grasses, loosening the dirt, adding compost from both Tía Roberta and Señora Rodriguez's piles, and planting the seeds that Doña Yolanda had kept hidden in glass jars for decades. Paloma wondered if the seeds were too old, but Doña Yolanda said they would be fine.

It was a slow work party because, besides Isa, Eugenio, and Paloma, everyone was in their forties or older, and it had been years since most of them had used shovels and hoes and garden rakes. But they'd done it. Each afternoon, when the sun was just beginning to cool, Paloma hauled water from Tía Roberta's rain barrel in two plastic buckets, and she watered the seeds gently.

Now water pooled on the surface of the soil, like a pond. Paloma reached her hand in and dug down with her fingers. Nothing. They'd planted the seeds somewhat shallowly, because farther down the earth was hard and made of clay. Paloma leaned back on her heels. She breathed deeply. The air smelled strange, like electricity and salt. She tried again, digging in at a different spot this time. Nothing. "No," she said. Her voice hung drily in the air. She looked at her fingernails. Two brown moons. She tried again. Nothing.

This was why she'd been afraid to look. This was why she hadn't run out there first thing in the morning. She'd felt it. Known it.

That afternoon, Isa and Eugenio dropped by to see the damage.

"We need to make a barrier or something. To keep this from happening again," Paloma said.

"But what kind of barrier?" Isa said. "I've never heard of anything like that."

Eugenio stared silently at the mud.

"It could be a windshield, or something," Paloma said. "With a roof for rain. Something you could put up when a storm's coming in."

"That's a good idea. But how could we afford that?" Isa asked.

"We can get funding from Medicina Mas Allá."

"It won't work," Eugenio said. "Doña Roberta was right. This is not a good place for it."

"That was a big storm. They won't all be like that," Paloma said.

"Some have been worse," Eugenio said.

"But there's nowhere else to build it." Paloma knew it was unfair of her to get upset. She was the one who would be leaving soon; the one who had a way out.

"Yes. We should leave it," Eugenio said. "This is not worth the time."

"It was your idea," Isa said.

"And look at it. *Se murió.*"

"I started telling people about it," Isa said. "People who came into the *farmacia*. They all seemed interested. 'Much better than growing sugar cane,' they said. I told them how beautiful it would be. How much we planted. Rows and rows of plants." She placed her hand over her mouth.

"It's okay. It'll be fine. We'll replant it, just like Tía Roberta always does." Paloma put her arms around both of them, and pulled them into a hug. "It'll be fine," she said. "Just fine."

That night, Paloma couldn't sleep. She asked her phone for the news. The wildfires had finally mellowed in California, but the drought was going strong. It was predicted to last until winter.

Paloma turned over onto her stomach. She pulled the sheets over her legs to keep the mosquitoes away. "What's the news in Blue Mar?" she asked.

"Blue Mar. Current reports indicate that early yesterday morning, a hurricane made landfall on Blue Mar Island. It is currently ranked as a Category Two. Of the 200 island residents, it's estimated that 20 were injured, and 10 were killed as a direct result of the storm. Property damages have been catastrophic, with more than half the island's structures destroyed. A statement by Planet's executive director—"

Paloma exited out. She tried to call Laurel, but there was no answer. She texted her, and then tried to call again. The phone rang, and rang. Paloma stood up. She looked out the window, at the silver earth, at the cloud-heavy sky. Still ringing. Still ringing. "Come on, Laurel. Answer." No. It went to her video message. She called her parents and asked if they'd heard from her. They hadn't, and they knew nothing about the hurricane.

"I told her not to go," her mom said. Her voice cracked with panic. "We'll keep calling her. Or else I'll call that man who's always on the news. *Ese hombre.* Schraffen or whatever his name is."

Paloma couldn't sleep. She sat at the edge of her bed and tossed her phone between each hand. She couldn't stand the stillness; the silence. She escaped to the citrus grove, but it was quiet there too. Mosquitoes bit her calves, and her shoulders, and her neck. There were more than ever because of the mud, and because the wind had slowed after the storm. She walked in circles. Where was the moon? Where was anything, under this thick, blank sky? Yes, where was anything? Anything at all? She ran to the chain-link fence where Galleta usually waited for her, but she wasn't there. Of course not. She was asleep. Paloma leaned back against the fence. She sat on the mud. The mosquitoes flocked to her sweat. She brushed away as many as she could, and then she checked her phone again. Still nothing.

CHAPTER
TWENTY-ONE
LAUREL

THE WIND AND THE OCEAN BECAME ONE. Together, they crashed over the plastic pavement, one-two, the beating of a heart. Laurel squinted against the rain. The drops fell sideways, or perhaps up from the sea. The ground slid beneath her like a ship. She kneeled, and covered her eyes, and thought of grass. The big blackbirds in the dirt fields. The old rainforest trees by the ocean.

"Here!" Mauricio grabbed her arm and tried to lift her up. The wind knocked over them, through them, as it would through branches. "Grab my hand!"

Laurel clung to him. Each muscle in her body tightened. She hunched forward, and, together, they ran. "It's too hard to see. Where is it?" she asked, yelling, screaming, but her voice was carried away by the wind. Something shattered in the darkness. A metal panel blew past them—wet, blind, and searching for the sea. Mauricio's hand left hers. Her eyes popped immediately open, and she found him on the ground; he'd slipped and landed on his back. She gripped his shoulders and hoisted him up. "I don't see it anymore," she yelled again, right in his face.

"The lights," he said. He pointed through the gray-black darkness. She saw them again—the lights of the Administration Building; the only lights on Blue Mar. All the houses were dark or destroyed, and even the blue path-lights were broken. There was nothing else. Only the shaking floor and the joining of sky and sea.

"We should've stayed in the house," Laurel yelled.

"It's our best shot—" Mauricio pointed again to the light. The faintest of suns. Nothing but a star.

Time slowed. Had the Administration Building always been that far away? They jogged along, their heads down, their feet waterlogged.

The wind picked up. They ran faster. Water dredged up toward their knees, so cold that it burned.

Suddenly, a flash of light. Laurel felt the hair on her arms rise. One of the wireless electricity units had exploded. She couldn't tell how far away it was. Close enough. Too close. It continued to spark in a shallow, salty puddle.

Farther off, something blue flickered, branching out like veins of lightning. A woman screamed. Then, all at once, the flood rose to Laurel's waist. She panicked and kicked, until she was treading water. The water rounded up, then back down, like a wave. "Mauricio!" she cried, but he had disappeared. Laurel kicked toward the light, until she made it to ankle-deep flooding.

A hand gripped her shoulder. She turned to find Augusta, her hair limp and straight from the rain. "*Ven. Ven!*" They rushed into the Administration Building. All at once the wind was silenced to a dull thud against the walls. Laurel squinted into the flat, yellow lights. Augusta hugged her.

"*Donde está* Mauricio?" Laurel asked. She looked around the room. Bodies. People. Overturned desks. Damp tile floors. "*Donde está?*" Laurel pulled away, back toward the door, but Augusta grabbed her arm.

"*Cálmate.* You cannot go back out." Augusta's honey eyes locked onto hers.

"Where's Jacinto? And Silvana? And Marta?"

"Doña Silvana and Marta are here, we came together, but Jacinto is not."

"We have to look for him. And Mauricio. A big wave came—"

"It is more dangerous—" Augusta switched to Spanish. "It's more dangerous each minute. The storm isn't at its worst yet. This is the only place that's not flooding."

"We can't leave them out there."

Augusta stared at her, unblinking. The walls rattled. Another group of people walked in, dripping, soaked through, and pale from the cold. One man had a red gash on his forehead. The front of his shirt was soaked in blood.

"This is how my parents died," Augusta said. Her mouth opened and closed, and then settled in a frown. "We're safer in here."

Laurel shook her head. "I have to look for him." She started toward the door.

"Laurel, don't go out there!" Augusta called, but it was too late. Laurel pushed her way through, out into the salted air. The wind knocked into her stomach. She doubled over. All of this, all the air, it smelled like rain on pavement, but also like something chemical—burnt plastic; something that had melted. She squinted. A man with no shirt stopped in front of her.

"Are you okay?" he asked, his eyes black, without pupils. She nodded, and patted his shoulder, and continued on.

Where should she look? "Mauricio! Jacinto!" she yelled. The ocean answered in dark, loping curls. "Jacinto! Mauricio!" A tide of floodwater trickled ahead in a steady stream. A weak place in the plastic had collapsed into a shallow crevasse—a riverbed. For some reason this didn't surprise her. It seemed right. Like it had always been there. She stooped close to the ground for a moment. The sea and the wind spoke an ancient language, a language the color of clouds before rain. Laurel felt their murmurings deep within her own body, within the hollow place in her chest. She closed her eyes to take a break from squinting. As she opened them, she looked across the thickly flooded plain, across the shallows, where the sky had come to rest, and to a caved-in rooftop. On it, there was something white, and round. Suddenly, it leaped off the roof. At first Laurel thought it was debris, some piece of fabric carried wildly by the wind, but then it changed direction. Two great wings soared over her head. It was a bird—*the* bird— the one she'd seen following the currents above Blue Mar. The white seabird. "Wait," Laurel yelled, stupidly, desperately, but her voice could not escape the wind. She watched as the bird tangled itself in the clouds, as the warmth of its body faded into darkness. She felt, suddenly, more alone than ever. The wind felt like rocks thrown against her skin, and her feet had grown numb in the floodwater. She sloshed through the rising ocean, back toward the Administrative Building. The island shook again. She felt like she was standing on the back of some hunched creature that at any moment would stand up and rise.

"Laurel!"

Hands gripped her shoulders. It was Mauricio, soaking wet, his face a scrape of sallow moonlight. They hugged, both of them flushed, and shivering.

A wall of rain blew into them. Laurel fell down to the plastic earth. She could see nothing but white mist. Her hands and knees submerged in the black water. Something flew over her head. A sheet? A plastic bag? The sea bird? She shivered, and tried not to breathe the burnt chemical smell. She waited until the wind quieted, just slightly, and then she and Mauricio ran the final stretch to the Administrative Building.

Augusta was waiting for them near the doorway. She asked about Jacinto. "We didn't see him," Laurel said in Spanish. "We couldn't see anything. But he might arrive any time now," she said, but she wasn't sure. This was just the beginning.

Mauricio was pulled away by a co-worker, and Augusta drifted off to find Silvana. Laurel wandered off alone and huddled numbly against an open stretch of wall. For a long time, she simply stared, shifting her gaze from person to person. The room was humid with wet hair, and with the breath of hundreds of people. Outside, the wind barreled into the building in great, wild gusts.

Laurel took out her phone. It was, supposedly, indestructible. Maybe she could record a message. Then, even if Blue Mar was swallowed by the sea, her phone would set sail, and drift, and drift, maybe forever. Maybe it would finally meet soil again. Maybe someone would see her message, and hear her voice, and know that she had been alive.

"Can we take a video?" Laurel asked her phone.

"Would you like to send a video message?"

"Shit. It's broken."

"Would you like to send a video message?"

Laurel looked more closely at the screen. She had a small, weak connection to the satellite service.

"What? How?" She hadn't had service back at the house.

"Would you like to—"

"Yes, yes, send a video message."

"Who will be receiving this message?"

"Paloma," she said, her hands shaking. "Send this to Paloma."

She leaned in toward her phone and left a long message, and then sent another to her mom, and another to her dad. Laurel was surprised none of them picked up. Maybe they were all busy, and immersed in normalcy. Or maybe the service was just being slow. Or maybe her videos weren't being sent after all.

Just in case, Laurel saved a copy of the messages to her phone, so at least her words could someday drift long and far out to sea.

Laurel wasn't sure what to do next. She sat against the wall. Eventually, Augusta joined her.

"A boat, they say," she said. "*Un barco.*"

"What, to rescue us?"

"*Sí.*"

"No—we need more than that," Laurel said in Spanish. "We need a plane."

"Marta said that planes can't land on Blue Mar. The ground is too bad. Too rough. And it's too far for helicopters or water planes to fly over from the mainland."

Laurel shook her head. "They could do it if they wanted to."

Augusta was quiet for a moment. "Well at least they won't be able to build their stupid eco-resort, huh?"

"Not for a long time." Laurel laughed, a laugh propelled by fear, and adrenaline, and the feeling of having survived.

It wasn't long before the two of them fell asleep, their heads crooked, their backs upright against the wall. Laurel dreamed of nothing—quiet, and darkness. The next morning, when she awoke, a strange liquid rolled through her chest. Phlegm? Water? Whatever it was, it crinkled with each breath, and it tugged on her lungs like a weight. She coughed into her hands, trying not to wake Augusta.

Somehow the administrative building had endured the hurricane. Everyone huddled on the floor, arm to arm, leg to leg, all squished into one room, with their damp blankets, and their phones on flashlight mode, waiting.

Laurel stood up from her blanket. Her head throbbed. This was a terrible time to be getting sick.

Mauricio appeared at her side. "They're not telling me anything," he whispered.

"They didn't even tell you when the boat's going to get here?"

"No. They kicked me out. They kicked everyone out, except for Will and Riley. They're talking to Schreifer on the phone right now."

"Why isn't the coast guard here? The marines? Whoever the government sends for emergencies?"

"I don't know. It's expensive to get out here. And we're not legally part of the United—"

Laurel coughed again—wildly, deeply, until she couldn't breathe.

Mauricio's eyebrows wrinkled with concern. "That sounds bad. Maybe you should go see the medics."

"They have bigger things to worry about. It's just a cough."

"At least drink some water. The stash is in that room over there."

"That's okay." She wasn't thirsty. Suddenly she was just unbearably tired. Maybe she had a fever. Her face felt swollen. She sat back down on her blanket.

"Here, I'll get you some."

Laurel closed her eyes. Seconds later, Mauricio kneeled in front of her, holding a cup of lukewarm water.

"Are you sure you're okay?" He squinted into her eyes.

"Fine. I'm fine." She took a sip of water. It burned her throat. "By the way, do you have a battery pack? My phone's low."

"No. But I'm sure someone has one. I'll ask around later." He sat down next to her, with his legs crisscrossed. He leaned his head against the wall.

"You know what? I threw some of the fish into the ocean," Laurel said suddenly.

"What? Why?"

Laurel laughed.

"When?" Mauricio asked.

"Yesterday. Just before the storm hit. I picked up a few and threw them out into the ocean."

"Why would you do that?"

"I wanted to set them free."

"Why? You hate those fish."

"I don't hate them. I hate what's been done to them. I hate how sad their lives are. How everything about them has been changed just so we can eat more of them—"

"You know what you did? You put GMO fish in the wild. If they mate with other fish, those genes will spread. All the fish will be genetically modified."

"They try to make them sterile, don't they?"

"I haven't heard that."

"That's what they do with most of the cows."

"Well, either way, the other ones are gone too. Most likely they got pulled out by some giant waves."

"You see? You see that? Now they're all free."

"Or dead." He sighed. "It's all done, I think. This is how the experiment ends."

"I think you're right," Laurel said. "So right." She closed her eyes. Hours later, she awoke feeling stiff. Her muscles ached painfully, and her chest felt swollen. She shivered. Her hands burned, hot, and blistery, and not her own.

"You okay?" Mauricio asked.

Laurel coughed again. "This is getting worse, quickly," she said, her voice small.

"I'll talk to the medic."

Augusta leaned over her. "Laurel, *estás bien?*"

"Sorry, I didn't mean to wake you up."

"*Qué te pasa? Con tu voz?*"

"My voice?"

"*Estás enferma?* You are sick?"

"*Sí.*" Laurel placed one hand on her throat and the other on her chest.

"All this cold. Here." Augusta draped her blanket over Laurel.

"*Gracias,*" Laurel said. Even under two blankets, she shivered rigidly, uncontrollably. Mauricio returned with the doctor—a young woman with glasses who Laurel had never met. She asked about her symptoms, and how long she'd been feeling like this. She looked at her seriously.

"This is unusual," the doctor said. "Symptoms usually don't become this severe this quickly, unless we're talking a stomach flu or something like that. And the stiffness—that's unusual." She ran her hands over Laurel's arms and legs. They felt hard, like metal. "Yes. There's some light swelling in there." The doctor stood up, shaking her head. "I can't say I know what this is, but let's keep an eye on it."

"Thank you," Laurel tried to say, but her voice no longer worked. The doctor pulled Mauricio aside. She leaned in close and whispered something—a secret. Mauricio nodded curtly.

Night faded into dawn. Cell phone lights turned off. All around her, people groaned and rolled over and conversed loudly in Spanish. Laurel remained under her blankets. The room smelled like sweat and body-heat, but, still, she shivered.

"*Agua?*" Augusta asked. She tipped a cup to Laurel's lips.

Augusta said something to Mauricio in Spanish. They talked for a few minutes. Laurel hadn't heard Mauricio's Spain-Spanish accent in a long time. The administration did everything in English. How had that happened, Laurel wondered? Why English? Why not Spanish, when almost all of the residents spoke Spanish?

She closed her eyes again. She felt like she was floating on the ocean. Like she had always been there, on her back, staring at the thin, papery clouds. Suddenly, out of nowhere, out of nothing, a cow swam by, paddling and panting like a dog. Laurel looked into the cow's eyes. They were the same dark brown as Abuelo's. The cow continued on, and disappeared.

Laurel treaded water. Her muscles ached. The waves spoke— they asked to pull her under. She could not answer.

Then—water over her head. Salt in her throat. Rubbed red and raw. Cold. Bones. She felt her bones. Finally the sky surfaced above her. Everything was water. Where was the—where was the land? She swam in a circle. Her eyes burned. Rain hung on her eyelashes. Another wave pushed her under. She tried to swim up but she couldn't find it in the darkness. Her chest tightened. She kicked frantically. Air, then. Air, just for a moment. Everything felt clear. Such a beautiful gray—silver and green. The wind on her face. Waves rising and falling. Hills. Soft, smooth hills.

Another wave. It pushed her down even farther this time. When she surfaced, the world spun. Fog, spray, dust. Ahead of her, she could see the land, pale in the distance. Yes, she could see it. She could see it all, just then. Everything.

CHAPTER TWENTY-TWO PALOMA

PALOMA WATCHED THE OCEAN CAREFULLY. This was her favorite time to go out to the old beach, at the peak of night, at low tide. Tonight, the half-moon cast its soft, yellow light on the water. Everything was still, and quiet, like the night had never been seen before, like she was the first human, the first one to see the stars hiding alongside the moon. The waves were calmer at night. They, too, wound down for sleep.

Paloma turned back to the house. Panic sunk into her stomach—or was it dread? Fear? Whatever it was, it hurt. Her sister was missing. Laurel was missing. *Laurel.* Paloma had been trying to keep busy the past few days. She tagged along with Eugenio and Isa when they went to the selva for more wood. She spent an entire afternoon plucking more plastic from the trees. She helped Tía Roberta till the soil in her garden. She read the

Spanish picture book Isa had lent her. The distractions worked until bed; until she was all alone in Tía Roberta's childhood bedroom, sitting there, listening, listening, to the dark, silent house, and holding onto the wooden horse Eugenio had made for her. Then worry smothered her. It covered her head like a heavy blanket. She slept maybe four hours each night, if that. Instead she went outside, or watched movies on her phone. Anything to keep her mind busy. She had to believe that Laurel was fine. There was no other option.

The next morning, Paloma crept outside at dawn. Fog rimmed the old rainforest trees, and nowhere else, like a small, singular cloud brought to earth. Paloma breathed in and out. In and out. Slowly, through her chest and stomach. She walked through the dewy grass and to the fence where Galleta usually waited. A few crickets chirped. Paloma tilted her head back. The sky blossomed to peach. In and out. The scent of manure and sea salt. More deep breaths. She had a plan for today.

She walked through the dust, to the south, in the direction of town. Suddenly she wished for a shot of tequila. Maybe two. Would *los pobres* be up? Would they be nice? Did she know how to say what she needed to say?

A fire cracked at the center of the hut village. Paloma took another deep breath, and then she stepped closer. Her feet thudded against the soil. The sharp smell of smoke reminded her of the wildfires back home. She walked faster and cleared her throat.

"*Hola?*" she called. Her voice was still raspy from sleep. She cleared it again. "*Alguien—está aquí?*"

Nothing. Paloma stepped in close enough to the fire that she could feel the warmth on her face. It wasn't wood burning, as she'd thought; it was a mix of many things—she could pick out cereal boxes, and old dishcloths, and the instruction manual for some appliance, either a food processor or a blender. Paloma was about to call out again, but then a voice rose from inside one of the huts.

A man walked out, hunched and shirtless. He spoke in a blur of Spanish. Paloma froze. She tried to pick out a word, any word, but she understood nothing. All this time with Eugenio and Isa, and everyone at Medicina Mas Allá, she thought she'd been learning so much. But now that she was on her own, with a voice that was fast and unfamiliar, she realized that she knew much less Spanish than she thought, and that everyone had been dumbing it down for her.

"*Hola,*" Paloma tried again, more slowly this time.

The man's eyes lingered on hers. He squinted. "*No hablas español?*"

She understood that. "*Un poquito.*"

He turned around without saying anything more, and lumbered back into the hut.

"Wait!" Paloma yelled. For a second she worried he might come back with a gun, but, no—he didn't come back at all. She was left with the crackling of the fire, and her own quick breathing. She stared at the soil. Why hadn't she watched those *telenovelas* with Laurel and Abuela all those years ago, instead of laughing at them? Why hadn't she taken four years of Spanish in high school? Why hadn't she practiced Spanish with her mom, and Abuelo? She could've been fluent by now, or at least close to it.

Paloma was about to head back toward the road when a woman stepped out from another hut. Her skin was lined and wrinkled, but her features looked young.

"*Inglés?*" the woman asked.

Paloma nodded. "*Sí,*" she said. She pulled an envelope from the pocket of her shorts. Inside were the squat, round seeds of a chayote squash, leftover from Doña Yolanda's stash. "We want to plant a garden."

The woman scooped the seeds from her palm and held one up to the light.

"I was thinking you guys might want to be part of it. We want to use some of your land, here, because it's a little farther back from the ocean. But, me and my friends would do all the planting, and all the hard work. And then we would all share the harvest." She motioned back and forth between herself and the woman, who continued to analyze the seeds. Did she really speak English?

"No hello, how are you?" The woman laughed. "What is your name?"

"Oh—my name is Paloma."

"Paloma. Nice to meet you. My name is Gloria."

"*Mucho gusto,*" Paloma said.

Gloria stared back down at the seeds. "We don't own this land. It is not ours."

"Whose is it?"

"It belongs to the woman, over there." She pointed north, toward the *finca.*

"Roberta? She owns this land, here?"

"Yes. Doña Roberta. You know her?"

Paloma smiled. "She's my *tía.*"

"Your *tía? Pero no hablas español?*"

"No. I'm from the U.S. I grew up there. I'm only half *Salvadoreña.*"

"Well. She's your *tía,* then this is your land, too."

Paloma felt a wave of guilt. "Not really," she said. "You live here. It's yours."

"I guess it belongs to all of us, huh?" She held up the seeds. "These don't grow here. The *tierra* is bad."

"But we have compost."

Gloria's eyebrows rose.

"Compost. It makes the soil healthier."

"It does?"

"Yeah. We planted seeds at Roberta's *finca*. Before the storm, they were growing just fine. The soil was bad there before, too."

The woman nodded. "Okay."

"Okay? We can plant here?"

"Sure. But we'll help. We can all help. There are ten of us here. It will be for all of us, huh? My husband used to work on the *hacienda* of a rich family. He was in charge of the orchards."

"I'm sure he knows a lot about plants, then."

"He does. Yes, he does. Me, I don't know as much about gardening. I was the cook, the one who made the food. And I learned English there. The mom was from an American family. They helped my daughter get to the United States. They were good people. Back then there were more good people. Yes." The woman nodded. She paused for a moment, and smiled. "Yes, we can do it. Why not? Let's raise the garden."

"Oh—yes. Yes! Okay. I'll tell everyone. I'll—come back." Paloma grinned. "You can keep the seeds. We'll bring more."

Paloma rushed back to the *finca*. Sweat ran down her forehead, down the indent between her nose and mouth. She let it drip. It was only nine in the morning, yet the sun had absorbed half the sky.

Galleta waited at the fence. "I'll be back," Paloma said. "Hold on." She flung open the front door. The whole house smelled like fried eggs and beans. "Tía!" she yelled. "Why didn't you tell me about *los pobres*? That's your property too?"

She waited for a response. But instead she heard a man's voice. Young. Familiar. Where did she know that voice from? She peeked her head into the kitchen. It was a young man with blonde hair and blue eyes, and tanned, golden skin. He spoke with a lisp, as though he were from Spain. She'd definitely seen him before, but she couldn't remember where.

"Tía?" Paloma stepped into the kitchen.

Tía Roberta clasped her hands over her mouth. Paloma rushed toward her.

"What's wrong?" she asked. "Who's this?" Tía Roberta shook her head and made a small noise, almost a hiccup.

"Are you Paloma?" the man asked. He spoke English without an accent.

"Yeah," she said. Then she remembered. It was the man from the boat. "Is Laurel okay?" she asked. Tía Roberta leaned heavily against the wall. Her hands remained over her mouth.

The man breathed deeply and glanced at the floor. When he looked up his eyes met hers. Paloma saw the sadness in them, the glassiness, the redness, the dull, weighty shock. She knew, even before he said it—Laurel was dead.

Paloma said nothing. She felt like she was no longer in her body. Like she was no longer real. For some reason her eyes drifted to the bookshelf. All those shells. One—a dark blue spiral—was coated with a light layer of dust.

The man continued: "There was nothing they could've done. It was one of those new diseases. Only three other people had ever had it before—"

"Had what?"

"The sickness. The virus. It's a new disease."

"But what was it? Was it exitosis?"

"No. Something else. I don't know the name. It comes on fast and strong. It's—there was nothing anyone could've done. Two other people on the island got it too. It was starting to spread around. It could've been an outbreak."

Paloma nodded. Outside, the chickens clucked. This couldn't be true. Laurel was still on the island. Or she was headed home, home to California. She'd be there any second.

"I can have someone call you about the funeral arrangements. Whenever you're ready."

Tía Roberta had become a statue. Paloma joined her. Hours passed. The man left them with his phone number. The chickens continued to chatter. Paloma wandered to the citrus grove. She sat on the grass. An ant stung her leg. She crushed it with her finger. It leaked green blood. She pulled a leaf from the lemon tree and used it to wipe her hands. Hours. Marisol's deep roar. Hours. Low sunlight. She squinted. The mosquitoes darkened. She returned to the house.

Tía Roberta's face was blotchy from crying, pinkish-red between her eyes and at the tip of her nose. "Mi querida. There are no words for this." She hugged her. "I talked to your parents. They know now."

They sat together on the couch. The night smelled like rain. Tía Roberta's tears rolled on, and on. Every so often Paloma shook her head. She couldn't cry. No. She felt cold and heavy, and angry, perhaps. Angry that Laurel had gone to Blue Mar in the first place. Angry that she'd left her behind. Paloma stood up. She needed to get her anger out, but how? There was no way. No place for it. It curdled inside her. Unbearable. Electric. All she could do was run outside, and lie on the grass and wait, and wait, and wait, and watch the bats fold and unfold over her head, and wait for the sun to rise like a dark forest flower. And then? And then? She couldn't even imagine it.

Her phone vibrated in her pocket. Just once. Probably a message from her parents. Slowly, achingly, she looked at the screen.

Video Message – Laurel. She sat up straighter. How was that possible? She looked at the time the message was sent – 11:45 PM, two weeks earlier. For the briefest, slimmest of moments, she'd thought that maybe Laurel was still alive, somehow. But no. The message just hadn't been sent until service was available. She threw her phone across the grass, and went back to staring, and waiting, and emptiness.

It wasn't until the next morning that she finally played the message. Her body was tight with mosquito bites, and chilled with dew from staying out all night. The backs of her thighs were imprinted with red marks from the grass. She felt drunk from lack of sleep.

"Okay. Here we go," Paloma said to herself. She played the video. Laurel's face appeared. Tanner, shinier, slimmer than when she'd left. Her hair was frizzy on top and damp on the sides. "Hey, Palomita. I know, I look terrible. There's a—there's a hurricane going on here. On Blue Mar." Laurel's eyes grew shiny. She sniffed. "It's, uh. I don't know. It's a lot. I guess you're probably by the ocean or something, or maybe you went back home already, but I just wanted to tell you—" In the background, the murmurs grew louder. It sounded like she was in a crowded room. Laurel's gaze lifted, and then she brought the phone closer to her face. "I just wanted to tell you that I'm sorry I haven't been a better sister. When I get back, things are going to be different. We're going to hang out when you're off on break, when you're home, you know. If you want to, of course. But, no, we're going to be real sisters. I'm going to be a real sister." Laurel sniffed again. "Being here, I realized—everything is going to shit, Paloma. You were right. It's like Mars. We should at least all be together when it crumbles. And, you know what? You know why we're here? To be low-wage workers for Planet's Blue Mar eco-resort. Yeah. That's why we're here. Not for a new society. No. But at least their plan is ruined, with this hurricane. The ocean is in charge, here. If you see it out here, how it's ripping up the island, it's obvious—the ocean's the most powerful thing in the world. It's like a god. We have no control anymore. We're small." She paused. "Anyway. Paloma, I'm sorry, and I love you, little sister. And hopefully—hopefully I'll see you soon." A quick, watery smile, and then Laurel hung up the phone.

CHAPTER
TWENTY-THREE
PALOMA

"PALOMA! OYE, PALOMA!" EUGENIO RAN TOWARD HER.

Paloma stood up. She dusted the dirt from her hands. "Eugenio? Shouldn't you be at the *farmacia*?"

"No!" He scooped her into a hug. "I had to tell you in person."

"Tell me what?"

"We got another offer."

"Where? From who?"

"There is a family in town that has land, but they have no money for seeds, and no money to fix the soil. If we share the food with them, they'll let us grow there."

"But—how did they find out about us?"

"Isa told them. When they came into the *farmacia*. She told them about *los pobres*, how good the food is growing there."

"Is their house far from the ocean?"

"Back toward the hills. Better than *los pobres*. It won't be flooded for a long time."

"That's perfect," Paloma said. "Perfect." She smiled and took off her gardening gloves.

"I talked to my abuela. She said you can work with us in the *farmacia*. We can't pay you very much, but you can have free *medicinas*. And you can stay at our house. If Doña Roberta ever can't take you anymore." He paused. "If you're staying."

"I am," she said. "I've decided to stay." She was old enough now to make that kind of decision for herself. Medical school wasn't for her. And she couldn't return to the United States, with its veil of normalcy; she couldn't live in a place where everyone's heads were turned. And, most of all, she couldn't leave without Laurel.

"*Qué bueno*," Eugenio said. He hugged her again, more tightly this time. "I couldn't imagine you leaving."

"Me neither." She smiled, a quick, short smile, and she brushed her hair out of her face. "You know what we could do, for the gardens? We could get food scraps from people in the community. We could make a big composting system. And more gardens."

"Someday, maybe. If people start to trust each other more."

"I think they will. I think they'll have to. It's either that or leave."

He smiled. "Maybe—maybe."

"Things will change. How they'll change is the question."

"You are so philosophical today," Eugenio said.

"It's true, though. Everything's going to change."

"You're right. It has and it will."

They stared at each other for a moment. "Come here. Look at how much plastic I picked up," Paloma said. She led him down to the rainforest trees. The shade felt good after an afternoon in the sun. "Remember all the plastic chunks that were here? All tangled up in the roots?"

"Where did you take them?"

"They're in a pile, up in the yard." She laughed. "But at least they're not here anymore."

"*Buen trabajo*, Paloma," Eugenio said, and he laughed, too, and he grabbed her hand.

They walked together in the sun-soaked water. The waves broke at their knees. The wind and the waves pushed and pulled, and stretched the world into movement. Paloma looked back at the shore. The trees swayed softly in the wind. One had browned after the storm. It would die soon. She pointed it out.

"That's too bad," Eugenio said.

"Yeah. Someday all of them will be underwater." Paloma stopped walking. She looked Eugenio in the eyes. "When the oceans rise, where will we go?" she asked. "What will we do? Gardens won't help us then."

"We will go wherever we can. To the mountains, or another town. Anywhere but the city. We will help people. We will be traveling healers. Or maybe Mas Allá will help us. And if not, we can go to *los Estados Unidos*."

Paloma laughed. "It's all going to fall apart," she said. "Even there."

"That's true. But nothing has ever been permanent. The Earth changes."

"It's all too fast," Paloma said.

"I know. I'm being philosophical, like you." He laughed. "I don't know. We should just enjoy it. Enjoy it while it's here."

"Yeah. And get ready. *Porque todo va a cambiar,*" Paloma said. The words felt sharp and full on her tongue. "*Todo va a cambiar.*"

But there were things that wouldn't change; things that would always be there. *Las estrellas. El sol. La luna llena.* And the roughness of grass, and the fullness of wind against the sea.

And the ocean would always be there, no matter how empty of fish it was, or how full of plastic. It would always be stronger than them. The place where life began.

Laurel was right. The ocean was a god—at once terrifying and beautiful, the thing that they could not destroy. That was how it had always been. That was how it would always be.

ABOUT THE AUTHOR

Francesca G. Varela is the award-winning author of four novels: *Call of the Sun Child, Listen, The Seas of Distant Stars*—winner of the 2019 Independent Publisher Book Award for Science Fiction--and *Blue Mar*. She holds a bachelor's degree in Environmental Studies from the University of Oregon and a master's degree in Environmental Humanities from the University of Utah, where she wrote *Blue Mar* for her final project. She calls Portland, Oregon home and is proud to be of half El Salvadorian descent. When not writing or reading, Francesca enjoys playing piano, figure skating, hiking, identifying wild plants, gardening, and traveling whenever she can.

WWW.FRANCESCAVARELA.COM

WL HOUSE BOOKS, an imprint of Homebound Publications, specializes in genre fiction: science fiction, fantasy, mystery, and thriller. Myth and mystery have haunted and shaped us since the dawn of language, giving wing and fleshy form to the archetypes of our imagination. As our past was spent around the fire listening to myths and the sounds of the night, so were our childhoods spent getting lost in the tangled branches of fables. Through our titles, we hope to return to these storytelling roots.

WWW.OWLHOUSEBOOKS.COM